BURNING FOR MORE

BOOK 1: BURNING FOR THE BRAVEST SERIES

KAYE KENNEDY

D1264244

DEDICATION

To my husband. Thank you for your unwavering support and for showing me what true love really is.

NOTE FROM THE AUTHOR

You're holding in your hands a little piece of my soul, and I can't thank you enough for choosing to read Dylan and Autumn's love story.

Fun Fact: I was a firefighter in a previous chapter of my life, until an injury sustained in a house fire put an end to that. I was actually the third generation of firefighters in my family. I grew up with a father who is now an ex-chief, and I told myself that I would *never* date a firefighter…but then I fell in love with my lieutenant.

After seven years together, we parted ways, but I took away a plethora of knowledge about the inner workings of the FDNY (that's the New York City Fire Department). When I decided to start publishing, I knew I wanted to write from experience and that's how the Burning for the Bravest series came to be.

I knew I could accurately depict the job, having done it myself, as well as the operations of the FDNY. Plus, the stereotype of firemen being sexy comes from somewhere, right? In this series, I stick as close to reality as possible, but I have used some creative freedom for the sake of the stories.

Note from the Author

I hope you enjoy reading this as much as I enjoyed writing it!

LOVE & HUGS,

Kaye Kennedy

KEY LOCATIONS IN BURNING FOR MORE

1. Autumn's Apartment
2. Dylan's Fire Station Ladder 65/Engine 13
3. Dylan's House
4. Hogan Brothers' Family Home
5. Autumn's Hometown
6. Jesse's Beachfront Town Home

*Kyle's Fire Station (Engine 11/Ladder 171) is a few blocks from Dylan's station

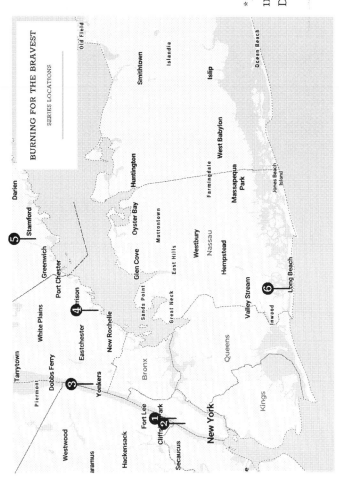

BURNING FOR THE BRAVEST

SERIES LOCATIONS

1

AUTUMN

I couldn't breathe.

The basic human function that kept people alive was my body's downfall. Confined to a hospital bed, I was vaguely aware of the beeping of machines to my left. The nasal cannula had been on for so long, it'd rubbed my nose raw. My chest felt like it was being crushed. It was as though, every few hours, someone would come and drop another brick on top of me, forcing my already compromised lungs to strain for oxygen.

Breathe, Autumn. Just breathe. I repeated what had become my mantra over and over again. The television was on, but I couldn't tell what was playing. I couldn't focus on anything other than the lack of oxygen in my body. I was too weak to function. They fed me through a tube because garnering the energy to eat was impossible. Oh, how I longed for a single bite of my grandmother's lasagna.

I was dying. Or rather, my body was dying. My soul, on the other hand, was determined to just—keep—breathing. Why? I couldn't tell you.

I was certain I still had a whole life ahead of me to live, but I wasn't sure where I got that notion from. I was alone, and I was a burden. How could someone as fragile as I was ever amount to anything?

Maybe I should stop fighting it. Clearly, my body was ready to throw in the towel, so why resist? The doctors had talked about putting me on a machine to breathe for me, but that seemed wretched. I could've put myself out of my misery if I just *stopped* breathing.

It'd be quick, or so I'd heard. There'd be a brief moment of panic followed by resounding peace. And peace sounded darn good. Another metaphorical brick fell onto my chest. Screw it. I was done fighting. If I had the energy, I would've pulled the oxygen tube out of my nose, but that much movement was so impossible, it was laughable. Laughing—yet another thing I couldn't bring myself to do—and let me tell you, life was vastly more miserable without laughter.

It took hardly any energy at all to stop breathing. Given how difficult the act of breathing was for me, I was surprised at how simple *not* breathing was. I was relaxed for the first time in years—and it was heavenly. The beeping of the machines was getting louder, but I pushed the noise away, not wanting to ruin the moment.

My lungs screamed in my chest, and my heart raced, but my mind was still. And it was magical. Not having to live every moment, counting my respirations, directing my body to inhale oxygen, was a much-welcomed break from what had been my reality for so long. The beeping was shrill in my ears. That must have meant I was close to the end. Finally.

The beeping penetrated my blissful moment of peace, and agitation flared up inside me. The frustration forced me to take a breath, but this was no ordinary breath. This air burned. My tongue, my throat, my lungs—they all screamed in agony as my body forced this toxic air out of my system. My moment of peace was gone, and that darn beeping was only getting louder.

My attempt at another breath failed just as miserably as the last one, and my eyes flew open as I hocked up dirty air. My eyes burned just as much as my lungs, and I suddenly realized I wasn't dreaming anymore. I wasn't in a hospital bed, I was on the couch, and my lungs were working just fine. I reminded myself that I was good now. I was healthy.

It had all been a twisted nightmare. It'd been a long time since I'd had one of those. I thought I'd moved on from those re-occurring dreams, where I was forced to re-live my past reality, but evidently, they still lurked in my subconscious.

If it had just been a nightmare though, why was I actually coughing and struggling to breathe? And why was I still hearing obnoxious beeping?

That's when I realized the apartment was on fire. And not a small fire either. The smoke was thick enough to blind me, and it was unfathomably hot. The beeping came from the smoke detectors screaming overhead. I shook my head in disbelief. Leave it to me to have a dream so close to reality, I couldn't decipher between what was really happening, and what was merely a figment of my imagination. It's like when you're sleeping and you have to pee, you dream about having to pee. Except this was worse. Much worse.

I sprang up off the couch as I pulled my sweatshirt up to cover my nose and mouth. I needed to get out of there. Fast. I couldn't see the door as I propelled my body forward, but I was blocked by a chair. *Wait, I don't have a chair there.*

I gasped when I remembered I was in my neighbor's apartment, not my own. The rush of smoke down my throat made me gag. Eli. I had to get Eli.

Ignoring the pain, I forced myself to cough out a scream. "Eli! Where are you?"

I dashed toward his bedroom, but my lungs rebelled against the movement. *This* was not how I was going to die. I tried to lunge toward his bedroom again, but I became light-headed and stumbled into a table. If I didn't get out in the next few seconds, I was fairly confident I'd lose consciousness and then I'd be of no help to Eli at all. My gut wrenched as I turned away from the boy's bedroom and propelled myself toward the exit. If I could just get some air, I could go back for him.

I cursed myself for not registering the smoke alarm sound sooner. I flung the door open and made it into the hallway, which was even smokier. Someone brushed past me, knocking me into the wall, but I forced myself to push forward toward the stairwell.

My lungs screamed for air. After what felt like an eternity, I pushed open the stairwell door, and as it slammed behind me, the air mostly cleared. I took a satisfying breath as I bolted down the steps. The lack of oxygen had made my vision fuzzy, and I wobbled on my feet. I would need cleaner air in my lungs if I was going to make it back up for Eli.

Being that we lived on the tenth floor, I had no doubt that I'd faint before I could get him out safely, but I was determined. If I could just make it down a couple of floors, I could inhale fresher air to clear out the smoke and stop myself from feeling so woozy. I made it to the eighth floor, pressed my back against the cool wall, and relished in the clean air. I told myself I'd take a few more breaths before heading back for Eli.

Before I could move, three giant men in fire gear barreled up the stairs toward me. One of them stopped upon seeing me. "Are you all right, miss? Do you need help getting out?"

I shook my head, as words were difficult, but relief flooded over me at the sight of him. Truthfully, I probably could've used his help, but it was more important to me that the men went up for Eli instead.

"Get yourself out of here then. Go!" He continued his quest up the stairs and I called after him, "There's a boy. Apartment 1005."

I prayed that he'd heard me and I told myself that they'd find Eli. I knew they would. They had to. That was their job, right? My legs carried me downward before I could even process the movement. I needed to get outside.

The cold air slapped me in the face and while the chill in my lungs had never felt so good before, I was fairly certain that I was on the verge of fainting. I was still struggling to see and my legs threatened to give out at any second. There were two fire trucks and an ambulance in front of my building, and I could hear more off in the distance, getting louder.

A man in a medic's uniform grabbed hold of my shoulders. "Ma'am. It's all right. You're okay now. You're safe."

Tears stung my eyes. I was going to survive.

2

DYLAN

Whoosh. Whish. Whoosh. Whish. I took a moment to remind myself to control my breathing. I'd just ascended nine floors of a Manhattan apartment building and my self-controlled breathing apparatus (SCBA) had to last long enough to get me through the fire floor and back, at least. Smoke started to fill the stairwell. The most recent status update had reported that the fire was on the tenth floor, and residents who had made it out claimed it'd already consumed at least three of the ten apartment units.

My company, Ladder 64, was the second truck company on scene, and we had orders to conduct a primary search of the five apartment units on the right side of the fire floor. Ladder 171 was currently conducting their search of the two apartments on the left side of the building.

"You ready?" I turned back to my squadmate, Frisco, who was at my heels carrying a hook and water can.

"Let's do this!"

With a set of irons—an ax and a Halligan—in my hand, we breached the stairwell door to the tenth floor. There was no water on the fire yet, which made for some gnarly conditions. The thick, black smoke was banked down to about three feet off the floor, and there was the unmistakable sound of flames crackling in the distance.

Frisco and I dropped to our knees to increase visibility and get out of the worst of the heat, which was trapped toward the ceiling. The hallway cut straight through to the rear of the building, and as we reached the door to the first unit, the crew from Ladder 171 exited the second unit across the hall, the body of a limp civilian in tow. Shit just got real.

Fighting fires certainly wasn't an easy job, but I fucking loved it. Running into a burning building elicited an adrenaline rush like none other. Though it was easier to get the job done when you focused on the task at hand instead of thinking about the destruction to life and property. However, when reality was thrust into your face as I'd just witnessed, it'd make anyone's eyes go wide and heart rate spike.

Frisco smacked me twice on the calf, indicating he was ready to breach the first door. I rose to my knees and jammed the Halligan between the door and its frame before handing the ax off to Frisco. After two swift hits from the back of the ax, the door gave way, and we crawled into the room.

With one hand on the right wall, we began our search, swiftly navigating around furniture, taking care to check under and on top of each piece. We sped through the apartment, looking for any signs of life, relieved to find it empty. The goal of a primary search was to efficiently, but quickly, search each room for the fire and victims. After the initial search, we'd retrace our steps in a more thorough secondary search.

As we exited the first unit, the engine company came on the radio. "The standpipe is frozen shut. It's inoperable." A circumstance we ran into more often than not in the January cold.

Frisco and I looked at each other. *Fuck.* We would be without water for a little while. Since the crew from Ladder 171 had to leave with the victim, we truly were on our own up there.

The familiar voice of Lt. Kyle Hogan, who was the officer-in-charge for Engine 11 that evening, came over the radio in response. "Well, then hurry the hell up and get your asses up that stairwell with a hose!"

He had a reputation for being a straight shooter with a bedside manner that could use some improvement. I didn't envy the men of Engine 11. Kyle was my older brother, and I'd been on the receiving end of his aggression more times than I could count.

Kyle's voice came over the radio again. "Ladder 64, update on the fire floor."

Being the more senior man in the pair, I hit the transmission button on my radio while Frisco and I cleared the second apartment unit. "Two of the five units on the right side are clear in our initial search. No sign of the fire yet, but feels like we're getting close."

We breached the third door in the hall as Kyle's voice permeated the air. "Ten-four, Ladder 64. We'll have water up to you soon."

As soon as the door to the unit opened and we crawled inside, there was the distinctive sound of the fire breathing as air whooshed over. "Close the door!" I shouted at Frisco, who slammed the door shut behind him. Fire fed on oxygen, and introducing more into the fire room could be disastrous. I looked up at the ceiling, but didn't see any of the telltale signs of a rollover or flashover, so I deemed it safe to proceed with the search.

I'd come to the realization that the apartments mirrored each other, meaning this unit should be identical in layout to the first one. If the fire had indeed made its way into three units, it was likely for the fire to be on the left side of this unit —where the master bedroom was—and in the two remaining units on this side of the hall.

"Frisco, let's start the search on the left."

Upon entering the first bedroom, the heat hit me like we'd run into a wall. There was definitely fire in that room. The scariest part was the thickness of the smoke. Blackness surrounded us and I couldn't see my own damn hand, let alone the fire, so it was possible we were inches from the flames without knowing it. Having no water and no visual, we retreated into the living room, shutting the door to the master bedroom behind us, hoping to contain it.

I hit the transmit button on my radio. "Fire located in the third unit from the stairwell on the right side. Contained in the master bedroom on the left. Continuing search of the unit now."

We crawled our way through the kitchen and over to the second bedroom in the back-right corner. Being it was shortly after midnight, the bedrooms were a priority for our primary search because any victims would likely be in bed.

Our radios squealed. "Ten-four. Engine 11 is three floors below, making our way up to you."

Looked like we'd be on our own a little while longer. If my logic was correct, we wouldn't be able to enter the remaining two units on this side of the hall until we had water. As we made our way into the second bedroom, a muffled cry made the hairs on the back of my neck stand up.

"You hear that?"

"Yeah, is that a baby?" Frisco replied, tension flooding his voice.

I did a quick scan of the room. There was no crib, only what seemed to be a full-size bed in one corner and a desk in the opposite corner, so it was weird to hear a baby crying. I held my breath in order to hear better without the sound of the SCBA clouding my ears.

"Sounds like it's coming from the closet." I rushed over to the door, which was open a crack, and I found a kitten visibly shaking with terror.

Thank, God.

"False alarm, it's just a cat."

Frisco and I both sighed in relief. The worst thing as a firefighter was to find a kid in peril. I didn't have the heart to leave the animal, so I scooped the kitten up and put it in the pocket of my bunker coat. I said a silent prayer that it'd be okay there for a little while because I couldn't leave the building just yet. We completed the search of that apartment and attempted to make our way to the next unit. Overhead, flames ominously licked the molding along the hallway as it searched for fuel, blocking our path to the four apartments in the rear.

I got on the radio once more. "Fire located in the back of the hallway. Access to four apartments is not possible at this time. Continuing search with the remaining unit on the left side."

My captain, John Andrews, came over the radio. "Ten-four, Hogan. Be advised, there's a woman down here saying there's an eight-year-old boy still inside."

Oh, fuck. A new sense of urgency filled me as we scrambled into the apartment across the hall, cautious that the fire could've easily jumped into that unit but motivated by the knowledge that there was a trapped kid somewhere. I prayed the boy wasn't in one of the apartments blocked by the flames. The smoke was thick, so I closed my eyes to heighten my other senses. Based on what I'd seen in the other units, I visualized the layout of the apartment. Keeping my foot on the wall, I swung my Halligan into the middle of the room, feeling for any victims. A major rule of truck operations was to never let a part of your body leave the wall, especially during a primary search when visibility was typically poor, so you didn't get disoriented and lost in a room.

"Hogan, look up!" Frisco shouted behind me.

There was a faint orange glow above us shining through the darkness. "Fuck," I cursed under my breath. The fire had jumped the damn hallway, and we were directly below the flames.

I hit the transmitter on my radio, "Be advised, fire confirmed in at least six of the units on the tenth."

We'd already cleared most of the apartment, save for one bedroom. At that moment, I heard one of the most terrifying sounds in firefighting—the distinctive hiss of fire breathing. My ass puckered as the flames crept along the molding on the ceiling in search of more oxygen. It was unmistakable, there was a rollover, meaning all of the gases on the ceiling had ignited, and the room we were in would be engulfed in flames within minutes if we didn't get water on it.

My training told me we should immediately exit the unit before we found ourselves trapped inside the fire with a mere water can to protect us. If the fire reached the door, we might not be able to get out, and because the engine company would attack the flames from the side of the hallway containing the exit, the fire would push toward us, and the department would be planning two funerals.

Except there was a boy still inside, and I didn't need another death on my conscience.

"Ready with water," came a voice over the radio. *Fucking finally.* The engine company was on the fire floor with the hose.

"Let's go!" Frisco shouted as he turned around to exit the unit, but something in my gut told me to risk it and check the bedroom. I couldn't ask him to break protocol and do the same, also putting his life in jeopardy, so I pushed further into the apartment, alone. That was the only accessible apartment left on the floor that hadn't been searched by us or Ladder 171, so I hoped the boy was in there.

I bolted into the second bedroom and immediately checked on top of the bed and under it, finding nothing. The engine came over the radio. "Water!"

My heart rate skyrocketed, and I forced myself to swallow the panic that was rising to the surface. I had to get out, or I'd risk being boiled alive. Just as I was about to exit the room, I thought about the kitten in my pocket and a voice inside my head told me to check the closet. I thrust open the door, and felt a foot.

Halle-fucking-lujah.

My heart jumped into my throat as I leaned down and wrapped my arms around the child, hoisting him up. I tried to stand since running was faster than crawling, but the fire laughed at that idea and the heat forced me back to the floor. Frisco came over the radio. "Hogan, where are you?"

The fear in his voice was unmistakable, but I wasn't able to grab my radio while trying to crawl and hold onto the kid, so I didn't respond. As I scurried through the apartment toward the exit, the familiar sound of the hoseline operating came from right outside the open door.

The flames overhead had quadrupled in size and were rapidly climbing down the wall, giving me no more than three feet of clearance. We weren't going to make it. I hurried into a corner and put the kid down, then settled my body in front of his to shield him as I got on the radio. If that's how I was gonna go out, I wanted everyone to know that at least I'd done everything in my power to save that kid.

"Shut down the line! I'm coming out of the third unit on the left with a victim."

I clutched the kid and waited to hear the engine company cease operations, praying we still had a few seconds to spare before the room was engulfed with us in it. The kid wasn't moving, and I feared the worst, but then a faint groan came from underneath me—the sound of hope. Without thinking, I took a deep breath and whipped off my helmet then heaved the mask over my head. I shoved it onto the boy's face and willed him to breathe. I didn't know if the smell of burning hair was coming from me or the boy, but the intensity of the heat on my bare head was excruciating. I jerked my hood up to cover my nose and mouth, and threw my helmet back on.

Was that reckless? Yeah, but I didn't want to carry out a dead kid. That meant more to me than my own safety.

"You're clear, Hogan," came over the radio, and before the transmission was complete, I'd already grabbed the kid and hauled ass out of the apartment. I pushed past the engine guys in the hallway as I willed my lungs to hold onto the tiny bit of oxygen left in them.

Just before making it to the stairwell, my body betrayed my mind and tried to take a breath, but all I got was smoke.

3

AUTUMN

*T*he smoke forcefully ejected itself from my lungs in a fit of coughing. The medic led me over to an ambulance and placed an oxygen mask on my face as I collapsed on the back step. Even though I was dizzy and my vision was foggy, at least the cool, clean air felt heavenly. Once the monitor was clipped on my finger, the medic started probing my chest with a stethoscope.

"Take deep breaths, ma'am," he instructed. I tried. He moved it across my chest. "Can you step inside the ambulance for me? I'm having a tough time hearing properly out here."

I stumbled into the back and collapsed on the stretcher. "Do you mind if I lift your sweatshirt so I can get to your back?"

I grumbled consent and sat up to give him access. The cold metal of the stethoscope sent a shiver down my spine and shocked me a bit out of my daze. He moved it to another spot, and then another. That's when I felt his hand go to the long, curved scar on the side of my ribcage, and just like that, my clarity returned. He removed the stethoscope from my skin.

"Ma'am, I'm going to take you to the hospital to get checked out."

He knew.

"Smoke inhalation isn't something *you* want to mess with."

The lack of oxygen had made me delirious, and I was cursing myself for wasting precious minutes.

I jolted up off the stretcher. "Eli!"

I pummeled through the doorway, getting as far as the steps before the oxygen mask tugged me back. I clumsily ripped the mask off my face and rushed toward the building's entrance, ignoring the protests of the medic behind me.

I approached the door, leaping over hoses, but was jolted to a stop by an arm around my abdomen. "I can't let you in there, miss."

I spun around and glared up into the face of a fireman wearing a helmet that read *Captain* on the front.

"I have to go back for Eli. Please, he's only eight." My voice oozed with desperation.

The man's expression became very serious. "There's an eight-year-old boy still inside?"

"Yes! I told the firemen on the stairs, but I don't know if they heard me. Please, I have to get him. He's my responsibility. We're on the tenth floor; he'll need my help to get out of there."

The radio by my ear made noise, but I was too distracted by my tunnel vision to decipher what was being said.

"Don't worry, we'll find him." He used his free hand—the one not wrapped around me—to hit the button on the radio pinned to his chest. "Ten-four, Hogan. Be advised, there's a woman down here saying there's an eight-year-old boy still inside."

I stared the man directly in the eyes and pleaded, "You have to find him."

His intensity mirrored my own. "We'll get him, miss. The best firemen in the city are in there looking for him."

The medic who had helped me interrupted, "Ma'am, we need to get you to a hospital."

"I'm not going anywhere," I barked. I wasn't going to leave Eli behind.

He sighed. "Well, at least let me get you back on oxygen."

The captain dropped his arm from around my waist. "We'll get him. Go with the paramedic and take care of yourself."

I slumped. "Fine."

I followed the guy back to the ambulance, and let him put the oxygen mask on my face. After a few deep breaths, I started to feel much better. The tightness in my chest was resolving—or at least it was overtaken by the worry in my gut.

"Last time I'm gonna say it, we need to get you to a hospital."

"I told you I'm not leaving," I snapped, which was rather uncharacteristic for me, but the guy was really pissing me off. "Eli is still in there. I *can't* leave him."

He nodded. "All right." He handed me the oxygen tank. "Leave this on until the tank empties, okay?"

"Sure." I cradled the tank on my lap, closed my eyes, and said a silent prayer that Eli would be okay. They would find him, and he would be fine.

My eyes snapped open. I had to call Janet and tell her about the fire. She'd want to be there for her son. My hand instinctively went to my sides, feeling for a pocket, but my shorts didn't have any.

I looked around the scene in front of me, as though the answer to my problem would appear. There were people everywhere in various states of distress. The whole building had been evacuated and tenants in neighboring buildings had come out to see what was going on as well. The street was flooded with people, reminding me of Times Square on New Year's Eve, except there was a much more ominous tone amongst them. Hoses cascaded out of the back of several of the fire trucks, and converged in the doorway, and all of the flashing lights lit the block in a red glow.

I made eye contact with Mrs. Allen, an older woman who lived at the end of our hallway, and she made her way over.

"Autumn, are you all right?"

"I'll be fine." I nodded. "Do you have your phone on you?"

She pulled it from her pocket.

"Do you have Janet's number? Eli—" Emotion caught in my throat and Mrs. Allen seemed to understand.

"Oh, dear. Yes." She fumbled with her screen before handing me her phone. "Here you go."

I hit send and put the phone to my ear, dreading the conversation. Janet picked up on the first ring. "Mrs. Allen, I heard there's a fire in our building—"

I cut her off. "Janet, it's Autumn."

"Oh, thank God! Autumn, I was trying to call you. Are you all right? Is Eli okay? I'm on my way; I'm only a few minutes out."

"I'm okay." I gulped. "Janet, Eli...he's still inside."

The guttural scream that came through the phone nearly broke me in two.

"I'm sorry, Janet. I tried to get him," I cried. "There was too much smoke."

"I'll be right there," she shouted and hung up.

I handed the phone back to my neighbor. She put her hand on my shoulder. "We'll pray for him. You need to have faith, dear. He'll be fine."

I prayed all right. I prayed Mrs. Allen was right because I didn't think I could live with myself if anything happened to that boy. It was my fault he was still in the building. If only I'd reacted sooner. My head drooped into my hands as tears fell down my cheeks.

4

DYLAN

I burst through the stairwell door, coughing uncontrollably, and found Frisco looking pissed. "What the hell, Hogan? You could've been killed!"

"I just ..." I coughed violently "...had feeling...kid...in that room."

Not wanting to waste any more time, I bounded down the steps. Frisco snapped to my side. "I get it, man, but you should've told me. You know I would've gone with you."

Frisco was a father, which was why I'd taken the risk on my own. I didn't have a wife and kids I had to get home to. If one of us was making that sacrifice, it had to be me.

We ran past two other ladder companies waiting in the stairwell on the floor below for the all-clear to resume searching the fire floor. "I know, but that could've gone...very wrong." I coughed out. "I wasn't gonna let you...take the risk, too."

Frisco let out a sigh. My logic was hard to argue with. "Well, at least I never would've told the engine we were clear for water if I knew you weren't right behind me."

"Let's get this kid out. You can...yell at me...later, okay?"

When we got down to the lobby, Frisco sprinted ahead,

rushing out of the building to flag down the medics. They met me at the doorway with a stretcher, and I placed the boy down on it, my lungs searing.

One of the medics gave me a once over. "Hey, man, you don't look so good, come to the ambo and let me check you out."

"I'm fine," I protested through a cough and waved him off. "It's just a little smoke." My adrenaline kept me going, and I wanted to get back in there and keep working.

Frisco interjected. "Get checked out, Hogan. You just took in smoke and carried a kid down ten flights of stairs. You look gray—and it's not all soot."

I coughed again, igniting the burning sensation in my lungs, and spat up black sputum. "Yeah, all right." I removed my SCBA and placed it on the ground beside me.

As I followed the medic over to the ambulance, I was stopped in my tracks when I spotted a woman jumping out of the back of another ambulance. She ripped an oxygen mask off her face, and ran over to the boy on the stretcher. "Eli! Eli, are you okay?" she cried. "I'm so sorry. I couldn't get to you. I tried. I'm so sorry."

Her rich brown hair was piled in a messy bun on top of her head, and she had on flannel pajama shorts and an NYU hoodie that was easily two sizes too big for her. Seeing her in such a state felt incredibly intimate. I was seeing her in a way only those closest to her probably had, and I didn't know whether to look away or comfort her. Her eyes glazed over with tears, and I felt drawn to her.

As I got closer, I figured she couldn't be older than twenty-three. Hadn't the captain said the boy was eight? She must've been a teenager when she'd had him. They lifted the stretcher into the ambulance and the woman's legs wobbled as she nearly collapsed on the ground behind it.

Just then, a woman wearing scrubs came running across the lawn. "My son! My son!" She pushed the woman I'd been watching out of the way, forcing herself into the ambulance behind the stretcher.

"Janet, I'm sorry," the younger woman shouted through her tears. Apparently, she wasn't the boy's mother. The brunette barely held herself together as the ambulance pulled away. My heart nearly broke in two at seeing her standing there alone, shivering and in hysterics. I walked up behind her and put a hand on her shoulder, causing her to flinch.

"Hey, it's going to be all right," I said in as comforting a tone as I could muster. Growing up in a family with four brothers had toughened all of our hearts, but I'd say I was always the most sensitive.

The woman turned and looked at me for a second, and I noticed her eyes were hazel behind her tears. She launched herself into my arms, throwing me off kilter. My arms hung at my sides for a moment, as I was unsure how to respond, but then I wrapped them around her and whispered, "It's okay. You're safe. Eli's safe, too."

Sometimes people just needed to be comforted, even if it's by a stranger. I enjoyed the feel of her there as she cried into my chest. She was more than a foot shorter than me and I felt an urge to protect her. Even through my bulky gear, the warmth emanating from the beautiful woman in my arms jolted something inside me, like I'd been struck by lightning. The tension in the pit of my stomach I never realized I had suddenly released. Something about holding *that woman* felt so incredibly right. She melded into my body perfectly, and I never wanted to let her go. I wanted to hug her until all of her pain went away.

And then I wanted to hug her some more.

As though she felt the electricity between us, too, she startled. She pulled out of my arms, backed away, and wiped her face with her hands. "I—I'm sorry. I don't know what got over me," she apologized through sniffles. "I didn't mean to—to—to invade your space like that."

I took a step forward. "Please, don't apologize, miss. It's really okay."

Up close she was even more attractive than I'd initially thought. She had this natural beauty about her. Her complexion was flawless, and she had these long eyelashes that highlighted the sparkle of green and gold flecks in her irises. Her cheeks were flushed, whether from the heat of the fire or the sting of the cold weather, I didn't know. And her lips...her lips were pink and slick, making my mind go to a dirty place. For a moment, all I could do was stare, mesmerized by her.

"Well, thank you. You're very kind to allow me to cry on you like that." She looked down, bashfully. "Do you really think Eli will be okay?" she asked, snapping me out of my trance.

Not wanting to make claims I had no business making, I simply said, "He seems like a fighter. He was responsive when I found him so that gives me hope."

She sighed, and her shoulders relaxed slightly. "I was watching him. He lives across the hall from me. His mom, Janet, she's a single mother and a nurse. She was working late so I made us dinner and got him ready for bed. I fell asleep on the couch, and when I woke up, there was so much smoke. I screamed for him and tried to get to his room, but I couldn't breathe." A pained look crossed her face. "I panicked and just ran out. If something happens to him..."

Tears ran hard down her cheeks, and without thinking, I reached out to wipe them. That time, she didn't flinch at my touch.

"You're so cold," I noted when I touched her skin. It was January, after all, and she wasn't dressed to be standing outside. Instinctively, I started to take off my bunker coat to give to her.

She gasped and threw her hands over her mouth. "Oh, my God! Lily!" Her head shook violently, and her tears fell harder.

A tinge of panic overtook me. "Who's Lily?"

She could barely get the words out through her sobs. "My kitten. Oh...God. I was...Eli...forgot."

With all the commotion with the boy, I'd forgotten about the kitten, too. As though Lily recognized her cue, I felt movement in my coat pocket. *Thank, God.* The last thing the woman needed was for me to pull her dead cat out of my coat. I wrapped the coat around her shoulders.

"Here, you need to get warm." I reached down and unbuckled the pocket, tenderly putting my hands in to retrieve the kitten, which was weak but miraculously alive.

"I don't suppose this is Lily?" I asked, extending the kitten to her.

The woman squealed with delight as she took the kitten from my palms and held her close, covering the meowing ball of gray fur with kisses. She looked me directly in the eyes and shook her head in disbelief. "You saved Eli and Lily?" It was a half question, half statement. "I truly don't know how to thank you."

Her gaze pierced my soul in a way I'd never experienced with any other person before. I suddenly felt extremely vulnerable, and I wasn't sure what to do about it. I shook my head and looked down, breaking the eye contact. "No need to thank me. I was just doing my job."

With that, she pulled me into another big hug, taking care not to crush Lily between us. She went up on her tippy toes, and kissed me gently on the cheek. "Thank you."

The breathiness in her voice gave me chills up my neck, and the skin on my cheek felt as though it were on fire—in the best way. That stranger affected me in a manner I simply couldn't comprehend. My mind ran with the thought of her lips on me and my dick stirred at the possibilities. Another bout of coughing snapped me out of the fantasy.

The woman put her hand on my shoulder, "Are you all right?"

I nodded, still coughing, not wanting to worry her.

"You should get checked out." Without waiting for my response, she grabbed my arm and led me toward one of the nearby ambulances. This woman, who had been an emotional mess just moments before, was suddenly in complete control. I was in awe of her.

"Excuse me," she commanded as she approached one of the medics on scene—this guy Steve, who I knew from going on various runs with his company. "Could you please take a look at him? He's coughing pretty hard."

Steve looked at her for a moment too long and I felt a tinge of jealousy in the pit of my stomach. "Yeah, sure," he replied. "But you need to get back on oxygen, too. If you refuse to go to the hospital, you at least have to stay on this for a little while." He handed her a mask, which she reluctantly took and placed on her face.

Steve turned his attention to me. "Have a seat, Hogan," he said, directing me to sit down on the back step of the ambulance.

I started to protest again, but the woman's gaze was piercing. She was very much in control of me. I gave in to her will and took a seat on the step. Steve listened to my lungs and got me started on oxygen before stating, "You've got some smoke in your lungs so keep this on for a bit, then I'll recheck you."

I nodded. The clean air filled my chest, cooling the burning sensation. The woman gave me a satisfied smile that I felt in my heart. *What is she doing to me?*

Noticing she still had the small kitten clutched to her chest, I pinched the mask off my face for a moment. "Hey, Steve, do you think you could check out the kitten? I had her in my pocket up there for a while."

The woman looked at me with adoration as she handed Lily off to him.

"Uh, I don't really know too much about animals, but the

medic in that ambo over there used to be a vet tech so I'll take her to him. You can wait here, and I'll bring her back shortly."

The woman nodded. "That'd be wonderful. Thank you." She took a seat on the step next to me, sitting close enough for our legs to touch. "You must be cold in just a t-shirt. Here, take your jacket back. I'll be okay."

She went to remove my bunker coat, but I placed my hand on her thigh, stopping her. The electricity that passed from her bare skin to my fingers was palpable, and the look on her face said she felt it, too. I warned myself to be professional as I fought the urge to let my hand glide further up her thigh.

"I'm fine, I promise. It was hot as hell up there, so this cold actually feels good. Please, you keep it on. You're certainly not dressed for winter."

"You sure?" she asked.

"Positive."

She smiled. "Thanks. I am actually pretty cold."

God, she was adorable. I let out a small laugh, and instinctively put my arm around her back, rubbing it with my hand to warm her. She looked up at me and grinned. We had a moment then. The chaos of the scene around us faded away, and it was just the two of us there together. Suddenly, I knew my life would never be the same after meeting her.

I was aware of what that woman was doing to my heart, and I didn't know if I could handle it. There was a reason I kept people at arm's length. People die and leave behind a trail of broken hearts, and the scars etched in mine still weren't healed. I wasn't prepared to create more wounds.

I removed my arm from around her back and extended my hand to her, breaking the silence. "I'm Dylan, by the way."

She giggled, shaking my hand. "I think we did this all backward, Dylan. We skipped the handshake and went straight to the ugly cry. But I'm Autumn."

"You could never be ugly—even crying." I risked crossing a line by flirting.

She blushed.

"But, hey, at least we got that part out of the way upfront. I hope to never see you cry like that again, Autumn."

I liked the way her name felt on my lips, and I couldn't help but wonder how *she* would feel on my lips.

Autumn gave me what I hoped was a flirtatious sideways glance. "Well, that sounds like you think you'll be seeing me again after this debacle of an evening, Dylan." She seemed to let the suggestion hang in the air for me to make the next move.

"A guy can hope. And perhaps our next meeting won't involve oxygen masks," I returned flirtatiously.

Kyle barreled over, breaking the moment. "What in the hell were you thinking?" he shouted.

I rolled my eyes, and the tension in the pit of my stomach returned. "I'm fine, Kyle, thanks for asking," I exaggerated my movements as I pulled the oxygen mask off of my face.

"It's lieutenant," Kyle corrected, oblivious to my sarcasm. "Now, I'll ask again, why did my men just tell me they almost killed you because your stupid ass stayed behind—without telling anyone—and put yourself behind the fire line with water flowing?" It was less of a question and more of a reprimand.

My brother was infuriating. He would've done the same thing had he been in my shoes. "I saved that kid," I shouted. "Would you have preferred I left him up there to die?"

Kyle shook his head, his face reddening by the second. "Not the point, Dyl."

"Excuse me, sir?" Autumn interjected. "Dylan saved my friend's son and my kitten. I'm certainly very grateful for whatever he did tonight."

Kyle looked at Autumn with widened-eyes, and his mouth hung open, leaving him momentarily at a loss for words. As if noticing her there for the first time, he cocked his head. I worried about him. Kyle hadn't dated since college, and even then, there was never anyone serious. I'd swear he was gay if it wasn't for the fact that I had evidence to the contrary. Our rooms growing up had shared a wall, and we were roommates for a little while after that. Let's just say he had a penchant for vocal women.

Kyle lived and breathed the FDNY, and it had made him impervious to the countless women who threw themselves at him at the bars on those rare occasions we got him to go hang out. As the eldest, Kyle had taken on a lot of responsibility after our dad had died, and I often wondered if my brother would ever *allow* himself to be truly happy.

Kyle returned his gaze to me, then back to Autumn, narrowing his eyes. Whatever was going to come out of his mouth next would not be friendly. And Autumn didn't deserve that.

"Who in the hell are you?" he spat bitterly in her direction.

Before I could jump in to defend her, she replied, "Just a grateful citizen." She held her own, but still tensed up beside me. "Um, I think I'll check on Lily," she said, understandably wanting to extricate herself from the conversation.

Autumn started to stand and remove her mask, but I placed my hand on her thigh, stopping her. I was afraid if she walked away, I wouldn't find her again, and as unprepared as I was for the things she made me feel, I was even more unprepared for her to walk away from me just yet.

"No, Autumn, stay. They'll be right over with Lily, I'm sure. And the *lieutenant* here is sorry for being so crass in the presence of a lady." I stared hard at my brother. "Aren't you?"

Kyle returned my stare and pointed his finger at me as if he were reprimanding a child. Through gritted teeth, he said, "This isn't over," before turning on his heels and walking away.

"Wow," Autumn exclaimed. "Is that your boss?"

I snorted. "He thinks he is."

"Well, he seems like a condescending ass," she stated.

I couldn't help the laugh that escaped my lips at her frankness. "You have no idea."

My heart softened. This complete stranger had just stood up for me when she had no reason to get involved in the first place. It was nice having someone in my corner for a change.

Just then, the medic returned with Lily wrapped in a blanket. Autumn jumped up and removed her mask as she took the kitten lovingly into her arms. "She's lucky," Steve said. "We warmed her up, gave her some water and oxygen, and she perked right back up. She should be okay tonight, but take her to your vet tomorrow, just in case."

"I will," Autumn replied. "Thanks again."

He nodded. "But please, I implore you, go see *your* doctor first."

Autumn tried to hide the embarrassment on her face, and I couldn't help but feel like I'd missed something.

She let out a desperate sigh and clearly tried to change the subject from her to me. "And how are you feeling, Dylan?" she asked.

I pulled my mask down. "Much better now."

Autumn gave me a questioning look.

"Really, I am."

Steve gave my lungs another listen. After a moment, he said, "All right, sounds clear. You're good to go back in."

Normally, nothing would make me happier than hearing those words, but this time, I hesitated, not wanting to leave Autumn's side. "Great," I said less than enthusiastically. I stood up and took my time pulling my suspenders back over my shoulders.

Autumn looked as saddened as I was that our impromptu evening together had come to an end. "Uh, here," she stated as she stood and removed my coat. "I guess you'll be needing this."

I reluctantly took it from her, catching a whiff of her flowery scent as I put it on. "Yeah, thanks." Not wanting to leave her out there in the cold, I asked, "Do you have some-where you can go? You won't get back in there tonight."

Autumn's hand flew up to cover her mouth as though it'd just dawned on her this wasn't like one of those fire drills at NYU where she'd stand outside for fifteen minutes, then get to go back to her warm bed.

"Yeah, I have—uh, a friend that lives down the block. I'll call—" She stopped, noticing she didn't have her cell phone. "Umm, I'll go over there."

I nodded, glad she could get out of the cold and into a hot shower somewhere safe. Then I thought about her in the shower, and my shorts under my bunker gear tightened in the groin.

"Good," I said, trying to scrub the image from my mind before I embarrassed myself. "I'll find you a ride to her house."

"His, actually." Her face flushed, and curled up as though she immediately regretted correcting me. "And that's really unnecessary, I—"

"Autumn, it's late, it's cold, and you're not wearing shoes. You're in no state to walk anywhere by yourself."

I was surprised by how much I cared about this woman who, half an hour ago, was merely a stranger to me. And I was *really* not happy that she was going over to another guy's house, but I had no right to stake a claim over her. Of course, she had a boyfriend. How could she not? A girl that beautiful didn't stay single for long. My heart sank at the thought.

Captain Andrews approached. "Hogan, you cleared for duty?"

"Yes, sir."

"Good. I need you to get in there for overhaul."

"Sure thing." I looked at Autumn, disappointed to be leaving her. "Captain, can you find someone to take this woman to her boyfriend's house? She's one of the residents on the fire floor."

He surveyed her. "Absolutely. I'll see if the battalion chief's driver can take her over." He directed his attention to Autumn. "See, miss, I told you we had the best firemen in the city up there."

She smiled ear to ear and snuck a sideways glance at me. "You were right."

He smiled back at her, and that jealousy monster welled up inside me again. *Get a hold of yourself, Hogan.*

"Grab a hook and head on up to the tenth. Frisco and Locuzi are already up there," Captain Andrews instructed.

Reluctant to leave, I nodded and looked at Autumn, knowing I had no choice in the matter. "Take care of yourself," I said, not knowing how else to end our moment together. I scratched Lily's head, getting a satisfied purr in return. "This furball, too."

I went to walk away, but she grabbed my arm, twisting me around. She gazed into my eyes again with that soul-piercing stare of hers. "Thank you again. Truly," she said. She seemed to be willing me to understand the depth of her gratitude.

I nodded, not sure how else to respond. That woman was dangerous for my heart.

"And, Dylan, he's not my boyfriend."

I smiled at her admission.

"I just thought you should know." She looked up at me with those sparkling hazel-eyes. "Be safe in there." She gestured toward the building with her chin.

"I will," I replied before turning back toward the fire. It was safer for my heart in that direction anyhow.

As I walked away, I heard my captain tell Autumn he'd make sure she got somewhere safely, and while I was grateful, I desperately wished *I* was the one keeping Autumn safe.

5

AUTUMN

$\mathcal{T}$he utter shock on Drew's face when I arrived at his apartment made me realize going there was probably a mistake, but I was freezing cold, reeked of smoke, and had nowhere else to go. I must have been quite a frightful sight as well, at nearly two in the morning, showing up in such a state.

"Hi," I said timidly, clutching my kitten to my chest. It took Drew a moment to register me standing in his doorway. I'd just woken him up, after all, and it'd been over a year since we'd last spoken.

"Uh, Autumn—hey," he stuttered.

"I'm so sorry to just show up like this in the middle of the ni—"

"Are you okay?" he blurted out, seeming to finally realize the oddity of my disheveled appearance. "Come in."

I entered his apartment with some trepidation. The last time I had been there was one of the worst nights of my life. I had thought we were going to get engaged that evening, but instead, I'd left with a broken heart.

Drew's voice brought me back to the present, his hand on my shoulder, and a look of concern on his face. That simple gesture was enough to send me over the edge again. I cried and struggled to catch my breath, and Drew pulled me into his arms. It felt awkward but familiar at the same time. The gravity of what I'd gone through was settling in, and I needed to let it all out.

After a few minutes of us standing there—me crying, him holding me and rubbing my hair, whispering platitudes to calm me—I took a step back from him. "I'm so sorry. I didn't realize I was going to get so upset." I thought I'd gotten it all out of my system already, but apparently, I hadn't.

Drew dismissed my apology with a shake of his head. "Autumn, what's going on? You're scaring me."

I took a deep breath. "There was a fire in my building." Saying it out loud finally made it feel real, and I rushed through the details of my ordeal, explaining everything to Drew. Well, maybe not *everything*. In this version, Dylan was far less sexy, but still very much a hero.

"He also saved my kitten," I exclaimed, lifting Lily up for Drew to see her. He went to pet her on the head, and she hissed, forcing him to jump back. "I'm so sorry. She's never done that to anyone before."

"No worries. It sounds like she's had a scary night. You both have."

I nodded. "When the fireman asked me if I had a place I could stay, I realized I didn't have my phone on me to call anyone. Britt's out of town, and your place was the closest, and I just found myself coming here without really thinking about it."

I would've much preferred to wake my best friend up in the middle of the night, but she was on a work trip and wouldn't be back until the next afternoon. So, there I was at Drew's.

"I'm glad you came over. Do you want me to take you to the emergency room?"

The sting I'd felt when Drew had broken up with me returned at that question. "No." I vehemently shook my head. "The paramedics put me on oxygen. I'm fine."

"You sure?" he asked. But the look of pity in his eyes was like a knife to my chest.

"Yeah, I am."

"Okay. Just making sure you're all right." He reached out and grabbed my free hand. "Your hands are frozen. I've got a few empty boxes, why don't I go set up a bed for..." He gestured at my kitten.

"Lily."

"I'll make up a bed for Lily while you go shower and warm up. I'll make you some tea and grab some of my clothes for you to wear. You'll both stay here tonight."

The tension faded away, and I couldn't conceal my smile as I nodded. It felt good to be taken care of by Drew again. I watched him bunch up a small quilt he had on his couch, shoving it into a large box along with a small bowl of water and some newspaper for Lily. I gently placed her in the makeshift bed, and she greedily lapped at the water bowl before curling herself up in the blanket.

Drew headed into the kitchen to make some tea, and I showed myself to the bathroom, where I took a much-needed shower. I didn't think a shower had ever felt so good before. Slowly, the feeling returned to my numbed limbs as the heat caressed them. I had to wash my hair four times before the smoke smell dissipated. I no longer smelled of fire, but I did smell like Drew, and just like that, a crack in my heart that had mended busted a few of its stitches.

I wrapped myself in a towel, then walked into Drew's bedroom, just as I'd done so many times before, but for the first time, I was starkly aware of my near-nakedness. Drew had laid out a pair of his sweatpants and a t-shirt for me, which I happily put on because the thought of warm, clean clothes was heavenly. I went back out into the living room, and he directed me to have a seat on the couch.

I looked around the apartment and noticed not much had changed since I'd left. The photos of us no longer hung on the walls, but otherwise it seemed to be the same. Drew had always been neat, and a bit of a minimalist, so I would've noticed signs of another woman being there. There were none.

"Here's your tea." He handed me the mug.

"Thanks."

I was suddenly very aware of the awkwardness of the situation. There I was, sitting on my ex-boyfriend's couch, wearing *his* clothes, and drinking tea out of *his* mug at two o'clock in the morning. His expression indicated he was in just as much disbelief as I was.

I broke the silence. "Thank you for letting me stay. I realize this is—" I struggled to find an appropriate word. "A little weird. Me just showing up."

Drew smiled. "It's definitely a surprise, but I'm glad you came here—that you felt you could come here."

Not knowing what to say, I curved my lips into a small smile and took a sip of my tea. We sat in silence for a few minutes, neither of us knowing what to say after not having seen or spoken to each other in so long. His shaggy brown hair was tousled from sleep and it was a bit longer than I'd remembered it, but otherwise he looked the same.

The tea warmed me from the inside, and I felt my eyelids getting heavier by the minute, having purged myself of so much emotion. I finished my tea and placed the mug on the coffee table.

He stood. "You must be tired." He went into his bedroom and returned with a pillow, which he placed on the other end of the couch. "You can sleep in my room and I'll stay out here."

"Drew, no, that's really not necessary. I'll be fine here on the couch."

"Don't argue with me, Autumn. You'll be much more comfortable in the bed, and after everything you've gone through tonight, you need to get some rest. I'm worried you were out in the cold for that long."

The look on his face meant business, and I was truly too

exhausted to argue, so I conceded. "All right. Thank you. I think I'll go lay down and try to get some sleep now if you don't mind."

"Of course."

I stood, and Drew stepped toward me, wrapping me in an awkward hug, neither of us really knowing what to do with our hands. He wasn't nearly as muscular as Dylan, but I still felt small in his arms.

"Good night," he uttered as we broke apart.

"Good night." I grabbed Lily, who was sound asleep in the box, and brought her into the bedroom, closing the door behind us. I climbed into Drew's bed, and was asleep before my head hit the pillow.

I woke up startled, forgetting where I was for a moment. The light had just peeked through the window blinds, and I realized I was in my ex-boyfriend's bed with my kitten curled up asleep on my stomach. The events of the evening came flooding back to me, and I squeezed my eyes tightly shut, willing it all to have been a bad dream. Well, not all of it. I'd like to keep that sexy firefighter in real life, but I wished the rest of it was nothing more than a nightmare.

The memory of Dylan standing in front of me holding Lily managed to take my breath away, making me gasp. When I'd thrown myself into his arms, his tremendous strength had wrapped around my small frame, and I'd instantly felt safe, like I was impervious to the world as long as I was in his embrace. Of course, I'd then realized I'd just thrown myself at a stranger, probably making him uncomfortable with my display of emotion, so I'd forced myself to vacate his arms.

As he'd removed his coat to give to me, I'd nearly come unglued at the sight of his cut biceps and his hard chest, which had stretched his t-shirt tautly across his body. But after he had handed me Lily, I simply had to be in his arms again. I'd kissed him lightly on the cheek, thankful for all he'd done for me that night, and I'd gotten a good look at my hero for the first time.

When he'd smiled at me, his white teeth were a stark contrast to his face, which had been darkened by the smoke. I'd fought the yearning to run my fingers along his stubble, tracing his strong jaw. His light brown hair was long on top and tapered down the sides. I could tell by the cut that he usually put effort into making it look good, but it had been disheveled from his helmet, which had sat on the ground by his feet. We'd locked eyes, and I couldn't help but stare. Those deep blues spoke to my girl parts, and I had nearly melted under his gaze. The thought of him alone was enough to heat me up between my legs.

I could hear Drew out in the kitchen making coffee, and the fantasy of Dylan that I'd conjured up disappeared. I propped myself up in the bed, and Lily meowed loudly at me, chastising me for disturbing her slumber. My head throbbed, my throat hurt, and my chest felt heavy—all reminders of the very real fact that the night before hadn't been a dream. I could seriously use some tea. And some water. Not necessarily in that order either.

I glanced around the room that had once been my own, but had become completely foreign to me. It'd been over a year since I'd been in that bedroom. The bedroom set was the same, but my things were missing from it. A stack of Drew's law books sat on the dresser where my perfume tray had once been. Most of all, it smelled entirely of Drew—a mix of bergamot and sea water assaulted my nostrils from the cologne I'd given him for a birthday long past. Any part of me that had been left behind was long gone.

As the morning light illuminated the bedroom, I wondered how I'd managed to sleep so soundly in that room—in *Drew's* bed—all night. An overwhelming need to escape washed over me. I threw the blankets off and stood up, preparing to put myself together and get the hell out of there. Then, I remembered I had no cell phone, no wallet, not even a pair of shoes. I doubted I even had a home to go to anymore.

I felt trapped.

I took a few deep breaths, trying to center my panicked mind. I could do this. I opened the door to the bedroom and found Drew standing there in his kitchen, shirtless. A part of me ached for what used to be, and could have been, but mostly, the anger over how he had broken my heart prevailed, and I was immediately hardened to his presence.

"Good morning," he said, holding out a cup of tea for me.

"Thanks," I said curtly. I didn't want to be rude after he'd so kindly taken me in, but I also couldn't forget what he'd done to me before. And since the emotional intensity of the previous night had subsided, the pain was all I could think about.

"How'd you sleep?" he asked, taking a sip of his coffee.

I shrugged. "Okay, I guess."

Truth was, I'd slept better than I had in months, but I wasn't about to admit that to him. I told myself it was due to his mattress being so comfortable, and because I was emotionally depleted. It certainly wasn't because that had also been *my* bed for the better part of three years and there was a part of me that missed it. No, definitely not that.

"So, do you want me to go to your apartment with you?" he offered.

"That won't be necessary." The words spilled out of my mouth before I even had a moment to process his question.

All I wanted to do was get away from Drew. I wanted nothing more from him. It was bad enough I was there in the first place. In retrospect, I probably should've slept on a park bench. Freezing to death would've been better than having to see him again.

He nodded, the smallest hint of hurt fleeting across his face.

I couldn't help but feel as if there was something between us. Not like I had wanted to get back with him or anything, more like there were things he wanted to say—for closure maybe? And as much as a part of me had wanted to hear him out, that was the last thing I needed. Getting over Drew had been one of the hardest things I'd ever had to do, and I regretted having gone back there.

He finished his coffee. "I was going to head over to one of the boutiques down the block to get you some clothes—"

"Thank you, but that's okay. I'll just put on my clothes from last night. I can change once I get into my apartment." I feared it had all been destroyed, but I wasn't going to let him know that. I'd figure it out on my own. Tension coursed through my body. I really needed to get out of there.

"Autumn, please, don't be like that." He sighed and shook his head. "Let me help you. You can't go anywhere in those clothes. It's twenty-three degrees outside."

I so badly wanted to argue because he had no right to tell me what I could or couldn't do, but he had me there. *Darn.*

"Don't you have to get to work?"

"I called my dad and told him I'll be in later."

Drew was a lawyer at his father's firm, so he likely had told his father what had happened and had easily gotten a pass on the morning. I hung my head in resignation and mumbled, "Okay, but I don't have my wallet." I felt like a child.

"Don't worry about that." He smirked. "I can take care of it."

"No, really. I'll pay you back once I can get my wallet."

He ignored me. "If you want to call your doctor, I can stop by the pharmacy and pick up replacement meds for you and some food for your kitten, too." He handed me his cell phone. "And make yourself an appointment, too. You really ought to get checked out after going through all that."

Slight panic hit me in the gut. "Yeah, I will. Thanks." *How could I have forgotten about my pills?*

He went into his bedroom while I called my doctor. When he came back out a few minutes later, he was dressed in his usual navy trousers and casual button down. He reached for his pea coat as he asked, "All good?"

"Yeah. He's calling them in now."

Drew nodded. "You still wear a small shirt, size twenty-six pants, and a size seven shoes?"

I nodded, my mouth agape, surprised he remembered my sizes.

"Okay, I'll be back shortly. Just make yourself comfortable." He grabbed his coat off the hook by the door.

The voice in my head laughed. Comfortable? Yeah, right. Not knowing how else to respond, I took a sip of my tea and muttered, "Umm, yeah. Thanks."

He strode out the door. I was finally alone in his apartment and I let out a breath, releasing some of my tension. Still standing in the kitchen, I looked around in utter disbelief that I was back there. I had vowed when I'd left that I'd never come back, and I'd been really good about it—until then.

It had been incredibly sweet of him to go out and get me clothes and pick up my meds, but I had to draw a hard line in the dirt. We weren't friends. I'd never be able to forget how much he had hurt me. In a way, there was a part of me that was still trying to get over it, and being around him wasn't in my best interest.

I glanced at the clock and started counting the minutes as I waited for Drew to return. I desperately needed to go home. If I had a home to return to, that is.

6

DYLAN

*A*fter having three days off, I was itching to get back at it, but first, I had to make it through lunch with my family. I got into my Dodge Charger and started the twenty-minute drive to my childhood home. I hadn't seen Kyle since the night of the apartment fire, and I knew he was going to break my balls about it, but skipping a family meal hadn't been an option. Still, I was in no mood to hear it.

I had no regrets. I'd done what I'd had to, and I'd saved that boy. I'd replayed the scenario in my head over and over, each time coming to the same conclusion. I wouldn't have changed a thing. If I had, that boy would be dead, and I wouldn't have been able to handle it knowing that I'd let him down. Not again.

I merged onto the Interstate, grateful that there hadn't been traffic. I had been late to our last family meal, and I hadn't wanted to upset my mother by showing up late again. I was the second of four boys, and since our dad had passed away, we all made an effort to be there for our mom. My dad had been an FDNY captain, and all four of us ended up becoming firemen, too. It got pretty complicated trying to get off work at the same time, but we coordinated at least once every two weeks, and all got together with Mom for lunch or dinner.

My youngest brother, Ryan, had just gotten off his twenty-four-hour shift that morning, and I was going in for mine that night, whereas Kyle and Jesse had the day off. Our mom had retired from her job as a high school principal five years earlier, so it was easier for her to adapt to our schedules. Kyle and I worked near each other in Manhattan, and our companies often went on runs together. Ryan and Jesse worked in Queens and Brooklyn, respectively, so I didn't get to see them as often. As much as we all griped about making plans, it was nice to see my brothers. Most of the time.

Our mother still lived in the house where we had grown up in Westchester County—Mamaroneck, to be exact. It was close enough to the city to be convenient, about twenty miles away, but far enough to be a quiet suburb. As far as places to grow up went, I'd say we'd been pretty lucky. We had lived minutes from the harbor and spent lots of time fishing and sailing on the Long Island Sound. I had actually really enjoyed living there—until my world had been turned upside down during my senior year of high school. Since then, I could barely tolerate being there at all.

The memory of that day crept up on me, making me nauseous. Jenna Lawson was the prettiest girl in my grade, and she had every guy in school drooling at her feet, so when my friends dared me to ask her out on a date our sophomore year, I never expected her to say yes...except, she did. We dated all through high school, and I could honestly say I'd loved her.

We'd planned to move in together after graduation while she attended Fordham University in the Bronx, and I got my required credits to get into the FDNY at Bronx Community College. After she graduated, we'd get engaged. She'd begin her career as an elementary school teacher while I established myself in the FDNY, climbing the ranks as my father had.

Then, we'd get married, move back to the suburbs, and start a family. It was the perfect plan.

Until it wasn't.

Whenever I went home, I'd take the long way to my mom's, avoiding the place where my life irrevocably changed. The place where Jenna had died.

Being a fireman was something I'd always known I'd wanted to do, but after losing Jenna, my desire to be on the job had magnified tenfold. I couldn't save Jenna—or my dad, for that matter—so I dedicated my life to saving everyone else.

After graduation, I moved in with Kyle in the Bronx to establish city residency and up my chances of getting a high ranking on the FDNY hiring list. I also was more than ready to get out of Mamaroneck and escape the constant reminder of what I'd lost.

It took years, but I eventually moved on. I'd had a couple of relatively serious relationships since then, although they never worked out. In the end, we'd been nothing more than friends, who had sex on occasion, and we'd split up on mutual terms. No matter how great those other women were, I'd never felt that spark I'd had with Jenna—and I was losing faith that I could ever love someone like I'd loved her. I'd pretty much resigned myself to the fact that I was already thirty and unlikely to ever find a woman I'd want to spend the rest of my life with.

But then I met Autumn and felt that spark again.

Ever since meeting her, I'd been incapable of thinking about anything else. There was just *something* about her. I'd felt more alive the past few days than I had in years. Which I realized was crazy because she was virtually a stranger. But I oddly felt like I *knew* her. I couldn't explain it. I was kicking myself for not getting her number or finding out a way to contact her, but with my captain standing right there when we'd parted ways, it wouldn't have been appropriate to ask.

Well, that, and her apartment had just burned down. Asking her out on a date wouldn't have been in the best taste.

I tried searching for her online, but without a last name and any details besides her having a kitten named Lily, it was nearly impossible to find her in a city of over three million people. I planned to try and find out more about that fire when I got to work, and at the very least, get the address for her apartment building so I could look her up that way. Maybe someone had information that could lead me to her.

I pulled up to my mom's house. I had been the last to arrive, but at least I was on time. As I entered the side door into the kitchen where everyone was gathered, the room went quiet.

"Hey, guys." I waved awkwardly before crossing over to kiss my mom on the cheek. "What's up?" I asked, knowing full well that they'd been talking about me.

Silence.

"Come on. What the hell did I do now?"

Kyle spoke up first. "I was just filling everyone in on how you nearly killed yourself. Again."

"That's not fair. I saved an eight-year-old boy," I retorted, then added, "And a kitten," not really sure why the animal was suddenly so important to me.

My mother quietly excused herself. She knew better than to get involved in our work.

"Kyle said you didn't evacuate when you should've," Jesse continued. "His guys opened up the line, not knowing you were still inside. You really want to put it on their conscience knowing they killed you?"

Jesse, like Kyle, worked in an engine company. His job was to get water on the fire and put it out. Ryan and I were in ladder companies, where our responsibility was to locate people and the fire, ventilate, then do overhaul (which was the technical term for putting holes in walls and breaking shit to make sure all the fire was actually out and not just hiding). We each had our own way of getting the job done, and our own perspectives on what those jobs entailed.

I did my job that night, and I damn sure didn't need their criticism. "I had *seconds* to get that kid out before the apartment was engulfed. I really didn't want his death on *my* conscience, knowing I could've saved him but left him to die a few feet away from me."

"Yeah, ever the fucking hero, Dyl," Kyle chimed in.

"What the hell is that supposed to mean?"

Ryan spoke up. "You take a lot of risks you shouldn't, that's all."

"Oh, so you would've just left the kid in there to die, Ryan? I call bullshit! You would've done the same damn thing."

"Not the point." Kyle shouted. "The fact is, this isn't the first time you've done something reckless on the job. One of these days, you won't be so fucking lucky and we," he motioned to himself and my brothers, "will be burying another Hogan."

Our father had a heart attack when I was sixteen. He'd collapsed in our driveway, which was where Kyle and I had found him over an hour later. We were too late. While he hadn't died on the job, the job was what had killed him. He had been there on 9/11, and while he had walked away from the rubble, he had also walked away with heart disease. On top of the three hundred and forty-three firefighters who'd lost their lives that day, over two hundred firefighters have died of 9/11-related diseases since. And that number isn't done climbing.

Bringing our father's death into any conversation was always the equivalent of pulling the trump card.

"Okay," I conceded, taking the high road. "You're right. I should've gotten out of there when Frisco did, but there was something telling me the boy was in there. I couldn't leave him. I'm sorry for taking the risk and for putting your men in that position."

Jesse patted me on the shoulder in acknowledgment that the discussion was over, and Ryan handed me a beer.

Always needing the last word, Kyle mumbled, "It won't bring Jenna back."

"What the fuck did you just say?" I was in Kyle's face with my arm reared back, hand in a fist. Everyone had that one line you simply didn't cross, and for me, that line was Jenna.

Jesse and Ryan sprang into action, one grabbing me, the other Kyle. Next thing I knew, I was in the driveway, getting into my car and pulling away.

When I got to the fire station—four hours early—I was overwhelmed with the desire to beat the shit out of something. I immediately went into the weight room and pounded the life out of the heavy bag until my knuckles bled. It made me feel significantly better, although a part of me wished I'd landed just one on Kyle.

I showered and offered to relieve one of the guys early since I was ready to go. Locuzi, my twenty-four partner, took me up on it, and I was ready to ride an hour and a half ahead of schedule. Locuzi and I traded shifts on the regular so we could work twenty-four hours instead of two consecutive days and two consecutive nights per week. This meant we never really had a chance to work together, but he was a good dude.

I was doing a truck check, making sure the SCBA tanks were full, when I heard the unmistakable voice of my buddy, Palmer. "Oh, my stars. Hogan the Hero in the flesh." He fanned himself with his hand, making a mockery of the Southern girls he had become infatuated with when he went to college at UNC.

I rolled my eyes. "Don't be jealous now."

"Jealous? Nah. I'm impressed. I wish I could save kittens,

too." He looked up at me with big doe eyes, his hands clasped over his heart.

"Tease all you want, Palmer. If you saw that kitten's owner, you'd have left my ass behind up there just to save that animal."

He gave me a sideways glance with a sly smile. "So I've heard. Autumn, is it?"

"Yeah." I looked at him, puzzled. "How'd you know?"

Unable to help it, I felt very protective of Autumn. God only knew what the dogs around the firehouse were saying about a girl that hot.

Jace Palmer and I had gone through the academy together, so he knew me better than any of the other guys in our station and I swear, at that moment, he could read the possessiveness on my face because the next words out of his mouth were, "I saw her." He looked at me, seeming to be waiting for me to take the bait.

I knew I should have just ended the conversation there before I revealed too much of my feelings, but all I had been able to think about for the past few days was finding her, and this might be the lead I was looking for.

"You did? Where? You weren't on duty that night."

"She was here," he responded simply, his hands on his hips.

He knew what he was doing, and I wanted to smack that smug grin off his face. "Care to elaborate?"

"Would you like me to?" he teased.

I threw my hands up. "All right, you got me. Yeah, I'm interested. Now will you please just tell me?"

He folded his arms across his chest, an expression of total satisfaction on his face. "She stopped by here earlier this afternoon with a tray of brownies for the—quote—'hero' who saved her kitten."

My heart skipped in my chest. She'd been *there*. To see *me*. And I'd just missed her. *Dammit!*

"Yeah, they were delicious, too." He winked. "I think the tray is still in the lounge if you want to lick it."

I crossed my arms and said, in the best deadpan tone in my repertoire, "Hilarious." I probably should have just left it at that, but curiosity got the best of me. "Did she say anything else?"

"Just that she loves you and wants to have your babies."

I punched Palmer in the arm.

"For real, though," he said. "We *all* really appreciate you saving Autumn's pussy." He elbowed me for emphasis.

I shook my head, covering my face with my hand, knowing the whole station would be fantasizing about her—*my* Autumn.

As if sensing I was done with talking about her, he patted me on the back. "Seriously. Good work. You're fucking insane, but I hear that boy survived because of you."

My skin flushed. It wasn't that I was embarrassed about it, but I'd saved that boy because it was my job, not because I wanted to be touted as a hero. As for the kitten? I chalked that one up to fate.

Palmer turned to go, but he stopped to look back at me. "Bianchi."

I looked at him, perplexed. "Excuse me?"

"Autumn's last name. It's Bianchi." He smirked, and left.

Autumn Bianchi. I smiled at the sound of it. That was exactly the break I was looking for, and I couldn't wait to get my hands on my phone to search for her.

The ten of us on duty sat around the table at six a.m., chugging coffee like we'd found water in a desert. We'd gotten our balls kicked in that night. A bullshit call came over shortly after my tour had started, and then they just kept coming. The truck had returned to the station at around two in the morning, and we had been back for all of twelve minutes before heading out again. We'd finally returned about half an hour ago. I would need a nap to make it another twelve hours 'til my shift was up. We all looked like hell.

"Is Pinelli coming in this morning?" Frisco asked.

Lt. Brewster, our ladder company's officer-in-charge this shift, grunted. "Yeah."

Frisco let out a whoop. "Fuck, yes. I need a bagel."

The guys coming in for the morning shift always brought in something for the crew for breakfast. Pinelli's family owned a bakery that he helped run in his off-duty hours, so anytime he came in, he always brought the best baked goods.

"I'd be so fat if I were him," Palmer chimed in.

"And broke, 'cuz you'd eat everything if you owned that place," I teased. "There'd be nothing left to sell to customers."

I've never met anyone in my life that ate as much as Palmer did. And I'd grown up in a house with four boys—all athletes, well over six feet tall. Our family's monthly grocery budget was higher than my mortgage.

Palmer lifted his shirt and proudly rubbed his abs. "Don't be hatin' just 'cuz I'm blessed with a metabolism powered by rocket fuel."

Mickey, one of the older guys on the engine, stood and lifted his shirt. "Yeah and this six-pack is sponsored by Budweiser." His stomach jiggled as he patted it.

We all laughed. I loved my job. What other jobs let you goof off with your buddies all day long and get paid for it? We busted each other's balls—oftentimes ruthlessly—but when shit hit the fan and our lives were on the line, every last one of us would die to save each other. The FDNY was a brotherhood unlike any other.

Ding! "Ladder 64, Engine 13—"

We all jumped to our feet and boarded our corresponding apparatus. It seemed there would be no rest for the weary.

7

AUTUMN

$\mathcal{M}$ ondays. If I were being honest, I'd never been a fan. Sundays ended the weekend, so Mondays always signified the start of a new week for me, and I'd always been uneasy about time passing. *This* Monday, though, was a good one. I had the day off to finish moving into my new apartment. I sat on the floor of my new living room, drinking a cup of tea from the café down the block, taking in my new surroundings. The space was mostly empty, save for the few things I'd been able to salvage from the fire. The kitchen, living room, and dining area were all connected, which made the place look bigger. I greatly appreciated the high-end finishes and the big window, which let in a lot of natural light. The two bedrooms branched off the living room and had a half-bath between them. The master bedroom had its own bathroom, which was a nice touch. I had my own washer and dryer, too. That was a requirement—I don't do laundromats. Overall, it was a great space.

Fortunately, I worked for a property management firm, and one of the perks of my job was getting to live in one of our buildings rent-free. The morning after the fire, I'd called my office and had explained the situation to my boss. I had started interning for the company during my junior year of college, and they had brought me on full-time once I'd graduated. I'd quickly worked my way up to one of the top positions, and my boss had taken me under his wing. "Like the daughter I never had," he always said. When I had told him about the fire, he'd made sure I was taken care of, giving me off until Wednesday, and he'd managed to get me into a nicer apartment than my last one. He'd even given me a very generous advance on my bonus so I could replace all of my things.

I was spending the day settling into my new building three blocks from my destroyed apartment. That apartment had symbolized my freedom because it had been the first place that was truly mine, and seeing it destroyed was like taking a punch to the gut. Thankfully, most of the damage had been sustained in the master bedroom, so I'd lost all of my clothes, but those were replaceable. My office—while it hadn't been in the greatest shape—had been spared from the flames, so I had been able to get my important files and some photo albums and books I loved—although, they reeked of smoke and I didn't know if I'd ever get that out. I had even managed to salvage most of my cookware from the kitchen.

I had gotten the keys to my new one-thousand square foot, fourteenth-floor apartment on Saturday, and I had immediately gone with my friend Britt to order some furniture. We had rented a car so I could pick up a new mattress, plus a few articles of clothing to get me through the next few days. I had a feeling I was really going to love my new place. I'd been able to find my same bedroom set, and I'd opted to go with a completely different look in my living room. My previous apartment had reflected a lot of Drew's minimalistic tastes, because that had been what I'd become accustomed to. This time around, I had gone for something more *me*. My new couch was comfortable, while still being chic. At least Britt told me it was chic.

I had also ordered a matching chair-and-a-half, too, which

was smaller than a loveseat, but bigger than a regular chair. I could already imagine myself curling up into it to watch *Dancing with the Stars* after work. I had a weakness for competition reality shows.

My new furniture was due to be delivered momentarily, and I while I waited, I was putting away all of the stuff I'd managed to salvage from my old apartment. As I unpacked the boxes, this overwhelming feeling came over me of how lucky I had been. Not only had I made it out of that fire alive, but so had Lily, and I had one person to thank for that.

Dylan.

Just the thought of that man made my skin tingle. Truthfully, I'd been thinking about him so much since we'd met, and no matter what I tried, I couldn't get the image of him standing in front of me out of my head, his face coated in soot, holding Lily in his big, strong hands. The way his biceps curved through his t-shirt, and that caring look in his eyes, tugged at my heart...and at my lady parts. Being around him had made me realize how much I missed sex.

When I had woken up on Sunday, I'd been overwhelmed with the need to see him. I'd tried coming up with excuses to go to his firehouse, but everything sounded lame. I had decided an offering of gratitude was sufficient enough, and next thing I knew, I was in my new kitchen baking brownies.

When I had showed up at Ladder 64, six blocks from my new apartment, there had been so many butterflies in my stomach that I'd felt like a giddy schoolgirl. I had been so nervous and excited about seeing Dylan again that it hadn't dawned on me he might not be there.

After leaving disappointed, I'd spent the walk home beating myself up. I had been so desperate to see him that I had painted this picture in my head of me showing up there, giving him brownies, him asking me out, and us living happily ever after. I had never considered it wouldn't go as planned. I had to devise a new way to find him because not seeing that man again simply wasn't an option.

The buzzer next to my door went off, pulling me out of my flashback of the day before. "Furniture delivery," the man at the front desk's voice came through the speaker. Over the next three hours, my apartment went from being sparse to actually being a home. Lily leaped up onto our new couch, meowing loudly. I had a feeling we were both going to be quite happy there.

I spent the rest of the day shopping for some new clothes, and as I was leaving Macy's, I opened the door to find Drew standing on the other side. I'd managed to avoid randomly running into him for over a year, and after what had gone down the other night, I somehow ran into him...in Herald Square of all places. One-million people commuted through that area on any given day. A *million* people. Seriously, Universe?

"Autumn," he said, sounding surprised. "Hi."

"Hey," I replied curtly.

"Replacing your wardrobe?"

I held up my bags. "Yeah. I couldn't salvage any clothes from my apartment."

There was sympathy in his eyes. "I'm really sorry to hear that."

I shrugged. "At least it's just stuff. It's replaceable. What are you doing here?"

He shifted on his feet, a telltale sign that what he was about to tell me wasn't going to be the whole truth. "I need to pick up a few things for work."

I gave him a look that said I knew better. "Really?"

"I forget how well you know me, Autumn." He shook his head and laughed. "Truth be told, I was actually here to pick up something I ordered." He paused as though he wasn't certain he should finish his sentence, but he did. "Something for you."

"For me?" I cocked my head.

Drew shifted. "With everything you just went through, I thought you deserved a little something to cheer you up."

I couldn't help the smile that escaped my lips. "That's very sweet of you, Drew."

He smiled back at me, and for the briefest second, I felt *something*. Not like I wanted to *be* with him, but for a moment, it felt good to be thought of and cared for in that way again.

"I was planning on delivering it to your office, but since you're here, would you want to go to Rowland's with me for a drink?"

Rowland's was a restaurant inside Macy's. Drew and I used to shop there often and go to Rowland's afterward to show off our new finds over a drink. The mention of this "norm" that was no longer our normal made my stomach flop. I should have politely declined and headed home because spending time with Drew was most certainly a bad idea, but my mouth spewed out, "Sure," before my brain could stop it.

Drew's face lit up with an ear-to-ear smile. "Great. You head on over and I'll be there shortly."

He proceeded past me and faded into the store, while I stood anchored in place for a minute, my mind racing. I could just leave. Granted, that wouldn't be the nicest thing to do, but it was what I should've probably done. I needed to leave Drew in the past. Or I could go and have that drink, prove to myself that I'd indeed moved on from that man, and then go home, satisfied that I finally got closure.

The latter won out, and minutes later, I found myself sitting on a barstool, my shopping bags gathered around my feet. The bartender greeted me, and I ordered an Old Fashioned for Drew—hoping that was still his drink—and a sparkling cherry lemonade for myself. I didn't drink alcohol, or rather I couldn't, so "going for drinks" to me meant getting a lemonade with soda water and a splash of grenadine.

When I had turned twenty-one and had started going out to bars with my friends, this bartender at one of our favorite places had come up with that drink for me. He had even put it in a champagne flute so I wouldn't feel left out sitting there drinking water. It had been a sad day when we went into the bar one night to find out he had quit. I never saw him again, but I thought about him every time I went out for "drinks."

Drew walked up and sat down on the stool next to me. I couldn't help but feel a little awkward being there with the man who had broken my heart, doing something we used to do together back when I was his and we were happy.

"Old Fashioned." He smirked. "You remembered."

I nodded, taking a sip of my drink, not knowing what else to say.

Drew covered my hand with his. "Thank you for agreeing to come here with me, Autumn. It really means a lot."

My cheeks flushed, and I hated my body for making me feel so vulnerable in front of him. "Sure," I muttered. I was at a loss for any other words. I fiddled with the hem of my sweater.

I'd made a mistake.

"How are you feeling?"

"Fine."

"What did the doctor say?"

I took a sip of my drink. "I didn't go."

"Really? Autumn, I don't think–"

I put my hand up. "Not your place, Drew."

He sighed. "You're right. I'm sorry."

The last thing I needed was a lecture from Drew about my health. He hadn't cared enough about it when we'd been dating, so he sure as heck had no right to suddenly care about it. I had thought about seeing my doctor, but I'd been feeling perfectly well since the fire, and the less I had to confront my condition, the better.

Drew changed the subject. "I'm not going to lie, Autumn, seeing you on my doorstep the other night certainly caught me off guard, but I'm glad you came over. I'm glad that you felt you could come to me."

"Well, I appreciate you letting me stay," I offered as an olive branch. Although, I was really thinking I hadn't run to him in my time of need in the way he believed I had. I'd been in shock and hadn't thought it through. It'd been an impulsive decision.

He took the shopping bag he'd placed on the chair next to him moments earlier and put it on the bar in front of me. "This is for you."

"Thank you." I smiled, touched he'd thought of me, but that little voice inside my head screamed not to open it and just leave.

I ignored her.

I dug into the bag to find a shoebox that contained a pair of my favorite Ugg slippers. Slippers that Drew always used to make fun of me for wearing because he thought they were ugly.

"I figured yours might've been ruined in the fire. I didn't want you to not have them anymore. Especially since it's winter. I know how much you love them."

I didn't know if it was my heightened emotional state since the fire, or if it was the pent-up emotion I'd been harboring since our break-up, but I leaned over and planted a kiss on Drew's cheek.

You idiot! that voice in my head screamed at me.

I pulled myself back, away from him. "I'm sorry. I don't know why I did that. Thank you for these. You were right, mine were destroyed."

Drew put his hand on my thigh, and my skin recoiled at his touch. "Please, don't apologize. Especially not for that." He squeezed my thigh. "Honestly, I'm the one who needs to apologize to you. I was an idiot. A jerk. A complete and utter ass."

Well, we agreed there. I wondered where the conversation was going.

"Seeing you the other night in my apartment—*our* apartment—wearing *my* clothes, made me realize just how stupid I was to let you go." He put his free hand on top of mine, which was perched on the bar. "I am so sorry. I wish I had a better reason to give you other than I was stupid. I didn't realize what I had—what we had—until I no longer had you. I threw away the best thing that has ever happened to me, and I'll never forgive myself for that, for hurting you."

My mouth went dry, and I was immobilized in my seat. He was still holding my thigh and my hand, but I couldn't feel his touch. My body was numb, and I was at a complete loss for words. I'd longed to hear him say those words for sixteen months, but actually hearing him say them...I didn't know what to do or how to feel.

"I can only pray you'll forgive me for abandoning you like I did. I promise I'll *never* do anything to hurt you again. I'll never be so selfish again. I'll be there for you always, as long as you let me because I love you. Please, baby, tell me I'm not too late. Tell me it's not too late for us."

He looked at me with those sad puppy dog eyes, and I was stunned. There were so many things I wanted to say to him. I'd literally fantasized about this moment where he'd come back groveling and I'd get my chance to stomp on his heart like he'd stomped on mine. With the moment upon us, however, I couldn't get the words out. Thoughts raced through my head.

Where was this man when I needed him?

Where was this declaration of love back then?

Why now, after all this time, was he having this epiphany?

Why, since we broke up over a year ago, has he not once tried to contact me?

How was it possible that he loved me now, when he'd told me on that brutal day that he wasn't in love with me anymore?

And how dare he. I'd cried too many tears over him.

I wanted to scream. I wanted to cry. I wanted to punch him in the chest. But I did none of those things. I mustered up every ounce of strength I had and calmly took a sip of my drink. I opened my purse, put a five-dollar bill on the bar, and collected my bags (including the slippers because as much as I was trying to take the high road, I really wanted those slippers, and let's face it, I'm human).

I looked Drew square in the eyes and said, "I'm not your baby anymore."

I stood up and walked away, telling myself repeatedly not to look back at him, despite the protests he lobbed in my direction as I left the bar.

My legs carried me quickly through the store and out onto the sidewalk where the cold air hit me, taking my breath away —a breath I'd apparently been holding since I had left Drew behind in the bar. I couldn't believe that had happened. I couldn't believe I had done that. I hailed a cab, not wanting to take on the responsibility of walking or navigating the subway home while in such an emotional state. I wanted to get as far away from there as quickly as possible. As my cab pulled away from the curb, Drew burst through the doors, looking around frantically. For me, no doubt. I let out a sigh of relief.

Holy smokes. That. Just. Happened.

During the ride back to my new apartment, I heard sirens coming toward us from up ahead. Hearing sirens in New York City was commonplace, and typically, I wouldn't give it a second thought, but as the source of the sirens approached, I realized the front of the truck *read Ladder 64*, and my heart did a flip. As it passed by my cab, I craned my neck to look up, and sitting there, in the window seat, was Dylan.

My lungs involuntarily seized for a few moments. He was so much sexier than I remembered. My heart leaped as I recalled the moment when he'd pulled Lily out of his coat pocket. The pride on his face gave me butterflies in my stomach. As the truck sped past, I said a silent prayer that wherever he was heading, he'd be kept safe.

Mere moments before, I had been freaking out. The man who caused me the biggest heartbreak of my life had just proposed we get back together. But, in one instant of seeing Dylan's face, all of the panic in my gut had dissipated, and instead, a huge smile took over my lips. I groaned as I imagined what his lips would feel like.

That voice inside my head set off warning bells. I'd developed feelings for a man I didn't even know. This had heartbreak written all over it, yet I didn't care. I wanted to risk it. For Dylan, I wanted to risk it. And at that moment, I was too excited to feel scared.

8

DYLAN

*T*hat was one of the most brutal tours I'd ever worked. I couldn't wait to get home, eat dinner, watch the hockey game, and collapse on my bed for the next sixteen hours — at least. We had run around for what felt like the entire shift. There hadn't been anything major, just a bunch of bullshit calls, but sometimes, those were worse than actually catching a job.

I showered before leaving the station and went to grab some takeout from my favorite Chinese restaurant — well, my favorite outside of Chinatown — a few blocks away before driving back home to Yonkers. I ordered my usual Kung Pao Beef and sat down in a chair, chugging a Coke and willing myself not to fall asleep before my food was ready. As I sat there, I reflected on my day, bitter about not having the time to really investigate and find out a way to contact Autumn.

A few of the guys had made some cracks about her showing up at the station the day before looking for me, and it had taken every ounce of self-control I had not to punch them in the mouth for the way they had spoken about her. Me having "saved Autumn's pussy" was apparently their favorite topic, and knowing the guys were lusting after my girl made my blood boil.

Okay, okay, she technically wasn't *my* girl, and I had no right to stake such a claim over her, but every time the guys mentioned how hot she was, and how delicious her brownies were, knowing full well they weren't talking about the baked goods, I wanted to punch them.

I wanted to slap myself in the face until I snapped out of it. I'd never felt so consumed by a woman that quickly before. I needed to find her. I wouldn't be able to let it go until I did, and I planned to exhaust every avenue. I pulled out my phone and typed *Autumn Bianchi + Manhattan* into the search bar. Unfortunately, the service in the restaurant wasn't great so it was taking forever to load the results.

I pictured her in my mind's eye, clear as day, standing in front of me in those shorts and wrapped in my bunker coat, *my* name written across her back. She was so unbelievably sexy. When we had been sitting there on the back of the ambulance, our thighs touching, my arm around her back, I had so badly wanted to kiss her to find out if her lips felt as soft as they looked. Though I don't think my captain would've approved, so it was probably for the best that we'd both had oxygen masks on.

Mr. Chen, the owner of the restaurant, interrupted my fantasy and pointed at me. "Yours almost ready." Then I heard him call out, "Autumn?"

My heart stopped. I swear to you, my heart actually stopped beating for a few seconds. I looked around to see if I could find the woman who would answer. And I did. I could only see her from behind, but I knew, without a doubt, it was her. Her ass was unmistakable. Standing there in the flesh, right before my eyes, was the woman I'd been daydreaming about. I jumped to my feet, suddenly wide awake, and pushed my way up to the counter through the crowd.

I reached my arm past her and handed Mr. Chen my credit card. "I've got hers, too."

Her head snapped around, a look of annoyance and something else—fear?—on her face for just a moment, but it faded into a smile when recognition set in. That big, beautiful smile I'd longed to see for the past four days.

"Dylan?" she said, her eyes wide with surprise.

I flashed her a grin. "Looks like we're meeting again, after all, Autumn."

She placed her hand on my arm, and electricity jolted through my whole body. The other night hadn't been a fluke. Our connection was real. She must've felt it, too, because she quickly pulled her hand away. "You really don't have to pay for my food. You've done enough for me. In fact, I'll pay for your dinner."

She reached into her purse, fumbling with her wallet. It looked like I might be under her skin in the same way she'd gotten under mine. God, I hoped so.

"Too late. It's already done," I said.

"Well, thank you," she replied, before pointing at my chest. "But next time, I'm paying."

I couldn't contain my grin. "Next time, huh?"

She blushed. Clearly, she hadn't realized the implication of her statement until after she'd said it. "I always settle my debts. And now I owe you three. One for Eli, one for Lily, and now one for dinner."

I laughed. "You don't owe me, Autumn, really. That being said, if you *thinking* you owe me means I get to see you three more times, then it's a deal." I held my hand out for her to shake.

She shook her head and laughed, taking my hand. "Deal."

My fingers tingled for several minutes after she pulled her hand away from mine. Her soft skin was cold from having been outside, but the heat between us was unmistakable.

Mr. Chen interrupted us, handing my food over the

counter. I took it and, not wanting the moment to end, blurted out, "I was planning on taking this home, but seeing as we're both here getting takeout, would you want to have dinner with me? If you don't already have other plans, that is." My heart beat rapidly in my chest, willing her to say yes. Before she could answer, I added, "If you say yes, we can count this as repayment for one of those debts you claim to owe me."

She giggled. I'd never get sick of hearing that sound. "Sure, I'd love to have dinner with you."

I looked around the small restaurant, not seeing any available tables. *Think. Think. Think.* I wasn't about to blow the opportunity because we had nowhere to eat.

She beat me to it. "Looks like this place is full, but my new apartment is two blocks from here if you'd like to go there. All my new furniture was delivered today. We can break it in."

My cock twitched at the thought of christening her new bed, her new couch, her new desk, hell, her whole apartment. Behave, I warned myself. This woman was different. This woman was so much more.

Her face reddened, as though she realized how I'd taken what she said. "I mean —"

"Sounds great," I interrupted, saving her the embarrassment of having to backpedal.

I grabbed her takeout bag from her, and she immediately protested, but I wasn't wavering. I felt like I was in middle school again, carrying the pretty girl's books to her class. We briskly walked the couple of blocks back to her place, as the wind had really picked up, whipping us with a bitter cold.

She shuddered. "God, I can't wait for spring. It's just so flipping cold out."

"It's not that *flipping* cold," I teased at her choice of words.

She cocked her head. "Are you making fun of me?"

I couldn't hold back my laughter.

She responded by playfully punching me in the arm. She wrinkled her nose, making a face at me, and it was the cutest thing I'd ever seen. "As I was saying, you've got to admit, this winter has been brutal."

Truthfully, the cold hadn't phased me. "I kinda like it."

"No way. It's, like, thirteen degrees outside, not counting the wind chill." The appalled look on her face made me smile.

"I guess I've never really minded the cold. I used to play hockey and I go skiing a bit."

She looped her arm in mine and tucked her body against me as though it were the most natural place for her to be. It felt right.

Her teeth chattered. "I've never been skiing before."

"We'll have to change that." Presumptuous of me, perhaps, but I knew this was only the beginning of us.

She tried to disguise her smile, but I caught it. "I'm not convinced hurling myself down a mountain at high speeds in the cold winter is a good idea."

"You won't even feel the cold after your first run."

"Yeah, because I'll be an icicle." She wrinkled her nose.

I laughed. "No, because your body warms up pretty quickly from exertion."

"If I'm going to willingly be outside in the snow, it's because I'm sipping tea in a hot tub."

The visual of being in a hot tub with Autumn in a bikini, her legs draped over mine while flurries fell around us, sent blood rushing to my cock. I was in trouble with this one.

"Sign me up for that. When do you want to go?" I hadn't expected her to agree to go anywhere with me, but a part of me wished she would.

"We haven't even made it to our first dinner together and you're planning a vacation?" she replied, seemingly amused by my antics.

"Planning ahead." I shrugged. "You said you still owe me two."

"That I do."

When we arrived at her building, she dropped my arm and

sprinted to the door. She waved at the doorman and I followed suit as we made our way past the reception desk and into the elevators. It was a nice building. Really nice. The lobby was marble and there were several fresh flower arrangements scattered throughout. I wondered what she did for a living to afford a place like that. Even with overtime, I wouldn't be able to touch that place on my salary.

As we rode the elevator up to the fourteenth floor, I imagined what it'd be like to ride her in that elevator. Her back up against the mirrored panes. Legs up around my waist. Her hands holding onto the bar to support herself. Me pinning her to the wall with my hard—

Maybe going back to her place wasn't the best idea, after all. I was crazy about her, and I didn't know if I could trust myself to be a gentleman. I needed to keep my mind away from anything sexual.

"Thank you for bringing those brownies by the station, by the way. That was really nice of you."

She grinned. "You're welcome. I'm glad you liked them. I was worried they'd be too sweet. I read the recipe wrong and accidentally added too much sugar." She blushed as she looked down at her feet. It was cute.

"Not at all. They were perfect." I didn't have the heart to tell her the other guys had devoured them before I'd even gotten there. Damn, I wanted to devour her—have her sweet juices run down my chin. That's all the sugar I'd need. Just the thought was making me hard. I moved the takeout bags so they blocked my awakening erection. I didn't want to scare her off before spending any real time with her.

She retrieved her keys from her pocket as the elevator approached the fourteenth floor. We walked up to her door, and she hesitated for a moment before putting the key in the lock. I leaned over and whispered in her ear, "I promise I'm not a serial killer."

She laughed. "Oh, and you would tell me if you were,

would you?" She turned the key in the lock, and then swung the door open.

"Ask Lily. She can vouch for me." I closed the apartment door, instinctively locking it behind me. While I was glad to be there with Autumn, I hoped she didn't make a habit of inviting strangers into her home. I might need to talk to her about that.

She had a small entry way that opened up into a large open-concept room. The apartment was mostly bare, save for furniture, but that hadn't been a surprise given that she'd just moved in and had to replace her things. Again, I wondered how she afforded a place like that. The address alone was expensive, but from the looks of it, she had a two bedroom, which put her in a whole new required income category—one I couldn't touch. It intimidated the hell out of me.

Autumn scooped a familiar ball of fur up off the floor. "Lily? What do you think? Is Dylan a serial killer?"

Lily meowed on cue.

"Sounds like a 'no' to me." I walked through the apartment to put our dinner down on the kitchen island before going back into the living room area to pet Lily. "Hey, girl, remember me?" Before I could finish my question, she leaped out of Autumn's arms and into mine. We both broke out in laughter. "I'll take that as a yes."

"Definitely a yes." She grinned.

Lily purred loudly in my arms as I stroked the top of her head with my finger. Autumn took off her coat and headed over to the kitchen island to lay out our Chinese food. I bent down and whispered to the kitten, "I hope your mom likes me as much as you do." She licked my nose. I'd never been a cat person, but I suspected that was about to change.

I caught Autumn looking at us with a huge smile on her face. "What?" I asked slyly, knowing full well that if you won over a girl's pet, you were in.

"I can't believe how much she likes you. She isn't that affectionate with anyone else besides me."

I shrugged. "We're bonded. She did ride in my pocket during a traumatic event, after all. No big deal."

Autumn came over and gave Lily a kiss on the head, and she placed her hands over mine. "You're our hero."

She looked up at me with those big, sparkling, hazel eyes, and my heart raced in my chest. Autumn's mouth opened slightly, and her breathing got heavier. I knew that look. Desire coursed through her just as it did me. Even Lily stilled in my arms, as if sensing the passionate tension in the air. It took every ounce of self-control I had to not bend down and kiss Autumn.

No, the voice in my head warned, *don't rush with her.*

For the first time since we had met, I got a good look at her body. That first night she had worn a baggy sweatshirt, and at the restaurant she had been wearing a bulky jacket. In that moment, however, she was wearing dark skinny jeans and a V-neck cashmere sweater that hugged her curves in all the right places. The swell of her breasts poked out of her low-cut neckline. They were perfect handfuls, just begging for my grasp. Her narrow waist curved down to her hips, which I imagined gripping as I pulled her down on top of me.

My cock jolted in my pants, and I forced myself to break our intense eye contact. "Shall we eat?" I asked, needing to interrupt that moment of closeness between us before I pushed too far and scared her away.

She slid her hands off mine and took Lily from me, placing her down on the couch. I pulled the stool out for Autumn, and she thanked me before taking her seat at the kitchen island while I took my place next to her.

"Thanks for laying this out," I said. "This is a much nicer way to have dinner than I'd originally planned. Better company, too."

She blushed. "Next time, I'll cook us a proper dinner."

"Deal," I said before taking a sip of my water. "Unless

you're not a good cook, in which case I'll gladly get us more takeout."

"Ha. Ha. I can cook. Thank you very much." She wrinkled her nose at me.

"What do you like to cook?" I asked, before taking a bite, which reminded me of how I hadn't had any time to eat that day. I was suddenly starving.

"Italian, mostly. Some Latin dishes, too. I make a pretty good mofongo."

I put down my fork and turned to look at her. "Mo-what-o?"

She giggled and broke it down for me. "Mo-fon-go. It's a Puerto Rican dish with plantains and chicharrons."

"Oh." I nodded, not wanting to sound stupid again.

As though she knew me already, she offered up, "Chicharrons are fried pork skins."

My eyes went wide, and I pushed my plate back. "Why don't we just throw this out," I indicated the Chinese food, "and you can make that instead?"

I was certain I'd never get tired of hearing her laugh. "Sounds good, doesn't it?" she tempted me.

"Sounds incredible. How'd you learn to make that?"

"My…housekeeper was from Puerto Rico. Alma. She taught me several traditional recipes when I was a kid. I loved cooking with her."

I noticed her hesitation and made a mental note to ask her more about it later, once we weren't strangers anymore. "Well, you should definitely make that for us sometime."

"Maybe I will." She winked. "If you're lucky."

"Maybe I'll let you," I retorted. "If you're lucky."

She smiled big, showing off the tiny wrinkles in the corners of her eyes. That woman had me mesmerized by her beauty and enthralled with her playful personality. There was intimacy in sharing a meal together in her home. It could've been awkward, but it wasn't. Far from it. She was easy to be around, and I felt like I could talk to her. Like I could be myself. I hadn't felt a connection like that with someone since Jenna. At the realization, guilt welled up in my throat. I knew Jenna would want me to move on and be happy, but the thought of replacing her made me nauseous.

The relationships I'd been in since Jenna had been good, but no other woman had compared to her—which, inevitably, was why none of them had worked out. It was also probably why I'd been okay with dating those girls in the first place. I knew I wouldn't be betraying Jenna.

Out of a desperate need to wipe those thoughts from my head, I changed the subject. "Speaking of lucky, this is a really great apartment. How'd you manage to find one so quickly?"

"I work for a property management firm, so I actually get to live in one of our units rent-free."

My pride silently celebrated. "That's one hell of a job perk."

She nodded. "For sure. I called my boss Friday and told him what happened. He had this place secured for me by that afternoon."

"That's awesome." I swallowed my bite before probing for more. "What do you do there?"

She dabbed her mouth with her napkin before placing it back on her lap. "I'm the Director of Property Management and Leasing."

"Sounds fancy."

"Yeah, I guess." She shrugged. "I'm one of the highest-ranked people at the firm, just below the C-Level executives. I worked really hard to make my way up in the company pretty quickly."

"I bet. I know this goes against all etiquette, but if you don't mind me asking, how old are you?"

She reached for her water. "I'm twenty-five."

I tried not to feel intimidated, but truth be told, I was a little. "That's very impressive, Autumn."

Her smile fell for a split second before she replied,

"Thanks." Her hands fidgeted with the bottom of her sweater. Clearly, she was uncomfortable with being complimented. I wondered why that was.

"I feel like there's more to this story," I pressed.

She sighed, her shoulders slumping slightly. "I don't normally talk to people about this, but not everyone in the company appreciates having me as their boss. It can be difficult at times, being so young and having people twice my age working under me."

I nodded, appreciative that she decided to share that with me. "That's shitty, but understandable. My big brother doesn't take me seriously." I laughed. "So I'd imagine being in that situation in a corporate setting is tough."

She fidgeted with her sweater again, rolling the fabric between her fingers. "Unfortunately, I'm kind of used to it."

"Why is that?"

She paused before responding, as though she were weighing whether or not to answer me. She looked down at her lap and smoothed out the hem of her sweater with her fingertips. "I graduated high school at sixteen and went straight into college, so I've always been looked down upon because of it."

"Sixteen? Wow."

"I was homeschooled most of my life and really pushed myself through my education." Her face flushed a little.

I hadn't meant to embarrass her. I truly was in awe of her. "Being homeschooled must have been interesting."

She snorted and vehemently shook her head. "No. What was interesting was going to college after having spent the better half of the preceding decade being homeschooled."

"I'm sure it was." I nodded, imagining what a shock that must have been for her. "Did you go to NYU?"

She angled her brows. "How'd you know?"

"I'm psychic."

"Seriously?"

I couldn't keep a straight face. "I'm messing with you. I noticed the sweatshirt you had on the other night."

"I actually believed you for a second."

I leaned closer and dropped my voice. "Maybe I am a little psychic. I said the other night I'd be seeing you again."

"And here we are."

I nodded. "Told you."

She giggled. That was quickly becoming my favorite sound. She intrigued me and I wanted to know everything about her.

"So, how'd you get into property management?"

"Kind of by accident, actually." She dabbed her mouth with her napkin. "I got an internship with my company when I was eighteen, and I've been there ever since. Turned out I was good at it, and I like working with people. I'm also not stuck at a desk all day, which is wonderful. And I have plenty of fantastic coworkers."

"But?"

"How'd you know there was a but?"

"Guess I'm getting good at reading you."

She stared at me for a beat, as though she were trying to figure me out, before she continued. "Nancy, she was the Director before me, retired last summer, and I got promoted into her position. There are definitely people in the firm who are not happy about it."

"Screw them. Sounds like you earned it."

"I do my best."

She was incredible. Her humility was a turn on, and she was obviously brilliant. I should've been happy as a pig in shit that she had wanted to get to know me, but there was no way she'd ever be happy with a simple fireman. *How does she not have a boyfriend?* A woman that sexy and successful had to have guys throwing themselves at her. I was up for some healthy competition, but I was a fireman, and while I'd say I was fairly smart–I kind of had to be, having a principal for a mom–I'd never been described as the intellectual type.

Maybe I wasn't the kind of guy Autumn was looking to be in a relationship with. Maybe she just saw me as a few fun nights. That thought made my heart hurt. She'd never been mine in the first place, but it suddenly felt like I was mourning the loss, anyway.

"Dylan." She stopped me from overthinking. "Everything okay? You look like you zoned out there for a minute."

Shit. She'd caught me. "Sorry." I willed my brain to come up with something clever, but I went with honesty. "I'm just trying to understand how a woman as beautiful and successful as you are could possibly be single."

That playful smile danced across her face again. "Who said I was single?"

Fuck, I was confused. "You told me the other night that you didn't have a boyfriend."

"I believe I said the guy whose house I was going over to was not my boyfriend."

I wiped my hand over my face; how could I have messed that one up so badly? I thought she had been flirting back with me, but I guess that was her personality. Or maybe she was only being nice because I saved her cat? I shuddered at the thought.

My chest hurt. "I'm so sorry. I misunderstood. Of course, you have a boyfriend. I apologize if I've made you uncomfortable, I thought—"

She busted out laughing. "Dylan, I'm kidding! I couldn't resist." She put her hand on my arm. "You look so upset, though. I'm sorry. I was just messing with you."

My arm burned beneath her hand, sending goosebumps up to my shoulder, and I didn't want her to ever let go. She had gotten me good, all right. I couldn't be upset about it, though. I was too relieved that she was kidding. And, it turned out I liked her playfulness.

I shot her a grin. "You're lucky you're cute, Autumn."

"Does that mean you forgive me?"

I shrugged.

"No?" she asked in a lower, more seductive tone. The nervous girl who'd been sitting next to me moments earlier was gone, and a hint of the woman-in-charge I'd seen the night of the fire emerged.

My heart thundered in my chest. "I'll think about it."

She stood up, but instead of removing her hand from my forearm, she trailed her fingers tenderly up my bicep, positioning herself behind me and then covering my shoulders with her hands. She leaned over, her breasts pressed against my back, and whispered in my ear, "I'll make it up to you."

Chills crawled up my spine as I felt every breathy word in my body.

She continued in that low, seductive voice that dripped with desire. "You must be tired and sore after working all day. I'll have you know I give fantastic massages."

I moaned as she started kneading my shoulders with her hands. It felt so fucking good. I didn't know which was better: the massage or simply knowing it was *Autumn* touching me. My cock stirred under my jeans, and if she kept touching me like that, it'd be only a matter of minutes before I was fully erect. But stopping her was out of the question. After the tour I'd just suffered through, her fingers kneading my sore muscles felt unbelievably good. I couldn't remember the last time a woman had offered to give me a massage. Autumn's touch was nothing short of magical.

"You're so tense. I'm going to grab some lotion and we'll work out a few of these knots."

Before I had a chance to protest, she'd already removed her hands and was off toward the bathroom. I took that moment alone to adjust my cock and tuck it up behind my waistband. I could hear Autumn's footsteps approaching as I quickly pulled my sweatshirt down over the exposed head.

She grabbed my hand from my lap, and I froze for a

second, worried she'd feel my erection and know how hard *she'd* made me. Thankfully, she didn't notice.

"Come on." She pulled me away from the kitchen island and led us into the living room. "Take a seat in this chair, it'll be more comfortable, and I can get better leverage to work out those knots."

I didn't want her to stop, but a part of me felt bad that she was doing this. I should've been taking care of her. "You don't have to, Autumn. It's okay, really."

She looked up at me, doe-eyed. "Does that mean you forgive me?" she asked teasingly, lightly touching my chest.

I sighed at the pleasure from her touch. "Of course."

"Good. But I'm not finished with you yet." She pushed my chest, forcing me to sit down in the oversized stuffed chair that sat perpendicular to her couch.

I bit down on my lip. She was driving me wild, and it was taking every bit of my restraint to keep me from scooping her up in my arms and having my way with her right there on her living room floor.

She was behind me again, but this time, instead of grabbing my shoulders, she ran her fingers over the top of my head and through my hair. I thought she was going to massage my scalp, but then she surprised me and pulled my head back, so I was looking up at her.

She bent down, lowering her face dangerously close to mine as she whispered in my ear, "I'm going to work these knots out for you, Dylan." Her fingers found that tender spot at the base of my skull. "And you're going to let me." She pushed my head back up and started massaging my neck.

I had chills over my entire body. That sweet girl I had gone home with earlier had another side to her I didn't expect. But I liked it. *Really* liked it. I was getting a glimpse into why she had been promoted to being a boss at only twenty-five years old. She had a shyness about her, but she also had the ability to be in control. I was all about it.

Whatever she was doing to my neck made my eyes roll to the back of my head, and I groaned. "God, that feels unreal."

I could practically feel her smiling behind me as her fingers dipped beneath my sweatshirt and skillfully moved over my shoulders. Tension I'd been holding onto for God knows how long began to melt away.

Autumn's voice penetrated my state of bliss. "This would be much easier if you took your sweatshirt off."

Without hesitation, I yanked it over my head, only remembering at the last possible second that my dick was standing up out of my pants. I quickly tossed the shirt over my lap, hoping I was fast enough so that Autumn didn't see anything. I was thoroughly enjoying the moment and didn't want to scare her off.

"Much better," she said, sounding satisfied. She popped open the cap on the lotion bottle, and I heard her rub her hands together before returning them to my bare shoulders. The lotion felt warm and helped her hands glide over my body.

I moaned. "You're killing me."

"Sounds like you like it, though."

"I do." I snorted. "Too much."

She bent down again and whispered in my ear, "No such thing as too much."

"If you were in my head right now, I think you'd disagree."

"Oh, would I?" she purred. "Why?"

"Trust me."

"You want more, don't you?"

My cock twitched. "So much more."

Her hands moved over my shoulders and rubbed the top of my pecs, just below the collarbone. She bent her mouth down to my ear and whispered in a low, primal tone, "Then it's not *too much*."

That was it. There was only so much self-control I could have, and I'd hit my limit. I spun my torso, wrapped my arms around her, and pulled her up and over the back of the chair, to cradle her in my lap. I was done playing her game.

She gasped and looked up at me, her mouth slightly ajar. The lust burning in her eyes matched my own. I held her in my arms, our faces only inches apart.

"Still not too much?" I whispered, practically growling.

She shook her head slightly, almost imperceptibly, and that was all I needed. I closed the gap between us and placed my forehead on hers, our lips millimeters apart, so close it felt as though we were taking the same breath.

"How about now?" As I formed the words, my lips softly grazed hers. I was too close to see her response, but I felt it. Her tongue slipped slightly between her lips as her teeth sucked her bottom lip into her mouth. She let out a small sigh that bordered on a moan, shattering my self-control.

I claimed her lips, sucking her top one between my own. She felt soft and plush, our kiss gentle for only a moment before she deepened it, wrapping her hands behind my head and pulling me down onto her harder. Her tongue came out to explore, and I let it dance with my own as I moved one of my arms up her back and into her hair, gripping it and holding her firmly against me. I never wanted it to end.

Kissing Autumn felt unlike anything I'd ever experienced. It was as though my body needed the seal of her lips on mine to breathe, yet, at the same time, I was breathless. Kissing this woman was something I was *meant* to do. Like I was put on this earth just to be with her. My heart clenched in my chest, suddenly overwhelmed with my feelings for her. I wanted more. So. Much. More.

And then I thought of Jenna.

The connection I had with Autumn scared me. I wanted it—wanted her—but I didn't want to disrespect what Jenna and I'd had. I kept my women at a distance for that reason, but Autumn threatened to crawl under my skin and call it home.

As badly as I wanted to go beyond that kiss and claim

Autumn's body as mine, I knew that had to wait. I couldn't rush with her. If our kiss were any indication, sex with Autumn would be more than just a casual fuck. It had to be. I didn't know if I was ready for that.

As painful as it was, I gradually toned things down and, loosening my grip on her hair, pulled our lips apart. If we kept going as we were, I might regret it, and I couldn't let things get out of control that night.

I held her against me still, her forehead on mine, both of us panting. I was at a loss for words. That kiss...hell, there were no words to describe it.

Autumn broke the silence with an exaggerated "Wow."

I let out a small, breathy laugh. "Yeah..."

"Before you ask, no, that was not too much." She brought her hand up to my face and traced my lips with her fingertip. "In fact, I think we should do a lot more of that."

I gave her a quick peck. "Me too, sweetheart." I forced myself to pull my face away from hers. "But not tonight."

Her smile dropped a little. "Why not?"

Because you scare me.

I took a long breath in. "At the risk of sounding like a total pussy, I don't want to rush this." Her smile returned, even bigger than before, and I knew I'd made the right decision. "I don't know about you, but nothing about that was normal for me. There's something about you that's...different. More. I felt it from the second you first touched me the other night when we met, and that kiss...that kiss was..." I searched for the words to do it justice, coming up short again.

"Wow?" she offered, a twinkle lighting up the corner of her eye.

"Yeah." I laughed. "Wow."

9

AUTUMN

*M*y alarm sounded and I silenced it, choosing to lay in bed a little while longer. I thought about the night before with Dylan. It had honestly been one of the best nights of my life. That might sound sad since we just stayed in and ate take out, but touching him had turned something on inside of me that I'd never felt before. I'd felt powerful. I didn't know what had come over me to make me so bold, but I'd had to get my hands on him, and the massage was the best idea I'd been able to come up with. And kissing him? Kissing him had been the most natural thing in the world coupled with the force of a volcanic eruption.

When he had stopped us from going beyond that kiss, every physical part of my being wanted to protest, but when he had said those things about not wanting to rush it, I'd melted. Some girls liked those tough alpha males, but Dylan was an alpha male with a sensitive side, and it was so incredibly sexy. Truth was, if we'd gone further, I would've embarrassed myself, so I was glad we stopped. The memory of that kiss would stay with me until I could see him again.

I grabbed my phone off the night stand and smiled when I saw Dylan's name on my screen.

Dylan: Good morning my beautiful girl xxoo
Me: Hey Handsome
Dylan: I'm gonna bring over a pizza later. What kind do you like?
Me: Anything with sausage
Dylan: You got it
Me: And no anchovies! Yuck!
Dylan: Extra anchovies. Got it.

Our banter came naturally, and I really enjoyed it. When he had gone to leave at the end of the night, there had been no way I was letting him go without having plans to see (and kiss) him again, so I had asked him to come back the next day and help me set up the internet and mount the television. He'd gladly obliged, and knowing I'd get to spend the day with him had turned me into a giddy teenager. Except, I had never dated as a teenager, so I imagined that's what it was like to fawn over your first real high school boy.

While I put myself together for the day, I continued to reminisce about the night before. I was proud of myself. Dating Drew had only reinforced the belief my parents had instilled in me: I was fragile. But I didn't want to be that fragile girl anymore. Dylan brought out a persona I'd secretly fantasized about being: the woman in control. I'd been able to tap into that side of me while I was at work, but it wasn't something I'd utilized in my love life before.

I recalled how this big, strong man had melted under my touch and that gave me the confidence I desperately needed. I'd woken up feeling like a completely new version of myself. A better version. The more I'd rubbed Dylan's shoulders, the more desire had pulsated from his body, which had only fueled me further. I'd taken control, teasing him until he couldn't restrain himself any longer. *I* had done that. And when he'd kissed me...God, when he'd kissed me! I'd felt like I was in another dimension.

Granted, the only guy I'd ever kissed before Dylan was Drew, but what Dylan and I had blew any connection I thought I'd had with Drew out of the water. Dylan was a man. There was nothing tentative about the way he'd kissed me. No, it had been unapologetically strong, claiming me. It'd been so unbelievably hot. I wanted more. No—I *needed* more.

I wondered if he hadn't stopped us from going further, would I have? The desire I had felt was so overwhelming, I seriously would've had a hard time turning him down, but would I have been okay going there with him so soon? Letting him see my scar?

My best friend had no problem with casual sex, and she certainly wasn't shy about sharing the details of her escapades with me. Britt made it sound easy. When I had told her about Dylan while she'd helped me move, she'd suggested that I pursue a physical relationship with him. Although she was a little less lady like in her suggestion. She'd said firemen were every woman's fantasy. I had to admit there was something appealing about the no-strings-attached thing, but I struggled with the idea of actually going there with someone.

The more I thought about it, the more I realized how grateful I was that Dylan had stopped our kiss from taking us further. While I'd been more confident than ever last night, I was pretty sure my fear would've won out in the end, and I would've had to stop things. Truthfully, I didn't know how I would've done that, so thankfully, I hadn't had to deal with it, and I could still ride the wave I was on, feeling confident and powerful.

At noon on the dot, the intercom next to my door buzzed, the doorman telling me Dylan arrived. I straightened the velvet mini skirt I was wearing and adjusted my bra, lifting my boobs so my cleavage looked just the way I wanted it to. When Dylan knocked on my door, I was already standing with my hand on the knob. I took a deep breath and counted to five before opening it. I didn't want to seem too desperate.

"Hey," I said casually as I pulled my hair over the front of my shoulder. He was even sexier than I remembered. He was freshly shaven, which showed off his sexy jawline, and he looked refreshed. Until that point, the only times I'd seen Dylan had been when he was tired from work, and while he had looked good then, too, this was even better.

His smile stretched from ear to ear. "Hey there." He entered my apartment and bent down to kiss my forehead. Warmth spread through my body. "Did you order a pizza with extra anchovies?"

I put my hand on my hip and cocked my head. "Hilarious."

After placing the box down on my kitchen counter, he unzipped his jacket and hung it on the back of the chair. His plain black V-neck shirt clung tightly to his torso. The sleeves cut at the perfect line on his bicep, and his pecs filled out the front of the shirt, making me desperately want to touch his chest. The thought made me suddenly aware of the warmth between my legs.

I turned around to close and lock the door, and heard the jingle of Lily's collar behind me. When I turned back around, she was rubbing herself against Dylan's legs. "It is seriously impressive how affectionate she is with you."

He bent down and patted her head. "Well, I hope she doesn't get jealous of her mama."

I folded my arms. "Oh, yeah?" I asked. "Why would she be jealous?"

In the next instant, Dylan crossed the apartment and wrapped me in his arms, lifting me off the ground. "Because of this," he uttered before pressing his lips to mine. His lips were slightly cold from having been outside, but his mouth was soothingly warm. He pulled my bottom lip between his, and I traced his top lip with my tongue, tasting him.

When he put me back on the ground and pulled away, I tossed my head back and groaned.

"Sorry," he said, his hands finding my hips. "I just couldn't wait to do that again. It's all I've been able to think about since last night."

"Me, too," I admitted. I held my eyes closed for a beat, breathing in his scent of cedar and spiced orange. When I opened them, I looked straight into his intoxicating blue eyes and got lost in the tenderness there.

His hands caressed my hips, and I saw his gaze dip down to my breasts for a fleeting moment. I liked being desired by Dylan. I reached for him and glided my palms over his chest, which was warm and hard under my touch.

"Feel free to do *that* anytime you want." I bit my lip. That man's ability to turn my desire up to a stratospheric level in just an instant was remarkable.

"Don't say that," he teased. "Or we'll never get anything else done today."

"An entire day in your arms doesn't sound so bad to me."

He lowered his forehead to mine. "You're something else, Autumn, you know that?"

I lowered my head, not wanting him to see me blushing. I was very aware of my rapid pulse. My body reacted to Dylan in a way that was unfamiliar, but I liked it. I glanced back up at him. "I think you're the special one, Dylan."

Lily meowed at our feet, making us both laugh and step back from our heated embrace. "Looks like Lily agrees with me." Not giving him a chance to argue, I asked, "Shall we eat while it's still hot? Or are you one of those cold pizza people?"

"Not gonna lie, I've been known to have cold pizza for breakfast on more than one occasion."

I grunted. "And just when I was thinking you were perfect."

"Sorry to disappoint." He flashed a smile in my direction, making me forget all about his pizza faux pas.

"Well, I'm eating my pizza properly. *Hot.* If you care to join."

He followed me across the room to the kitchen. I noticed

the six-pack sitting on the counter next to the pizza box and tensed. I wasn't prepared for *that* conversation. I watched Dylan open one of the bottles and extend it out to me. "I wasn't sure what kind of beer you liked, so I just went for a light lager."

I hesitated for a second before grabbing the bottle. "Thanks." I was too chicken to tell him I couldn't drink—too afraid I'd lose him before he was even mine to lose.

He clinked his bottle against mine and took a swig. I smiled back at him nervously before lifting my bottle to my lips. I took a tiny sip of the golden liquid, the bubbles tickling my throat on the way down. We ate the pizza, with sausage and peppers —my favorite—as I listened to Dylan tell me about why he was convinced the pizza place he went to was run by the mob, but their pizza was simply too good to care about that. He finished off his beer and grabbed another, offering to open a second one for me, which I declined.

"Do you not like this kind?" he asked, motioning to the nearly full bottle in front of me.

I forced myself to take another sip and swallow before replying. "No, it's good. Just savoring it, I guess."

I'd never had an alcoholic drink of my own before. I'd had sips of Drew's on occasion, and I actually found beer to be quite tasty. It really was a shame I couldn't have it. But in that moment, I was allowing myself the pleasure. What harm could one beer really do?

I'd like to say *we* hooked up the internet, mounted the TV, and hung some artwork, but really, Dylan did it all while I super-vised. Watching his muscles bulge slightly as he twisted the screwdriver made me noticeably warm between the legs. I kept imagining being underneath his chiseled body, those strong arms pinning me to the bed, while he buried himself deep inside me. *Where had this sex kitten come from?* I liked her. I finished my beer as I fantasized about being intimate with the tantalizing firefighter in my living room.

Dylan passed me another beer to replace my empty bottle, and I didn't say no. I'd never been drunk before, and I had to admit, I really liked the way I felt–loose and carefree. I wanted to feel more of that. I snapped out of my inner conversation and glanced over to find Dylan staring at me, a huge smile on his face.

"What?" I asked, wanting in on the secret.

"You're staring at that beer like you're about to declare your love to it. I'm a little jealous."

I laughed so hard I snorted, which only made me laugh harder as I collapsed on the couch. It must have been contagious because Dylan started laughing along with me. By the time I got myself back under control, I'd forgotten why I was even laughing in the first place.

"Dylan," I took another swig from the bottle, "I think I'm a little drunk." I laughed again because, apparently, laughing was what drunk-Autumn did.

Dylan came over and plopped himself down on the couch next to me, swinging my legs up over his lap. "You don't drink much, do you, sweetheart?"

"You caught me." I swallowed another sip. He took the full bottle from my hands, and I protested. "Hey, that's mine."

Dylan stopped me by placing a finger over my lips. "I think you've probably had enough. I don't want you to be so drunk you feel like I've taken advantage of you."

His pupils were dilated, and I saw the lust burning in his eyes. "What if I want you to?" I uttered, brave from the alcohol. "Take advantage of me, that is."

He moaned in response, and his hardness twitched under my thigh, which only made me wetter. He ran his fingers up my bare leg, stopping at the hem of my mini skirt. He gripped my thigh in his hand, his massive palm swallowing my leg up. I felt invincible under his touch. He rubbed my upper thigh, his thumb sneaking just under my hem. I was certain that he could feel the heat emanating off my sex, burning for him.

"God, sweetheart, you drive me wild. I know I said I want to take things slow, but if I'm being honest, I've never wanted anyone as much as I want you right now."

His words caused my breath to catch in my throat. The fact that a man like him could possibly want a girl like me was unbelievable in itself, but the sheer magnitude of his desire truly made me feel like the powerful woman I'd always wanted to be, but was too afraid to become.

"I'm all yours, Dylan," I whispered, my words dripping in lust and fueled by his desire.

"Fuck, Autumn," he growled as he wrapped his arm around my back and swiftly pulled me toward him, never taking his other hand off my thigh. He lowered his face to mine, stopping just before our lips touched. I felt his hand shift closer to my inner thigh and his fingers inched a little further up until my skirt rested on his knuckles, and the walls of my warm, wet center contracted in response to his closeness.

"I've been watching you walk around in this skirt all afternoon, and I've been craving to know what's underneath it."

I allowed my thighs to fall apart, giving him better access. "Why don't you go ahead and find out?" I whispered against his lips.

His mouth collided with mine, not gentle like before. This time, he was telling me just how much *more* he wanted, and I was so ready to give it to him. He sucked on my lips with such intensity, it felt as though I would become a part of him. His tongue darted into my mouth, in search of my own, and my core contracted in response. He kissed me like I was his lifeline, pulling him to safety from the wide-open sea. My heart exploded at the thought. I didn't just *want* this man. I *needed* him. With every fiber of my being, I needed him.

As though he could read my mind, he inched up further between my legs, stopping just inches from the apex between my thighs. He broke our kiss and looked me dead in the eyes. "Are you sure this is okay? I meant what I said last night. I don't want to move too fast. And I know you're tipsy, I don't want to do anything you'll regret."

The genuineness in his words and in his gaze warmed me. "I think the only thing I'll ever regret is not having you sooner."

And I meant it. That man awakened a part of me that'd been lying dormant inside forever, and now that I'd found him, I'd never let him go.

Dylan's lips met my neck as his fingertips brushed gently against the crotch of my lace thong. I tossed my head back and moaned.

"Damn, sweetheart, you are so fucking wet," he growled through his teeth as he rubbed his fingertips over my panties. His hand retreated, and before I could protest, he pulled me up and repositioned us so I was on his lap, straddling him.

I leaned down, and while I kissed him, I felt his hand move between his legs, adjusting the bulge trapped in his pants. I hiked my skirt up to my hips, my panties fully on display, so I could spread my legs far enough to lower myself onto him completely. He let out a moan, and his audible satisfaction encouraged me to grind myself against him. Dylan felt so big against my wet folds, and I ached for more of him. His hands came around and grabbed onto my ass, his fingers working their way under the strap of my thong and up to my hips, helping me move back and forth on top of him.

He broke our kiss and leaned forward, nestling his face in my breasts. His tongue ran up between the crease of my cleavage. "Fuck, sweetheart, I just want to devour you. I want to taste you...all of you."

It was so hot. He alternated between nibbling and licking along my exposed breast line, and I locked my fingers together behind his neck. His lust made me realize I'd never felt so wanted before. I loved every bit of it. Dylan's hands traveled up from my hips and along my sides, then he passed over my scar. Instinctively, I tensed and froze.

And he noticed.

Dylan looked up at me, concern in his eyes, and something else — like he was worried he'd hurt me or pushed me too far. "You okay?" he asked, as his hands slipped out from under my shirt.

I could breathe again. I nodded, unable to form words, tears threatening to sting my eyes. And just like that, my newfound power retracted, deep within.

Dylan pulled my hands off his neck and held them in his own. "What's wrong? Did I hurt you?"

"No," I whispered almost inaudibly through gritted teeth. I didn't know how I was going to get out of that one. I wasn't ready to tell him the truth yet because I was selfishly terrified of losing him, but I had to tell him something.

I spat out the first excuse that came to mind. "I think you're right. I drank too much." I scooted off his lap and hung my head, ashamed. It wasn't a total lie — I had drunk too much. I drank. Period.

He reached his hand out, and tipped my chin up to look at him. "Hey, it's okay, sweetheart. I'll wait. As long as it takes for you to be ready, I'll wait."

The earnestness in his eyes made me want to cry. I wanted this man with every fiber of my being, and there I was, screwing it all up because I was afraid. Afraid that once he knew the truth, he'd leave and break my heart. Just like Drew.

10

DYLAN

*A*utumn looked like she was about to cry, and I desperately wanted to go back in time and not touch her like I had. I should have been stronger. Things were different with her. I had to take it slow, but flirting with her all afternoon—watching her hips sway under that tight skirt—had worn down my defenses. I was a man who knew what he wanted. And I wanted her.

She was a little drunk, and I worried she'd think I was taking advantage of that, when that couldn't be further from the truth. I felt like a total prick.

"I'm sorry," she whispered, not meeting my gaze.

I needed to convince her that I wanted more than just her body for a good time. "It's okay. Really. I shouldn't have tried to go further with you when I knew you were tipsy. That's on me. I'm the one who's sorry."

She shook her head intensely. "No, Dylan. I wanted that, really I did. And I still do—just maybe on a day when I'm more clear-headed."

I lifted her hand up to my lips, kissing the back of it. "I'll wait as long as you want. I don't know what it is about you, but I know what we have is something worth waiting for."

She was worth it. Sure, it freaked me out, but the unexplainable connection we had was too irresistible to ignore. I knew if I hadn't given us a shot, I'd live to regret it.

She leaned forward and planted a soft kiss on my lips. "Thank you."

I stood up. "Shall we finish hanging up your artwork?" I gestured toward the stack of paintings and photographs piled in the corner.

"Sure." She stood and pulled her skirt back down. I caught a glimpse of her lacey black thong and knowing how wet it was made me bite my lip to hold back a moan. I would wait however long it took because I absolutely needed to know how she felt under my tongue and wrapped around my dick.

"I'm just going to use your restroom first." I gestured awkwardly at my erection that needed adjusting.

Her cheeks flushed, and she stammered, "Oh, uh, sure. Go ahead."

When I got to the bathroom, I shut the door behind me and pressed my back against the it, releasing a long-held sigh. She'd gotten to me. And it wasn't just our physical connection. She'd made me smile and laugh more in the past twenty-four hours than I had in weeks. Her intelligence, albeit a little threatening to my ego, was a serious turn-on, and our witty banter made me playful in a way I hadn't been since Jenna.

Jenna...

Hi, J, it's me. I really hope you're okay with this. I want you to know I'm not replacing you. I could never do that. This one seems special, though, J. I don't know what it is about her, but I feel like I need to pursue this. If this is the right thing to do—if she is the right one—send me a sign. Let me know you're okay with this. Love you.

I offered up a silent prayer in my head with the hope of calming some of the guilt stirring in my gut. I wanted to spend more time with Autumn and get to know her better. Clearly, our physical chemistry was off the charts, but I wanted more than just that with her. I wanted a real relationship. I'd nearly given up on the idea of getting married and having kids, but with Autumn, I thought I could open that door again.

I finished up in the bathroom and went back to the living room where I found Autumn sitting cross-legged on the floor wearing yoga pants and a cozy sweater, sipping from a water bottle. I couldn't help but smile. I liked seeing her like that, in her element, relaxing at home. It reminded me of the night we'd met.

She had a painting sitting in front of her of a girl dancing in a field of sunflowers. She was staring at it so intently that I didn't think she'd even realized I'd come back in the room. I sat down on the floor next to her, and she turned to me and smiled, placing a hand on my leg. "Thanks for helping me today. And thanks for being so cool about...you know."

I shrugged. "Happy to do it. I mean it. I'm just glad I get to spend more time with you. And don't worry about 'you know,'" I said, poking fun at her choice of words—or lack thereof, rather—making her laugh and breaking the tension from our emotionally-charged interaction earlier.

"I really like you, Dylan."

I smiled. "I like you, too, Autumn. A lot." I bent down and kissed the top of her head. "Do you know where you'd like to hang that one?" I asked, gesturing to the painting on the floor in front of her.

She sighed as she ran her hand over the top of the canvas. "This piece has been hanging in my bedroom since I was a little girl. Randomly, two weeks ago, it fell off my wall and the frame cracked. I took it to get fixed and hadn't had a chance to pick it up–thank goodness–because if I had, it would've been destroyed in the fire. I lost everything in my bedroom."

I put my hand on her shoulder, wishing I could take the pain of that away from her.

"This painting is a reminder of the beautiful world out there beyond these walls. I've always admired how free she looks, standing in that field, dancing among the flowers without a care in the world."

"That's lovely. I see what you mean."

She grinned at me. "It wouldn't feel right to hang her anywhere other than my bedroom."

And off to the bedroom we went. She picked a spot on the wall and laid back on her bed to admire it. She patted the mattress and looked up at me, waiting for me to join her. I hesitated.

She noticed. "I just want you to see it from here."

I laid down beside to her and looked up at the painting, centered across from the foot of her bed. It'd be the first thing she'd see when she woke up and the last thing she'd see before going to bed. At least that's what she said when she'd told me that's why she wanted me to hang it there.

Autumn scooted herself over until she was up against me. She lifted my arm around her back, and she laid her head on my chest, her arm across my abdomen. "Don't get awkward on me now, okay? I just want to be close to you."

Holding her close sent a warm sensation throughout my body. I'd never been much of a cuddler, but I felt the intimacy in it with Autumn, and I knew I'd be lying in bed alone later, craving that moment. The fear that'd crept in earlier had subsided. I got in my head too much sometimes. What Autumn and I shared was real, and the feel of her tucked into me felt right. I had to remember that.

"There's nothing awkward about this, sweetheart." I held her close and breathed in her smell, an intoxicating mix of coconut and gardenias. I tried to memorize how the weight of her head felt against my chest, and how the warmth of her arm draped across me made me feel...safe. I didn't know what to make of that.

Her voice interrupted my thoughts. "So tell me, how'd you get into firefighting?"

"Well," I murmured. "It's all I've ever wanted to do. My

dad was FDNY and my brothers and I all wanted to be, too. So now we are."

"Really? How long have you been a fireman?"

"Seven years. I was twenty-three when I got called up. My brother Jesse and I actually took the same test and ended up in the same hiring class."

Her finger traced my abs. I don't think she even realized she had been doing it. "Do you guys work together now, too?"

I shook my head. "Jesse was assigned to Brooklyn and he's been in the same house ever since. I went to Manhattan. I started off in the engine, but I moved across the floor to the truck three years ago."

"What'd you do before that? Did you go to college?"

"I got my Associates at Bronx C.C. I knew I was gonna be a fireman and that's all the schooling they required."

"That makes sense."

I was relieved my answer hadn't disappointed her, but still thought I needed to impress her. "While I was in college, Jesse and I started a small moving company together. We pooled our money and got a little donation from our mom to buy a truck. The business sustained us through college and our first year on the job."

"That's wonderful. Do you still do that?"

"No. It became too much for us. After a year of commuting to Brooklyn, Jesse decided to move to the south shore of Long Island to be closer to his firehouse, so he pulled out of the business. I kept things going with my youngest brother Ryan for a while, but when he started at the fire academy, we decided it was best to let the business go."

"Well, given that being a fireman was your goal all along, I'd say that was sensible. You had to follow your childhood dream."

"Yeah. I guess you can say that."

"I love that." She sighed. "Not a lot of people get to do what they dreamed of doing as a child."

I contemplated her words for a moment, realizing how lucky my brothers and I truly were. "Yeah, I suppose you're right. What was your childhood dream job?"

A forlorn look took over her. "I wanted to be a travel journalist. I watched the Travel Channel a lot, and there was this show where this woman traveled the world, did a bunch of amazing things, and told the audience about her experiences. I wanted to do that. On camera, in magazines, didn't matter. I just wanted to see everything, do everything, and tell everyone about my experience."

"Where's your favorite place you've traveled to?"

"Um." She tensed. "I haven't."

"You haven't what?" I asked, perplexed.

"Traveled."

I sat up a little to look at her. "What? Really? You wanted to be a travel journalist, but you haven't traveled?"

"Pathetic, I know."

"No, I'm just surprised."

"My parents never let me leave Connecticut. It was tough enough getting them to agree to let me go to school at NYU. I went to Atlantic City with my girlfriends for spring break our senior year of college, but that's the furthest I've gone from home."

I couldn't help but notice how sad she became.

"I guess that's why I loved that show so much. I could visit all those places without actually leaving home."

I didn't press her, but I knew there was more to that story, and I hoped she'd tell me when she was ready. In an effort to lighten the mood, I asked, "Where do you want to go most in the world?"

"Italy," she blurted out without hesitation. "I want to immerse myself in the culture, the language, the food. I just know it'll be fabulous."

I loved the way she lit up when she talked about it. "Italy, huh? Okay, one day I'll take you there."

She lifted her head from my chest and looked up at me. "I'd really love that." She kissed me tenderly, and I felt the emotion behind her lips. This meant a lot to her, and I promised myself I would do whatever I had to do to make her dream come true.

She pulled back and rolled over onto her stomach, her arms crossed on my chest, supporting her head, that way she could look at me while we talked. "Where's the coolest place you've ever been?"

"My mom was a history teacher before she became a principal, so she was really big on taking us on trips that had something educational to provide. We traveled mostly in the U.S. and have been to a couple of places in Europe, but I'd have to say Greece was my favorite place. Athens is pretty something."

"Shut up," she exclaimed, taking me aback.

"What?"

"I have always been obsessed with Ancient Greece and Greek mythology. *The Odyssey* was my favorite book in college. When I was a kid, being an only child, I was left to my imagination a lot. I used to read stories about the gods and goddesses, and I'd go off into dreamland pretending to be one of them. I'd love to visit there one day, too. If I weren't Italian, Greece would be number one on my bucket list."

"Well, then I'll take you there, too."

She smiled ear to ear. Hell, I'd buy an airplane and take Autumn all around the world if it meant I got to see that smile for the rest of my life. She laid back, and I noticed her staring at the painting of the girl, a distant look in her eyes. I remembered what she'd said before about how that painting had reminded her of the beauty out there in the world, and I understood it more after what she'd just told me. She craved more. Autumn wanted to experience the world, but there was something holding her back, and I desperately wanted to know what that thing was.

"I have to go back to work tomorrow." She sighed.

"Are you busy Friday night?" I rolled over onto my side.

My finger traced the outline of her waistband where a thin strip of her skin was exposed.

"No plans. What'd you have in mind?"

"I'd love to take you out on a date."

Her face lit up. "I'd like that."

"There's a really good Italian restaurant on the east side with the best homemade pasta and meatballs you'll ever have in your life. It might not be Italy, but we can pretend for the night."

She pulled my head to hers. "Sounds perfect."

Autumn kissed me again, running her fingers against the grain of my hair, holding me tightly to her. Even though she took this kiss to a deeper level, that was as far as I was going to let it go. I savored the taste of her mouth on mine—the softness of her lips against my own.

The way she held me so tightly was like she was trying to fuse us together, body and soul. She needed me as badly as I needed her. I'd do whatever it took to make her mine, because I knew my life would never be the same without her.

As I drove over the Throgs Neck Bridge heading to Long Island to meet my brother Jesse, I checked out the Manhattan skyline, in awe of how small it looked from that distance. Overlooking the city made me think about Autumn, sitting at her desk, across the water I was currently suspended above. Okay, if I were being honest, I hadn't been able to *stop* thinking about Autumn. The memory of spending the previous day with her put the biggest smile on my face.

The next few days without her would be brutal. I was looking forward to taking her out on a real date, though. Get her dressed up and show her off. All right, all right, she wasn't exactly mine to claim—not yet, anyway—but having her on my arm would make me the envy of every man in Manhattan.

We'd have a nice dinner, and hold hands across the table. When finished, I'd help her with her coat, and she'd give me a thank you kiss that promised more later. I'd take her out for a nightcap, and we'd sit at the bar, her hand on my thigh, possessively but sweet. Maybe we'd dance to a song or two, and allow the rest of the bar patrons to melt away into the distance. It'd be just the two of us, in our own little world.

Damn. When did I get so soft?

I pulled up to my brother's place in Long Beach. The crashing of the waves was audible before I even got out of the car. Jesse loved to surf, and he'd rented this ridiculously expensive waterfront townhome so he could go out in the waves any time he wanted. We tried to talk him into saving money by buying a place further from the ocean, but he seemed content to throw away twenty-six hundred dollars a month to be on the beach. Maybe that's why he had studied so hard for the lieutenants' test. He could use the pay bump.

I missed seeing my brother. It had been a strange transition once Jesse had moved away. We'd gone from being together all the time to really only seeing each other at our family meals and on occasional nights out. I'd always been closest to Jesse out of all my brothers, since he was only sixteen months younger than me. We had been on the same hockey team together from the time we were kids, all the way through high school—the only exception being the three non-sequential years we fell into different age divisions. We had played lacrosse together in high school, too. Even made it to the playoffs twice, and we had been regional champions my senior year.

Those were some fun times.

I knocked on his door twice before twisting the knob and letting myself in. Jesse had this bad habit of leaving his door unlocked all of the time.

"Yo, Jes," I shouted, announcing my presence. He had eighties rock blaring on the stereo.

"Be right out."

I opened his fridge and helped myself to a beer before propping up against his kitchen island to admire the view of the water through the glass balcony doors in his living room. Jesse's place was certifiably a small bachelor pad lacking style, but this view was all the place really needed to make it look good.

Jesse emerged from his bedroom wearing dark grey dress pants and a lavender button-down.

I looked down at my jeans and cursed. "Fuck, man, you didn't tell me this thing was going to be that fancy."

"I told you it's a fundraiser at the yacht club. What'd you expect?"

"Yeah, but it's a *fire department* fundraiser." I shrugged. "I wore my nice jeans and thought that might even be too much."

Jesse shook his head and pointed toward his bedroom. "Go change."

Luckily, we were the same size. I swapped my jeans and my polo for some navy slacks and a white-and-blue pinstriped button-up I found in my brother's closet. When I walked back out, Jesse was already by the door, putting on his jacket.

"Come on, bro, we're gonna be late. You were supposed to be here thirty-minutes ago."

"I'm sorry. You're the one who decided to move here. Long Island traffic is a bitch. It took me nearly two-hours to drive forty-miles."

We got in his pickup truck and drove the five-minutes to the yacht club. "So, tell me again what this fundraiser is for?"

Jesse had taken the lieutenant's test a little over a month ago, so he was finally starting to resume some kind of social life after months of having done nothing but study. It was nice to have my brother back.

"You remember Tim Erikson?"

"That guy you were surfing with at that volly picnic on the beach you dragged me to last summer?" When Jesse had moved to Long Beach, he had joined the local volunteer fire department. I guess the FDNY wasn't enough for my smoke-breather brother.

Jesse rolled his eyes at my *volly* comment. That's what guys on the job called the volunteers. I wasn't hating. Hell, the job had to get done, and the fact that they did it for free was pretty commendable. That being said, I had to at least pretend to hate them. It was kind of a thing between us paid guys and the volunteers. Truth be told, if I lived in a volunteer town, I'd probably be one of them, too. Just don't tell Jesse. It was too much fun to rag on him for it.

"Yeah. His wife has been battling cancer, and she's been out of work for a few months now. They have three young kids and really need some money, so dig deep into those pockets tonight, brother." Jesse patted me on the shoulder to hammer in his point.

I felt bad for the guy. I couldn't imagine going through something like that. Immediately, I thought of Autumn. I couldn't bear to see her suffer through something like cancer. I shook my head to get the image out of my mind.

We pulled into the parking lot and made our way inside. I actually knew quite a few of the guys there. Not just from going to some Long Beach Fire Department events with Jesse, but there were several guys on the job there as well. Long Beach was a popular place to live for a lot of FDNY guys because of its close proximity to the city. There were a lot of women at the event, too. Normally, I'd be thrilled at the prospect of not spending the night alone, but I had no interest in even flirting, not unless Autumn magically appeared. I was kicking myself for not inviting her.

I bought some raffle tickets for the 50/50. Although, let's be honest, when you bought 50/50 tickets at that kind of fundraiser, you were really just donating money because if you won, you gave the money back to the cause. I had been bidding on a vacation to Mexico in the silent auction, already envisioning a trip there with Autumn to escape the cold weather, when Jesse came up and slapped me on the back. "Come on, it's almost time for the live auction."

I went to head back to our seats when Jesse stopped and steered me in the other direction, toward the stage. "Where are we going?"

"Don't be mad. I signed us up for the auction."

I stopped and turned to look at him. "What auction?"

"The Bachelor Firemen Auction."

I stared at him for a beat while my brain processed what he'd just said. "You did what?" I growled, my hands balling into fists.

"I knew if I told you, you wouldn't have come, but it's for a really good cause so just be a good sport about this. Who knows, you might even meet someone." He winked and pushed me forward.

"I don't want to meet someone, Jesse," I hissed. "I have a girlfriend."

He stopped and rapid-fired questions at me. "You do? Since when? Who is she? Is it serious?"

I was not prepared to talk about it yet. Hell, Autumn wasn't even my girlfriend, though I had no doubt that's where we were heading. If I told Jesse the truth, I knew he wouldn't understand, and he would totally rag on me for dating a girl I met at a fire. That was a big no-no, especially if you saved them or someone they love. They got this hero-worship thing, and relationships based on that rarely ever worked out. It wasn't like that with Autumn, though. We had a real connection, but I didn't expect Jesse to understand that. His definition of a relationship was when he slept with the same girl more than once.

I gave him as much information as I was willing to divulge. "It's still new, but yeah, it's serious."

He studied my face for more. "What's her name?"

I hesitated for a second, not remembering the full conversation we'd had at my mother's house the other day. If Kyle had said something about Autumn, Jesse would easily put two and two together. Truth was, though, I really thought I had a chance at a future with this woman, and I figured honesty would be best. "Her name is Autumn Bianchi."

"Sounds hot. How'd you meet?"

"In the city." I wasn't lying. Rather, I was being intentionally vague. Thankfully, the music started up, ending our conversation.

We stood on the side of the stage with the other "Firefighter Bachelors," that's what the emcee called us, getting all the single women to go wild in the audience. The auction was starting. The emcee already had the roster, and my name was on it. There was no getting out of that one.

"Sorry, Dyl. I didn't realize you had a girlfriend, or I wouldn't have signed you up. It's just for fun, though, okay? For a good cause."

I nodded. I hoped the girl who won a date with me saw it the same way—just for fun—and wouldn't be looking for anything more.

The photographer came by to take photos of each of us while we were waiting, and I asked her to snap one with my cell phone. I loaded the photo into my messages and sent it to Autumn.

Me: Wish you were here
Autumn: Wow! With you looking like that, I wish you were HERE. I couldn't do what I want to do to you in public. People tend to frown upon that sort of thing.
Me: I'll gladly take a rain check
Autumn: Can't wait for Friday
Me: Me too sweetheart

The emcee called Jesse's name, and I prepared myself for the show. Jesse had never been shy, and being in the spotlight was definitely his element. He'd have no problem hamming it up for the crowd. I saw my brother go over and whisper into the emcee's ear. *What was he up to?*

A second later, the emcee announced, "Well, ladies, you are in for a real treat tonight. Firefighter Hogan here apparently has a brother in the auction, too. Let's bring Dylan Hogan of FDNY Ladder 64 up to the stage for a double date auction. That's right, ladies, pick one of your girlfriends and get ready to go out with *two* FDNY firemen!"

The women cheered, and Jesse looked at me with a big smile and a wink. That stunt was his way of making me more comfortable with the situation. I wouldn't have to go out with a girl on my own, we could go as a group, and I would feel a lot better about that.

I made my way up to the stage and over to my brother, playfully punching him in the arm. He took that as a cue to show off his biceps. More screaming from the crowd. I had to admit, it was kinda fun, but as I looked out into the crowd of women, the only face I wanted to see was Autumn's.

Jesse and I pulled in the most money during the auction, raising four hundred and eighty dollars for the Eriksons. The best part, though? Our dates were Betty and Kathy—two sisters in their seventies, widows whose husbands were members of LBFD. That date, I could handle. Even Autumn would approve.

Once the fundraiser started to wind down, I had one of the guys drive me back to Jesse's townhouse so I could head home. My brother had decided to stay and chat up the pretty girls who were runners-up for dates with us.

As I crossed back over the bridge with a view of Manhattan, I thought of Autumn lying in her bed a few miles away, and even though it was late, I really wanted to talk to her. So, I called her, simply to hear her voice.

11

AUTUMN

I'd never been so excited for a Friday before in my life. It was my first real date with Dylan. Not seeing him the past few days had been torture. I missed his presence in my apartment. Lily did, too. She seemed to mope around quite a bit. We talked on the phone every day, but nothing compared to actually seeing that man.

Truthfully, I'd been obsessively looking at the photo he'd sent me of himself from that fundraiser. He was so sexy all dressed up, and I couldn't wait to see him for our date. Around lunchtime, a beautiful bouquet of roses was delivered to my desk at work. The card simply said:

Just thinking about you.
♡ *D*

The smile on my face couldn't have gotten any bigger. All the girls at work wanted to know who they were from. I'd never gotten flowers at work before. I texted Dylan a photo of me in front of the bouquet, holding one of the roses.

Me: Thanks for making a girl feel special

Dylan: You are special
Dylan: But those aren't from me...

My smile fell, and my face got red and hot from embarrassment. I'd just sent the guy I was dating a photo of flowers some other guy had sent me. *Shit.* But I wasn't seeing any other guys, so who could they possibly be from? I thought for a second, and my heart sank when I realized who D was. Drew. What could I possibly say to smooth over that blunder? I racked my brain, coming up with nothing, but knowing I had to respond to Dylan.

Me: Sorry, I assumed they were from you. The card was signed just 'D' and I thought it stood for Dylan.
Dylan: Secret admirer, eh?
Me: I guess so
Dylan: Looks like I'd better step up my game then. I'd hate to lose you over a bouquet of roses.
Me: I'm fairly confident you have nothing to worry about in this competition
Dylan: Well fairly isn't quite good enough. Perhaps our date tonight will solidify your confidence.
Me: I have no doubt it will

Was this man the best or what? I'd rubbed it in his face that another guy had sent me flowers, and he turned it around into a game. I wouldn't allow myself to stress about Drew. I chose to ignore him, and I gave the roses to my assistant, along with instructions that if Drew ever called or came by, she was to say I wasn't in.

I left work a little early to treat myself to a blow out before my date. My stylist, Rico, said I looked "muy sexy" with all the extra volume he had added to my hair. I went home, did my makeup, and tried on no less than thirty outfits. I decided on a simple black, cowl-neck, knit dress that dipped down just low enough to show off a hint of cleavage. I finished the look with small hoop earrings, knee-high heeled boots, and red lipstick.

Rico was right. I was *muy sexy*.

Dylan arrived right on time, and I met him downstairs, so he didn't have to struggle with parking. When he saw me, he jumped out of his car to open the door for me, but he paused to check me out first.

"Wow, sweetheart, you're stunning."

I smiled, pleased with myself. "Thank you. You look rather handsome yourself."

He leaned down to give me a quick kiss before opening the car door for me. We drove over to the east side, which took longer than it should have because of Friday night traffic, but I wasn't complaining because Dylan held my hand the whole way.

When we walked into Cucina Della Mamma, the smells hit me in layers, and my stomach grumbled. My nose picked up the scent of fresh bread, rich ricotta, and homemade gravy. Yes, gravy, not sauce. I'm Italian, don't argue with me.

I was in heaven.

The hostess took our jackets before showing us to our table by the fireplace. The restaurant was terribly romantic with its low lighting and instrumental soundtrack. Excitement bubbled up inside me at knowing I was there with Dylan. A bottle of prosecco was already chilling in a bucket on the table. I would have to tell Dylan at some point that I didn't drink, but it was so sweet of him to have planned ahead, so I figured a little bit would be okay.

The rich, red linen tablecloths and white cloth napkins gave the place a Valentine's Day feel, but it complimented the large mural of the Italian countryside, which spanned the length of the back wall. It gave me wanderlust.

Our waiter greeted us with a plate of bruschetta and fresh Parmigiano Reggiano. He opened our prosecco and poured a tiny bit into my glass. "For you to taste, my lady."

I lifted the glass to my lips, the bubbles tickled my nose, and I took a sip. It was delicious, but I truly hadn't known what it should taste like anyway. He poured the rest of my glass before serving Dylan. Dylan raised his into the air. "To the first of many evenings together," he said and clinked his flute against mine. *I could get used to this.* Sitting across a table from the most attractive man I'd ever met in my life, sharing a delicious meal, then going home to make passionate love—

I was getting ahead of myself. But have I mentioned how sexy he was? And how sweet? It was hard to believe he was real. And he liked me. *Me!*

Dylan ordered for us: antipasto salad and spaghetti with meatballs served family style. I didn't know why, but having him order for me was a serious turn-on. I didn't think it would be, but it made me feel...taken care of, I guess.

The food was just as good as it smelled. No, it was better.

"How did you find this place?" I asked in awe between bites.

"I told you it was the best thing outside of Italy."

"You weren't kidding. My nonna would've loved this place. She was a great cook. I have a book of her recipes. That was actually the first thing I went to look for when I went back to my apartment after the fire. I was so worried it would be gone, but thankfully, it survived. Although, it does still smell like smoke. How the heck do you get that out?"

"Lemons. But I don't think I'd try that on paper." He shrugged. "It works great on my hair, though." We both laughed. "Just give it some time to air out. Maybe put it on your balcony on a day when you know it won't rain."

"Good idea." I nodded, savoring another bite.

"What's your favorite recipe of hers?"

I didn't even have to think about my response. "Stuffed artichokes. They're simply the best. Garlic, breadcrumbs, cheese...you really can't beat it."

"I know we just ate, but that sounds so good right now."

"I'll have to make them for you sometime."

"I'd love that." He shifted his body forward in his seat. "It sounds like you were pretty close with your grandmother."

I dabbed my mouth with the napkin. "I was. She died shortly after I left for college. I miss her every day. She was kind of my person."

"I'm sorry to hear that." Dylan covered my hand with his, a look of understanding in his eyes.

I shrugged. "Such is life."

Dylan nodded. "You said you're an only child. Are you close with your parents?"

I shifted in my seat and took another sip of prosecco. Dylan had refilled my glass earlier, but I was nursing it. "Not exactly." I wasn't ready to explain it yet, so I treaded carefully with my word choice. "They can be too much to handle sometimes."

"I can relate. Sounds like my brother Kyle. I love him, but he can be a lot to handle too." He took a sip of the cabernet he'd ordered with dinner.

"You've mentioned him a few times. He sounds like a tough person to be around."

"After my father died, he felt the need to take over that role in the family. He can be very obnoxious, but I know it's always because he cares about us. Too much sometimes. I think he forgets about taking care of himself. I worry about him; he takes life too seriously." He paused for a second, and I could tell he was hemming over his next words. "You've met him actually."

"Your brother?"

"Yeah, he was there the night of the fire."

"Really? Who was he?"

"Do you remember sitting on the back of the ambulance and that lieutenant came over and screamed at me?"

"That ass is your *brother*?" I asked, more out of repulsion by the revelation rather than seeking an answer.

"Yup. You got to experience Lieutenant Kyle Hogan in all his glory."

"Wow. I wish I knew that then. I would've been much more insistent with him. I can't believe he'd speak to you like that. You saved a kid for heaven's sake, why was he being so obnoxious about it?"

Dylan shifted in his seat, and I could tell he was unsure of how to respond. "I don't agree with how he handled it, but he did have a valid point. I took a pretty serious risk to save that boy."

I considered his words. "But you're a firefighter. Your job is inherently risky, isn't it?"

He nodded. "Sure is, but the risks we take should be calculated. Some risks aren't worth taking."

I was confused and didn't really want to know the answer to this next question, but I had to ask it. "So, you mean saving Eli was a risk you shouldn't have taken?"

He leaned back in his chair, appearing to be deep in thought for a moment. "Don't tell Kyle I admitted this, but no, I shouldn't have. My partner had just bailed, thinking I was behind him. There was a rollover, meaning I had a minute—if that—before the entire room was engulfed in flames. Honestly, I probably should have died in that apartment. We had no water on the fire, and I was trapped behind the firewall." He looked down, seemingly unable to meet my gaze. "But I couldn't leave him. I knew that boy was in there—I don't know how, I just did—and I had to save him. Even if it meant I died in the process."

I didn't know what to say to that. I was grateful that Dylan had saved Eli, but I was also terrified he'd taken such a dangerous risk. Was it the first time he'd done something like that? Would it be the last?

I had a connection with this man down to my soul, but in that moment, I wondered if I could handle being in love with a firefighter.

12

DYLAN

I could see the concern in her eyes, and I was worried I'd screwed things up. We were interrupted when the waiter came over to take our dessert order. I asked for the tiramisu with two spoons because, even though I was stuffed from dinner, I couldn't leave the restaurant on that note. I needed more time. And tiramisu was my favorite.

"I'm sorry, sweetheart, I don't know why I told you all that. I've been catching some flak for it lately, and I guess it's been bothering me more than I realized."

She looked at me for a moment before reaching her hand across the table to grab mine. "I'm glad you shared. I never want you to feel like you can't tell me something."

My heart did a flip. I was seriously falling for her.

"And, Dylan? Thank you. Thank you for saving Eli—for taking the risk." She stared down at her lap. "Because I don't think I would've been able to live with myself if you hadn't saved him." Her voice was heavy with emotion. "You succeeded where I failed. And, no matter what happens with us, I'll *always* be grateful for what you did—for Eli, for Lily, and for me."

I squeezed her hand. "Hey, look at me."

She tentatively lifted her head.

Seeing such raw emotion on her face made me want to jump over the table, wrap her in my arms, and hold her until her worries dissolved. "Sweetheart, you didn't fail. I had on protective gear and an air tank. Plus, I'm trained to work in those conditions. You didn't have any of that. I know you did what you could to help Eli. I also know what those conditions are like, and no matter how much willpower you have, sometimes you simply can't push forward. If you had tried to push beyond your limit, that day could've gone very differently." I took a moment to swallow the emotion welling up in my throat. "I may have needed to make a choice between rescuing you or rescuing Eli. So thank you. Thank you for getting yourself out and for letting me do my job."

I desperately wanted to kiss that pout off her lips, but I reminded myself we were in public. I rubbed the back of her hand with my thumb. "I didn't mean to scare you or upset you by bringing this up. Everything turned out just fine, so there's no reason to worry."

She nodded, a distant look in her eyes.

Please, God, don't let me mess this up.

We ate our dessert while she told me a funny story about work. Tensions melted away, and we went back to having a nice evening.

"Speaking of work, did you find out who sent you those flowers?" I'd been wanting to ask her about that since she'd sent me the photo earlier, but it had never felt like the right time. I was confident in the connection we had, but that didn't mean I wasn't a little jealous. It wasn't like we were exclusive. Hell, this was our first real date. She was perfectly within her rights to see someone else if she wanted. But I didn't want her to. I wanted her to be mine, so I needed to know where we stood.

She hesitated to answer, which told me she knew who sent them. My heart sank a little. I was really hoping my secret admirer theory had been correct.

She played with the hem of her dress sleeve. "Yes. I think I know who they were from," she admitted, before taking a sip of her prosecco. She'd barely had any, but I wasn't going to push her to drink, especially after the last time. "I'm pretty sure it was my ex-boyfriend, Drew."

"Oh," I blurted out, not really knowing what to say. That couldn't be a good thing.

"We broke up over a year ago, and I haven't seen him since. Until the other night, that is. It was his place I went to after the fire. I didn't know where else to go. I used to live there, too, so it was the first place that popped into my mind."

I listened intently, sensing it was hard for her to talk about. I was also pissed she had run off to her ex for help that night when I'd desperately wanted to be the one to take care of her.

She sighed, sounding exasperated. "He said breaking up with me was a mistake. He wants to get back together."

Another shot to my heart. "Is that something you want, too?" I asked, biting my lip.

"Definitely not." she exclaimed, making me relieved. "We were together for almost five years and," she swallowed, "I thought we were going to get engaged, but instead, he broke my heart. I can't forgive him for that."

Great. I was competing with a serious boyfriend, not just some fling. The guy clearly had to be a moron to let Autumn go, though, so I had that working in my favor at least. I'd never be that stupid.

"So the flowers are part of him trying to win you back?"

She sighed. "I suppose so."

"Well, the guy is an idiot for letting you go in the first place."

"You're too sweet, Dylan."

"I'm serious. I don't think I could date you for five years and not want to make you my wife before that."

She laughed and rolled her eyes. "That's quite a line, sir."

I laughed with her. "Not a line, I swear."

"Uh-huh, sure."

"Okay, fine, don't believe me. You'll see." I winked at her as I pushed back my chair and walked over to her seat. "Shall we move on to the next place?"

"Let's go," she said. I pulled out her chair, and once standing, she leaned up on her toes to give me a quick kiss. Even in heels, she was tiny next to me. I loved it. "Thank you. Dinner was amazing."

"I'm glad you enjoyed it."

We walked down to the next block where there was a whiskey and wine bar with live jazz music. The lights were low and forest-green velvet booths lined the exterior of the room, while several small round tables filled in the middle around an elevated stage where the band was playing. We found two seats at the carved wooden bar that stretched across the back, and ordered drinks: bourbon on the rocks for me and club soda for her. She said the prosecco at dinner was her limit. I didn't push, but I wondered if she had an issue with alcohol.

The music provided the perfect ambiance. It was sultry, which heightened my awareness of just how sexy my date was. She swayed to the sound, running her fingers through her long coffee-colored hair. I watched her, mesmerized by her body.

"Do you want to dance?"

She looked around. "No one else is dancing."

"So? It only takes two to dance. We don't need anyone else. Unless you plan on switching partners," I teased.

"I can't argue with that." She took my hand and hopped off the barstool. I led her over to the small dance floor in front of the band, and pulled her tight against me. We slowly drifted to the music, and the longer we danced, the more I felt her tension melt away. After a minute or so, she floated effortlessly across the floor, fully allowing herself to enjoy the moment.

I savored how she felt in my arms and against my chest. She was so small in my embrace, and it awakened my protective side. I could smell her familiar scent of coconut and gardenias wafting from her thick, wavy hair. It was intoxicating. A few others joined us on the dance floor, but it still felt like it was just the two of us.

I spun her around a few times before pulling her back into me. She ran her hands over my biceps, feeling me up, and I had no problem obliging by flexing ever-so slightly for her. Her touch made my skin erupt, giving me chills and making my hairs stand on end. The electricity between us ignited all of my senses.

After a couple of songs, the band took a break, and I nuzzled my head against hers. "Want to get out of here?"

"I thought you'd never ask," she whispered back, practically purring.

I planted a gentle kiss on her lips, leaving behind the promise of more to come, before grabbing our coats and leading her back to the car. The sexual energy between us was palpable, and I couldn't wait to get her home to really kiss her the way I wanted to without having to control myself because we were in public.

After parking my car in the garage at her building, we got into the elevator to head up to her apartment. As soon as the doors closed, she spun around and pushed me against the wall, taking me by surprise. With my shirt tangled in her fist, she pulled my mouth down to hers, kissing me fiercely as though my lips were giving her life. I wrapped my arms around her lower back, forcefully pulling her body into mine. Her hands snaked up to my neck and behind my head, holding me to her, extracting from me all the passion I possessed.

When Autumn was sexually charged, she became this confident vixen who enthralled me, making me want more. The elevator doors opened, and she backed away, leading me quickly and wordlessly to her front door.

13

AUTUMN

*W*ho knew dancing was such an aphrodisiac? I couldn't wait to get Dylan off that dance floor and into my bedroom. I thrust open my door with enough force for it to snap against the wall. Dylan's hands migrated up the back of my shirt before the door had even closed behind us. He turned me swiftly, pressing me against the wall in my foyer. I wrapped my arms around his neck, kissing him with all the fire in my soul.

Dylan ran his hand along my thigh. I took the cue and lifted my leg, hooking it around the back of his thigh and pulling his pelvis tightly against mine. In one swift motion, Dylan lifted me up by my legs, which I then wrapped around his waist. Suspended there, wedged between the wall and that man, I felt alive in a whole new way.

His groin was pressed up against mine, and his hardness was increasing by the second. I wanted him so badly. I wasn't going to let my insecurities get in the way again. The motion of his grinding hips rubbed me in just the right spot. Tearing my mouth from his, I tossed my head back and moaned. His lips found the spot where my collarbone and my neck met, sending me further into bliss.

Dylan's strong hands gathered beneath me as he dragged me away from the wall, fully supporting my weight. His strength was such a turn-on. I bent my lips to his earlobe as he walked us over to my bedroom and laid me down on the bed, positioning himself on top of me.

He kissed me with such intensity that I swear I could feel my heartbeat reverberating throughout my body. His hand moved from my cheek, down my neck, and across my chest, cupping my breast, squeezing firmly as though he were saying *this is mine*, before migrating down, over my abdomen, stopping on my hips.

His lips ceased their assault on mine, and he lifted his head, looking down at me. His eyes had darkened with lust, and his stare warmed me to the core. "You are so fucking beautiful," he moaned, his voice deep and sultry, his tone just above a whisper.

I bit my lip, meeting his gaze with my own desire-filled eyes. "I'm ready for you, Dylan. Please."

He groaned. "Let's see about that."

He slid down my body, positioning himself between my thighs. After pushing my dress up over my hips, he latched his fingers beneath the waistband of my thong, slowly sliding it down my legs, his eyes never breaking contact with my own.

He pulled my panties over my boots and paused for a second with his hand on the zipper of my left shoe. "I think we'll leave these on."

He gripped the heels on my knee-high boots to pull my legs further apart. After he swung my knees over his shoulders, he trailed kisses up my thigh.

A whimper escaped my lips.

He noticed. "I'm getting there, sweetheart. I want to savor every bit of you."

I tossed my head back over the pillow, arching my spine to give him easier access to my center. Once he'd fully covered my thighs in gentle kisses, I felt his breath over my bud, and I held my own breath in anticipation of what was to come.

When his tongue connected with me, I swear I went blind for a few seconds. My nerve endings fired, and I inhaled sharply. His lips moved expertly over me, causing all of my muscles to tense. My breathing turned quick and shallow. I moaned. And moaned. And moaned some more. I'd never felt such pleasure before. Ever. I was getting close to the edge.

"Don't stop. Please, don't stop," I begged.

His tongue worked quicker, and I felt his finger applying pressure over my opening without actually penetrating me. That was my undoing. My orgasm took hold of my body, and I writhed beneath him, riding his mouth until I came back down to earth.

"Wow," I breathed.

Dylan lifted his head, looking up at me from between my legs. His tongue traced his bottom lip before sucking it in behind his teeth. "Damn, sweetheart, that was so hot."

I grabbed him by the collar and tugged, pulling him up to me. I kissed him hard, tasting myself on his lips. My hands moved to the hem of his shirt and I lifted, pulling it up and over his head, breaking our kiss for only a second, before tossing his shirt off to the floor.

My attention went to the buckle on his belt, and I fumbled to get it open. Dylan rolled over to my side and had his belt, pants, and boxers off in an instant. I took a few seconds to admire his naked form. My gaze promptly went to his pelvis. I knew he was large from the times I had felt him hard against me, but actually seeing it was something else.

"Holy. Wow."

Did I say that out loud?

He smirked. "You like?"

Like a magnet, my hand reached for him, and I stroked his shaft, which was solid and ready for me. He groaned at my touch.

"I want to taste you," I said as I pulled myself up to move between his legs, but he stopped me.

"Not tonight. I need to feel you, and I don't think I can wait any longer, sweetheart."

He grabbed my dress and tossed it over my head. I took a deep breath to prepare myself. If the light were on, he'd see my scar, but with only the faint glow of the city bleeding in through the window, I hoped it was just dark enough to conceal it. Dylan's hand snaked around me, unhooking my bra, and he promptly tossed it across the room. He got on top of me again, this time lining his sex up with my own.

"Are you sure you're ready for this?" he asked, looking me in the eyes presumably to gauge my response.

"Hell, yes. I need to feel you, too."

"Do I need a condom? I'm clean. I was just tested for work a couple of weeks ago, and I haven't been with anyone since then."

I shook my head. "No, I have an IUD, and I'm clean, too."

I'd only ever been with Drew, so I hadn't had sex in over a year, although I left that part out.

His face lit up, as he rubbed his tip over my wet folds a few times before Dylan gently eased himself in, entering me slowly, allowing me to experience every incredible inch of him until he was fully seated between my walls. He was big, and my muscles ached as they stretched around his girth, but he filled me perfectly. I grabbed at his ass to hold him tightly inside me, savoring him.

"Oh, Dylan." I uttered, trying to make sense of the incredible pleasure.

"You're so tight and you're dripping wet, sweetheart. This feels fucking amazing."

He hadn't moved yet, and I needed him to. I needed him to take me. "Fuck me, Dylan," I rarely cursed, but there was no better way to describe what I wanted from him in that moment.

"No." He shook his head, and my stomach sank. "I'm not gonna *fuck* you. Not tonight." He lowered his mouth to my ear, and his warm breath sent shivers down my spine as he whispered, "Tonight, I'm gonna make love to you because, sweetheart, I am falling so hard."

A wave of emotion flooded my senses while I processed his words, and right then and there, I *knew*. I knew I was falling, too. Or maybe I already had.

14

DYLAN

I moved slowly, savoring being inside Autumn. *My* Autumn. She was warm and wet and so unbelievably tight. I didn't know how I would possibly make it last long. As I thrust myself inside her, I ran my hands up her abdomen to cup her breasts. Her moans told me she was just as into it as I was. My fingertips rolled over her nipples, making her gasp. I loved how responsive she was to my touch.

Her pussy stretched around me with each pump of my hips, and her muscles expanded and contracted around my shaft, sheathing me like we were made for each other.

It was perfect.

She was perfect.

My balls contracted, and I felt the pressure building, but I wasn't ready for it to end. I started reciting the ABCs in my head, trying to bring my focus away from how good she felt, but her moans made it nearly impossible to stay distracted. I managed to control my release for a couple of minutes longer, but eventually, I felt it rise to the surface—the point of no return.

"I'm gonna come," I muttered, and as I went to pull out, she crossed her ankles behind me, holding me inside of her.

"Come in me," she begged, and that was all I needed to fall over the edge.

I released inside of her, and I couldn't put into words how unbelievable it was to fill her up. A woman had never let me do that before. My cock twitched between her walls as she contracted them, milking me dry.

That was hands-down the best sex I'd ever had. I knew things would be different with her. Just as I knew she'd be worth the wait. Although, I was grateful I hadn't had to wait long.

I withdrew from her slowly before collapsing on the bed next to her. My whole body shook, and my pulse throbbed in my temples. Autumn lay panting beside me.

"That was…" She exhaled. "That was…"

"Wow?" I filled in the blank for her, just as she'd done for me after our first kiss.

"Yeah. Wow."

I rolled onto my side and ran my fingers down her cheek before placing a gentle kiss on her lips. "You're really special, Autumn."

She placed her hand on top of mine, pulling it down to her lips, where she planted a kiss on my knuckles. "I think you're pretty special, too, Dylan."

I held her in my arms for a while, as she rested her head on my chest. We laid there in silence, taking comfort in the closeness and listening to the sound of our synchronized breathing. I could've stayed like that forever.

I heard a mewing sound and felt pressure on the foot of the bed. It was dark, but I could make out the silhouette of Lily joining us. Not wanting my sensitive exposed parts to come in contact with the cat's claws, I reached over to the bedside table and turned on the light so I could find my underwear. When I did, I felt Autumn tense.

I flexed my chest, causing her to lift her cheek and look at me. "Are you okay?" I asked.

"Uh-huh."

I wasn't convinced. If she was self-conscious about me seeing her naked with the light on, she was crazy. Her body was perfect, and I immediately got angry at whoever it was that made her believe otherwise.

I spotted my boxers on the ground, so I gently shifted her off me and reached down to grab them. As I did, I noticed the large, curved scar on her side. It was fully healed and faded so it must've been old. I flipped onto my stomach so I could look at her. Then, I reached my hand out to touch her scar, and she recoiled, grabbing for the blanket to cover herself. *Was that why she'd tensed up when I turned on the light? She hadn't wanted me to see her scar?*

"Hey, it's okay, sweetheart, I won't touch it if you don't want me to. Does it hurt?"

She shook her head, unable to bring herself to meet my gaze.

"What happened?"

She brought her hand to her mouth and started to chew on her cuticles. This had to be something big. "I was in a car accident a long time ago."

I felt like I was going to throw up. Jenna's face immediately appeared in my mind. *Was this the sign I'd asked her for?* Jenna had lost her life in a car accident, and Autumn had a permanent reminder of her own.

J, would you really send me a sign this morbid?

Autumn was silent, not offering up any more information, and I was okay with that. My head was spinning, and the room seemed to darken around me. Suddenly, I was back in that car looking over at Jenna as she bled out before my eyes.

15

AUTUMN

*W*hy? Why did he have to see my scar? Why did he have to ask about it? And why did I have to lie to him?

If I'd told him the truth, this perfect thing we had going for us would be over. He'd look at me like everyone else had, with eyes laced with pity. Just like Drew, he'd think I was too fragile, and everything would be ruined. I'd be broken-hearted all over again.

We'd had the perfect evening. Our date had been extraordinary. The food, the dancing, that kiss in the elevator... I'd always wanted to do that, to feel that much passion with someone that I couldn't wait to get my hands on him. Our connection was indescribable. This had to be what it was like to find your soulmate, right?

And the sex? Oh, my word, the sex! No, I didn't even think I could call it that. I was pretty sure my soul had merged with his when our bodies did, and I would give anything to go back to that moment and not let it end.

But he had to ask about my scar.

And I had to lie.

I wasn't sure why I told him it was a car accident. I guess it seemed believable enough, and hopefully, he wouldn't ask me to elaborate. In fact, he wasn't saying anything at all.

I glanced up at him, noticing all the color had drained from his face, and there was a distant look in his eyes. It was concerning.

"Hey, are you okay?"

He didn't respond. I wasn't even sure he'd heard me. I reached up and touched his shoulder, and he jumped. "Dylan? What's wrong?"

He shook his head and cleared his throat. "I'm sorry. You mentioned your car accident and it reminded me of something traumatic I went through in high school."

I felt like a complete ass. Why'd I have to say it was a car accident? Granted, I couldn't have known this about Dylan, but I still felt guilty for triggering him. I flipped myself over and laid down on my stomach. I was still naked, and my scar was fully on display, but for that moment, I was okay with it. This man, who I cared deeply for, clearly needed some support, and I was happy to be around to offer it.

I linked my arm through his and urged, "Tell me about it."

He was silent for a little while, so I waited patiently while he gathered his thoughts. I didn't want to push. Heck, I had no right to push given that I was harboring a secret of my own.

Finally, he spoke. "I dated the same girl throughout high school, and we were in love." He paused, and I rubbed his forearm, giving him the time he needed.

"One night during our senior year, I was driving her home from school. It was dark. Roads were icy. A deer ran out into the street. I swerved. My tires skidded on the ice and that sent us barreling straight into a tree."

I gasped, imagining the horror of a moment like that. It was as though I was experiencing his pain, too.

He sat up on the side of the bed and I sat up behind him, giving him space. "The steering column pinned my legs, trapping me in my seat. I looked over to make sure my girlfriend was okay." He shook his head. "She wasn't. A branch had crashed down on the passenger side of my Durango, piercing the windshield." He inhaled sharply. "It impaled her in the chest."

My heart broke a little for him then. I knew a thing or two about trauma, having gone through my own. Experiencing it in any form—especially at a young age—was life-altering. He was lost in his thoughts. I moved to his side, and crossed my legs, angling my body toward him. I placed my hand gently on his thigh in an effort to bring him comfort.

He didn't flinch at my touch. He kept speaking, his voice trailing off with each sentence he uttered. It was clear he was reliving the moment all over again. Tears welled up in his eyes, but he didn't seem to notice.

"It was twelve years ago, but the look of terror on her face still haunts me. I used every ounce of strength I had to try and free myself so I could help her, but no matter what I tried, my legs wouldn't budge. I even punched my own damn thigh out of desperation. I was trying to break my femur so I could contort my way out of the seat. Nothing worked."

"Oh, Dylan."

"The sound of her gasping for air..." He shook his head, seemingly as if it would dispel the memory. "She saw me struggling to get free, so she reached her out to stop me. I held her hand. And I looked at her. We were both in tears. And she just shook her head."

His breathing became shallower, and his words sped up. I could see the vein throbbing in his neck. "I told her how much I loved her, and I pleaded with her to hang on. I just kept repeating that she was going to be okay, she was going to be okay, but we both knew that was a lie." He sniffled. "I was holding her hand as I watched her take her last breath. The blood was pooling out of her mouth and pouring out of her chest. Her eyes were still open, but she was gone."

Dylan hung his head in his hands. "And it was all my fault."

I squeezed his thigh tighter. I couldn't imagine what it must have been like for him to carry around that guilt all those years. I chose my next words carefully so as not to insult the deeply ingrained feelings he clearly harbored. "It sounds to me like it was an accident. Accidents happen."

He nodded slowly. "There was an investigation. I was exonerated, and it was ruled an accident. Still, I feel guilty, and I wish, *every day*, that it'd been her who had survived instead of me."

I swallowed hard to dispel the lump in my throat. "Dylan, I am so sorry. That's a terrible tragedy, but you can't blame yourself."

He stared down at his lap, and I reached out my hand to wipe his tears. I desperately wished I could take his pain away.

As we sat there in silence, taking comfort in our closeness, my mind processed what I'd learned. I knew what it was like to experience loss. I knew what it was like to witness a life at the end of its rope. I even knew what it was like to feel guilty for being alive.

Dylan had lost his dad *and* his girlfriend. Both losses were understandably traumatic for him. He'd found his father dead and then watched his girlfriend die. I couldn't imagine going through all that as a teenager.

Obviously, those losses had a profound impact on him, and my heart sank as I came to the realization that if we stayed together, I'd likely cause him to experience another painful loss. Everyone died eventually, but the odds of me dying, not just before him, but dying *young*, were pretty high. I couldn't put him through something like that again.

Soulmate or not, I had to let Dylan go.

16

DYLAN

The gray sky was threatening to snow on that dreary January day, as I drove to my mom's for dinner. I had almost used the weather as an excuse to get out of it, but I knew that wouldn't have flied because Jesse and Ryan had driven further. I simply wasn't in the mood to be social.

It'd been forty-eight hours since my first date with Autumn, and I'd barely heard from her since. I had to work early on Saturday, so I'd spent the night at her place and had gone straight to the firehouse in the morning, leaving before she was even awake. When we had gone to bed that night, she had been consoling me, and I honestly think that made me fall in love with her. Crazy, I know. It terrified me, too.

She cared about me, truly cared, and it felt so good to be cared for. It felt good to purge some of the hurt I'd been carrying around. Autumn had been so sweet and loving when I'd told her about Jenna. But I suspected I'd really screwed things up. I had cried...on our first date. *What the hell is wrong with me?*

I *never* cried. She probably thought I was a total pussy.

Autumn did something to me. I couldn't explain it. She made me comfortable. I could truly be myself around her, and I had wanted to open up to her. I'd never told anyone the details of what had happened in the car the night of the accident—not even my brothers. I'd felt like I could tell Autumn though. I had wanted to tell her. Sure, I could've said I was in an accident and left out the intimate details, but this voice inside my head had told me to put it all out there. So I had. And, truthfully, it had felt damn good. I'd needed to purge, and Autumn had made me feel safe enough to share.

The same thing had happened when I'd told her about what I'd done in that fire. I'd told her things I hadn't even admitted to myself yet. And I'd thought I'd screwed things up then by oversharing, but we'd pushed past it and ended up having an incredible evening.

Making love to her was unreal. I'd never experienced intimacy like that with any other woman I'd been with. Not even close. And then I had to go and fuck it all up by crying about Jenna.

I had called Autumn on Saturday while I was at work, but we'd only gotten to talk for five or so minutes before we'd been interrupted. I had to go on a run for a damn smoke detector that went off because the tenant had burned dinner. I'd tried calling her back, but missed her. She'd texted me in the morning saying she'd gone to bed early.

Earlier in the day, we'd texted a few times, but she wasn't as playful with me as she usually was. I missed our teasing conversation, and my stomach hurt because I knew *I'd* messed things up. I had met a woman I could seriously see myself having a future with, and I had to fuck it up by scaring her off. I had tried to see her that afternoon, before heading to my mom's, since she had to work the next day, but she said she already had plans.

When I pulled up, I noticed I was the last to arrive again. I'd procrastinated leaving my house until the last possible second. I sat in the driver's seat for a moment before having to head inside. I stared down at my phone, so badly wishing to see a new message from Autumn, but there wasn't one. So I texted her.

Me: Just got to my mom's for dinner. Call you after xxoo

I waited a couple of minutes to see if she'd respond, but no such luck. I sighed, stepped out of my car, and went inside. Everyone was in the kitchen putting dinner together before bringing it to the dining room.

"Dylan. There you are. We were wondering what was keeping you," my mother said as she mashed the potatoes.

I crossed over to kiss her on the cheek. "Sorry I'm late, Ma. I was doing laundry and lost track of time."

She looked at me with this knowing smile of hers, one that said she wasn't buying it. Before I could call her out on it, Ryan chimed in. "Laundry, huh? Is that what you're calling your new girlfriend?"

So that's what my mother's look was about. They'd been talking about me. My eyes darted over to Jesse, filled with daggers. "You told them about Autumn? What the hell, Jes?"

Jesse threw his hands up, but before he could speak, Kyle cut in. "Autumn, who's Autumn? I thought the old ladies' names were Betty and Kathy."

Fuck. My face flushed.

Jesse came over to pat me on the back. "Yeah, I told them all about our *charity dates.* You're the one who just spilled the beans about your girl."

Wordlessly, I grabbed the mashed potatoes from my mom and took them into the dining room in an effort to escape the inevitable discussion. The last thing I wanted to do was talk about Autumn. The rest of my family came in shortly behind me and found their seats at the table. Jesse handed me a beer.

As we started to fill our plates, my mother directed her gaze at me. "Well, are you going to tell us about her, or do I have to beg?"

I sighed. "There's not much to tell, Ma. It's still new."

"Autumn's a pretty name. What's her last name?"

Knowing what she was getting at, I said, "She's not Irish. She's Italian."

My mother sighed loudly, feigning disappointment. None of us boys had ever dated an Irish girl. Not on purpose or anything. It just hadn't happened. Our mother enjoyed making us feel like it broke her heart every time we started dating someone new who wasn't Irish.

Ryan spoke up, his mouth filled with food. "Italian chicks are hot."

"Ryan!" my mother scolded. "How many times do I have to tell you not to speak with your mouth full?"

Ryan gave her a smirk. My youngest brother had some growing up to do. His manners left much to be desired, but he was blessed with good looks, so girls practically threw themselves at him. Always had. He never had to work hard to impress.

"How'd you meet her?" Kyle asked before taking a swig of his beer.

"In the city."

He chuckled. "That's descriptive. Care to elaborate?"

I shook my head. "Not particularly."

"Why? Is it a secret?" my mother asked.

"It's not."

She echoed Kyle. "Then how did you two meet?"

I stared hard at my plate, dreading what was about to happen. "We met on scene at a fire."

Jesse leaned into me first. "Dude. *Never* date a victim. You know that."

"She got herself out. I had nothing to do with it."

Kyle looked at me with narrowed eyes. "*Which* fire?"

He knew.

"That apartment building. Thursday before last." I braced myself for what was coming.

I saw Kyle's mind turning. "The ambulance chick? The one with the cat?"

I nodded. "And she's not 'the ambulance chick.' Her name is Autumn."

"Even worse, Dyl. You saved her cat. You couldn't be more of a hero to her after that. You know how girls are with their pets." Ryan rolled his eyes.

"Wait a minute, didn't you save a kid that night, too?" Jesse interjected.

I nodded inconspicuously.

Jesse threw up his hands. "Great. You might not have rescued her, but you rescued her cat *and* a kid. That makes you an even bigger hero."

"Screw you guys. It isn't like that with her." I crossed my arms over my chest, already fed up with the conversation.

"I saw the way she looked at you that night. She had you up on a high pedestal, bro. You could do no wrong." Kyle shook his head, a look of disappointment on his face.

"You guys can think what you want. This isn't a rescue crush. We just—" I struggled to find the right word as I'd found myself doing a lot lately when describing this thing between us. "We clicked. She's different. Special. I really think she might be the one."

I don't know who was more surprised by my confession: me or them. Everyone was speechless. I dared to glance up from my plate and saw them all staring at me, shocked expressions on their faces. I hadn't spoken about a woman like that since Jenna.

Kyle broke the silence first. "You've known her, what? A week? Don't you think that's a little hasty?"

My mother glared at Kyle and we all felt it. "Enough."

We ate to nothing more than the sound of forks and knives on china for a while after that.

We were cleaning up after dinner when my phone pinged in my pocket, and as I'd been eagerly anticipating Autumn's reply, I smiled and pulled it out to check if it was her. It was.

Autumn: K

K? That was it? My smile fell.

"Uh oh, trouble in paradise already?" Jesse mumbled, coming up behind me.

"Screw you."

Ryan whistled. "Someone is sensitive tonight."

My mother poked her head into the kitchen. "Dylan, can you help me with something in the living room?"

My mother had always had impeccable timing. It was like she could feel when one of her sons needed her, and she magically appeared. I followed her into the living room and she sat down in her spot on the corner of the old couch that she refused to get rid of. She had let her shoulder length hair go completely gray, and it suited her.

"What do you need, Ma?"

"Sit down, dear. Let's chat."

I sat in the armchair adjacent to her. "What's up?" I asked, fully knowing what it was about.

"Tell me about her."

I took a breath in, gathering my thoughts. "She's incredible. Naturally beautiful, and I don't think she even realizes it. Inside, too, not just physically. She's witty, and she's extremely intelligent. Plus, she's got a serious career as a director at a property management firm. But mostly, she just gets me." I shrugged. "Frankly, I don't think I'm good enough for her, but for some reason, she wants to date me."

"Why would you say that? You're smart, too, Dylan. And you're ambitious. You started your own business when you were nineteen. It takes brains to be a fireman, too. Your father used to tell me about the calculations that you guys need to do." Anytime she mentioned my father, sadness flashed in her eyes. They had been soulmates, and I knew his death had been much harder on her than she had let on.

"Every day, you have to make high-pressure decisions with life or death consequences. I'd say you need a good head on your shoulders in order to do that." She put her hand on my arm before continuing. "You're exceptionally handsome, and you have the kindest heart of anyone I know."

"I think you're a little biased, Ma."

"A little bit, maybe, but that doesn't make what I'm saying false. That woman is lucky to have you, Dylan. So don't think you don't deserve her."

I couldn't help the smile that escaped my lips. "Thanks, Mom."

"I'm serious. Don't talk yourself out of a good thing."

I stared at her, processing what she had said. In every relationship I'd been in since Jenna's death, I had always kept the woman at arm's length. My mother had called me out on my self-sabotaging on multiple occasions.

She continued. "It's been a long time since I've heard you talk about someone so seriously. I can tell by the look in your eyes that this girl is special to you."

I nodded. "She is." I paused, afraid of the words I knew were coming next. "I think I'm really falling for her, Mom."

My mother covered her heart with her hand and smiled. "I'm so happy for you."

I sighed. "But I think I may have screwed things up."

"Why do you say that?"

I told her about the night of our first date, how I had opened up and had gotten emotional, and how Autumn had been acting differently ever since. "She's being distant. I think I scared her off." I bit the inside of my cheek. "Maybe the guys are right." I was finally vocalizing the fear I'd been keeping at bay for the past twenty-four hours. "Maybe she did have a rescue crush, and when I let my guard down, she realized I'm not this big strong hero she worked me up to be in her mind."

My mother shook her head vehemently. "No. Don't you let your brothers get into your head. You and Kyle are the only ones who've ever been in love anyway. They don't understand it."

Wait, what?

"Kyle has been in love?" That was news to me.

Her pale skin turned a rosy shade of pink. "Forget I said that."

"That's kinda hard to do, Ma."

"Well, you have to try. Besides, I don't think he even realized that's what he'd felt. It was a long time ago, so let's drop it."

I put my hands up in surrender.

"Good. Now tell me, how did your lady react when you told her about Jenna?"

I sighed. "She was amazing about it. Really. She was caring and loving and seemed to genuinely want to make sure I was okay."

My mother crossed her legs and leaned her elbow on her knee to support her chin as she got closer to me. "If she were into you for the wrong reasons, do you really think she'd take care of you like that? Or would she have made an excuse to end the evening?"

I thought about what she said for a moment. "I suppose you're right."

"When are you seeing her again?"

"I'm not sure. I wanted to see her today, but she had other plans. We haven't really had a chance to talk much since the other night. I told her I'd call her when I leave here."

She clapped her hands together. "I'll tell you what, I have a few of my shepherd's pies in the freezer. Take one and go surprise her with dinner tomorrow night. A woman loves it when the man takes the initiative and does something romantic."

I laughed. My mother always had a solution to everything. "That sounds like a great plan."

She patted my hand. "You've always been my most sensitive son."

I rolled my eyes.

"Don't think that's a bad thing, dear. It's actually your strength. Most women have to pull teeth to get men to show any emotion. I bet you Autumn is actually quite grateful you opened up to her." She swallowed hard before continuing, her voice laced with emotion. "And I'm really proud of you. I know how hard it is for you to bring up Jenna. It's quite nice to hear you talk about a woman like this again. I just want you to be happy and stop punishing yourself. You deserve to have the life you want."

A lump formed in my throat, but I swallowed down the emotion and pulled my mother into a hug. "I love you, Mom."

"I love you, too, son."

17

AUTUMN

I stared out the window of my private office overlooking Central Park, daydreaming. I couldn't bring myself to be productive, despite it being a busy Monday. All I could think about was Dylan. We had spoken on the phone for half an hour while he had driven home from his mother's house. He said he'd told his family about me. That was a big deal, right? I mean, technically, we'd only been on one date. Heck, we'd only known each other for a little over a week, and he'd told his family about me already.

I should probably be freaked out, but instead, I felt honored. I thought it was really sweet that he cared about me enough to tell his family, and I so badly wanted to let my happiness win, but I couldn't let it. Him telling his family meant he had serious feelings for me, which only solidified my resolve to end things with him, even if it meant breaking my own heart in the process. I couldn't let him have serious feelings knowing I'd only cause him more hurt. Dylan had suffered enough traumatic loss. I didn't need to add to that.

Even though I knew what I had to do, I really wished I didn't have to end it. I was falling for him. The connection we had was palpable—and I'm not just talking about in the bedroom. I thought if I had just tried to ignore him all weekend, maybe my feelings would go away. Turned out Dylan was a hard person to ignore.

By the time he had called me last night, I'd been weak. I'd missed him terribly, and my own selfish desire to talk to him outweighed my resolve to stay away. When he'd told me he'd spoken with his family about me, my heart had leapt, and I'd fallen even harder. I'd slept on it and woken up knowing that if I cared about him that much, I had to let him go. I couldn't be selfish, for his sake.

I swiped my phone off my desk and typed out a text before I could chicken out.

Me: Are you free tomorrow night?
Dylan: I'm working a 24. I get off at 6pm on Wednesday.

I couldn't drag it out, but I needed some more time to get the courage to end things, so later that night wasn't an option. It had to wait until Wednesday.

Me: After work on Wednesday then?
Dylan: It's a date

I sighed heavily. I was going to hurt him—which was exactly what I was trying not to do, but this kind of hurt was better than the kind of inevitable hurt that would come later.

Dylan: What are you doing tonight?
Me: Quiet dinner at home and a long hot bath
Dylan: Sounds perfect. You, wet and naked…

My thighs clenched at his suggestive choice of words. My body was powerless to his advances. I pictured Dylan in the tub with me, his hard muscles wrapped around my body, slip-ping over my soapy skin. I typed out and deleted my next text six times before having the courage to send it. I shouldn't have. I had no right to lead him on knowing I'd be ending things with him in just a couple of days, but I had a moment of weakness.

Me: It couldn't be perfect without you. Wet and naked together is way more fun
Dylan: God, sweetheart, you're getting me hard

I fought an internal battle: Did I keep the conversation going like I wanted to? Or did I end it like I should?

Me: I might not be naked right now, but I'm definitely wet.

I hung my head in my hands. I was weak. That man was my kryptonite.

Dylan: Well, if the other night was any indication, then you won't need a bath to soak in. I think you do a damn fine job of soaking yourself.
Me: I might need to replace my office chair
Dylan: I'd kill to be that chair right now
Me: Mmm, me too. I'd much rather be sitting on your face
Dylan: My tongue is ready when you are
Me: I don't suppose you are interested in touring an apartment right now? Like maybe you should call my office and mention that I come highly recommended by your friend and you insist on me personally giving you the tour.

It was official. I was going to hell. All thanks to my darn vagina.

Dylan: You're killing me. I'm helping one of my friends do some work at his house right now or I would absolutely LOVE for you to show me an apartment.

Dylan: But now that I know that's an option, I might be apartment hunting real soon.

Disappointment racked my body, but it was for the best. It would've been incredibly irresponsible of me to have sex with Dylan again, considering what I had to do.

But that didn't mean I couldn't fantasize about it at home later...in the tub...with my massaging shower head.

My office phone rang, and I heard my assistant answer it. "I'm sorry, Drew, she isn't in the office today."

I made a mental note to give her a raise. That was the third call from Drew she'd fielded, and she did exactly what I asked her to do about it, no questions asked. Yes, she definitely deserved a raise.

I got home from work and quickly stripped down before adorning myself with my red robe. The soft, silk fabric against my skin made me feel sexy and feminine. As I leaned over the tub to turn on the faucet, I heard a knock at the door. *Who could that be?* I wondered why the front desk hadn't buzzed my intercom to announce someone first.

I tightly wrapped my robe around myself and went out to my door, then got on my tiptoes to look out the peephole. Dylan's smiling face was on the other side. *No!*

I opened the door. "What are you doing here?"

His eyes lit up as they surveyed me in my robe. "Damn, sweetheart. You look sexy as hell."

He walked in and put the bag he was carrying down on the ground as he pulled the door from my hand and shut it behind him. Before I'd had a chance to even process his presence, he had me pinned to the wall with his hips, and his mouth devoured mine. I should have stopped him, but I didn't. I didn't want to. I was a selfish bitch with zero willpower to refuse that man.

I kissed him back, pressing my hips into his, feeling him grow between us. He groaned and pulled back. "I planned on having dinner before dessert, but I had no idea you were gonna answer the door looking like this. I think we might have to do dessert first."

He nuzzled his face into the crook of my neck, leaving a gentle trail of kisses along my collarbone. "Dylan," I moaned, trying to gain some control. "What are you doing here?"

He lifted his head to look at me. "I thought I'd surprise you. I brought homemade shepherd's pie."

My stomach grumbled. "You made shepherd's pie?"

"Technically, no. But it is homemade."

"Oh, yeah? By who?"

"My mom." He bent down to pick up the bag and bring it to the kitchen. "And now that I've heard it out loud, I realize how lame that sounds."

I shrugged. "Actually, I think it's sweet."

"It doesn't make me sound like a thirty-year-old virgin who lives with his mother?"

I laughed hard at that. "First of all, I happen to know for a fact that you, sir, are not a virgin. Second of all, I'm starving, so I don't really care where you got it from, I'm just glad it's here."

He started the oven and put the dish in. "Good, I'm glad. I wasn't sure if you'd be happy to see me or not. At least I know you're happy to see the food. That's a start," he jested.

"I'm happy to see you, too." I rolled my eyes. And it was true. I was happy to see him. Maybe I could allow myself just one more night. After all, I said I'd end things with him on Wednesday, so *technically*, we were still dating.

"I do have a question, though. How'd you get up here without the front desk buzzing me first?"

He popped the cork on a bottle of red wine and poured us each a glass. "The guy tonight is the same one from Friday, so he recognized me and said, 'Oh, you're her boyfriend.' I told him I was trying to surprise you with a romantic dinner, so he let me pass without buzzing you."

He handed me a glass of wine. I took it, ashamed I still hadn't had the courage to tell him I didn't drink. "My boyfriend, huh?"

He looked at me across the kitchen island. His eyes got serious and locked on mine. He nodded. "I didn't correct him either."

I didn't know what to say to that, but it made me smile. *Darn it.* I lifted the wine to my lips, an excuse to avoid having to respond. Then, thankfully, my phone rang.

"I have to take this." I excused myself and went into my bedroom. "Hi, Janet."

"Autumn, hi. How are you?"

"I'm doing all right. How are you? How's Eli?"

"Good. Good. He's been asking about you, and I was wondering if you're available for a quick visit tonight. We're near your apartment, and I know Eli would love to see you."

I thought about it for a second. After my conversation with Dylan last Friday night about how he'd taken a serious risk to save Eli, maybe if Dylan saw Eli, it might make him feel better about the whole thing.

"Sure, Janet, come on by. But you should know, I've been sort of seeing this guy and he's here."

"Oh, I don't want to intrude."

"No, no, you wouldn't be. But you need to know he's the fireman who saved Eli."

Silence.

"Janet?"

"We'll be there in five minutes." Emotion thickened her voice.

She hung up before I could say goodbye. I put clothes on and went back out into the living room where Dylan had made himself comfortable on the couch. He looked so natural there, just relaxing in my apartment.

"Everything okay?"

I nodded. "Yeah. Actually, I know you came here to surprise me, but I have a surprise for you."

"Oh, you do, huh?"

I grinned ear to ear. "Yup. I think you're going to love it. It'll be here in a few minutes."

Five minutes on the dot, my intercom buzzed. When I opened the door, Eli shouted my name and ran into me, giving me a big hug. I rubbed my hand on top of his blonde curls.

"Hey, bud. How are you feeling?"

"I'm totally fine. The doctor said I'm the toughest patient he's ever had." Eli puffed out his chest, looking proud.

Janet stood quietly behind him, staring at Dylan as though she were starstruck.

I turned to Dylan. "Dylan, this is Janet and her son Eli."

Recognition hit the second he heard Eli's name. The color drained from his face, and I thought maybe I'd screwed up by surprising him, but before I could say anything else, Janet ran into his arms, tears flowing freely down her face.

"Thank you so much. I honestly don't know how I'll ever repay you, but I am just so grateful for what you did. My son," she choked back her tears, "he's my whole world. Thank you."

"You don't have to thank me, ma'am. It's my job."

"No. Don't you be humble. Yes, it's your *job*, but you didn't have to risk your life to save my son. Except you did. And I can't thank you enough."

Janet released her grip on Dylan and turned to Eli, who

looked up at her with confusion. "Eli, this is the brave fireman who got you out of the fire."

Eli's soft brown eyes went wide. "Really?" He looked at me for confirmation, and I nodded with an encouraging smile.

He walked straight up to Dylan and gave him a bigger hug than he'd just given me. "Thank you for saving me, mister."

Dylan's Adam's apple bobbed as he bent down to be eye level with Eli. "You're welcome, little dude. Thanks for that awesome hug."

"Do you think maybe I could be a brave fireman one day? Like you?"

Dylan poked Eli in the chest. "I think you can be anything you want to be. You clearly have the brave part down already. I'll tell you what, if it's okay with your mom, maybe you can come down to my firehouse tomorrow after school and I can show you all the trucks. You can try on the gear and see what it's like to be a real firefighter. Maybe you can even stay for dinner with us."

"Really?" Eli bounced from foot to foot. "Mom, please can I go? Please, please, please."

Janet laughed. "Of course."

Eli jumped in the air and high-fived Dylan. "Yes!"

"We have to go now, though, Eli. You have karate in ten minutes."

Janet hugged Dylan one more time and gave him her number to coordinate Eli's visit. She also gave me a giant hug and thanked me for allowing them to meet *their hero*. They left and I turned to look at Dylan, not sure how he'd react to my surprise since we were alone.

My nerves got the best of me and I spoke first. "I'm sorry. I didn't think that through. I should have told you instead of—"

Dylan's mouth was on mine before I could finish my sentence. He wrapped his arms around me, pulling me so tightly against his chest I nearly became a part of him. He lifted his lips so he could look me in the eyes. "Don't apologize.

Thank you for that. I think I really needed to have that moment. I didn't even realize it, but you did. You already know me better than I know myself." He squeezed me tighter. "You're amazing, Autumn," he whispered into my hair as he kissed the top of my head. "Thank you."

Screw my plan. I wanted this. I needed him.

And that was the moment I fell in love with Dylan Hogan.

18

DYLAN

I was in love with Autumn Bianchi.

Laying in the bunk room, halfway through my twenty-four-hour shift, I relived Monday night with my girl. After Janet and Eli had left her apartment, we'd made love twice before dinner and once more before she had fallen asleep cuddled up against my chest. It had been intense, in the best of ways.

Being intimate with Autumn was an otherworldly experience. I was pretty sure when I came, I actually left my body and floated up to the stratosphere. She felt like she was made for me, stretching just enough so I could fill her perfectly. I couldn't wait to see her again in about twelve hours.

When she had surprised me with Eli and Janet, I didn't know how to feel at first. I was uncomfortable at being made into such a hero, but I really needed to see that boy to remind me of why I took such risks. Because of what I'd done, that kid would grow up and have a full life. Hell, maybe he would even become a firefighter himself and save someone else one day. He had seemed to really love his tour of the station the previous night, so that could be a real possibility. I had felt a renewed sense of purpose after that meeting.

And it was all because of Autumn.

I grabbed my phone and opened up my messages to text her, but to my surprise, I already had a message waiting.

Autumn: I can't wait to see you later

I smiled big. I wanted to wake up every morning for the rest of my life feeling that happy.

Me: I bet you I'm more excited to see you than you are to see me
Autumn: Doubtful. You're all I can think about.
Me: Ditto, sweetheart. I wish I was waking up next to you in bed right now
Autumn: Naked?
Me: Is there any other way?

A photo came through of her lying in bed. A sheet just barely covered her nipples. My morning wood twitched. She was so fucking sexy. I snapped a photo of the tent being pitched in my shorts and sent it over to her in response.

Autumn: I have big plans for him later
Me: Promise?

Before she could respond, we got a call. I shot her over a quick text before racing down to put on my gear and get in the rig.

Me: Gotta run. Have to operate with this hammer in my pants now. I'll leave you with that image xo

Once in the truck, I noticed Palmer staring from the jump seat across from me, a sly grin on his face.

I leaned toward him so he could hear me over the loud roar of the truck's engine and the blaring sirens. "What?"

He studied me silently for a few moments before speaking. "You're in love with her, aren't you?"

I answered him with a smile that said more than words could.

He snorted and nodded at me. "Hell, yeah, Hogan."

I'd confided in him about Autumn on Monday when I had helped him at his house. He hadn't really given me much choice since he'd seen me texting her, but I probably would've told him, anyway. He was one of my best friends, and while we ragged on each other a lot, it was out of love.

When I arrived at Autumn's apartment after my tour, the tantalizing scent of garlic and olive oil immediately assaulted me. My mouth watered.

"I don't know what you're making, but if you could figure out a way to bottle that scent, you'd be a very rich woman."

She laughed. "I don't know. I think it would just make people hungry all the time and then they'd be disappointed there was nothing to actually eat."

I thought about it for a moment. "I suppose you're right. I guess you'll just have to make me dinner every night instead." I came up behind her in the kitchen, admiring how cute she looked in her apron, and how great her ass looked in her jeans. I kissed her on that spot behind her neck she loved so much. "Hi, sweetheart."

"Hi." She looked up at me and smiled. "How was work?"

"Busy as usual. But at least we got some sleep last night."

"That's good. I hope you brought your appetite. I'm making Nonna's stuffed artichokes and ravioli Bolognese."

I grunted. "That sounds perfect. I'm starving."

We talked while she made dinner, and I imagined that being our life. I'd come home from work, and she'd make us dinner while we talked about our day. Maybe there would even be a couple of kids doing homework in the next room. Yes, I could do forever like that with her.

When it was time to serve dinner, I helped make the salad and laid out the place settings. After we had our ravioli, Autumn placed an artichoke in front of me that looked like it had come out of a magazine. And the smell…words couldn't do it justice.

I took my first bite, scraping the stuffing off a leaf with my teeth. Garlic, breadcrumbs, parmesan cheese, and olive oil assaulted my taste buds in the most wonderful siege imaginable. "Wow. This might just be the best thing I've ever tasted."

She smiled. "I'm glad you like it."

"No, I don't like it, I'm *obsessed* with this. You're going to have to make these at least once a week."

"No can do. They're a lot of work and Nonna only made them for special occasions. They won't be special anymore if we have them all the time."

"Does that mean today's a special occasion then?"

I could see her mind turning. "Well, it's the first time I've cooked for you, does that count?"

"I'd say that's special, but I don't know if it's Special Occasion Artichoke special."

"Then I guess today is a rare exception."

We finished our dinner, and I cleaned up while the chef rested her feet and relaxed on my orders. While I did so, an idea sparked in my mind. Since she had made us a special occasion meal, I wanted to make it a special occasion. It'd be a night she'd always remember. Once I had cleaned the final dish, I went over to join her on the couch.

I sat down and she immediately scooted over so that she was leaning against my chest, and I put my arm up on the couch behind her.

"I didn't think this through," she said. "Stuffed artichokes make for some very garlicky kisses."

We laughed, and I replied, "That's all right. At least we're both garlicky."

I took a deep breath, readying myself for what I was about to say. My heart was pounding out of my chest and beads of sweat formed on my palms. This was a huge deal for me. It was something I'd only ever told one other person before. I knew it was soon. We'd just met two weeks before, but when you know, you know. There was no rule book for love.

I brushed her hair from the side of her face and tucked it behind her ear. "Autumn, I was thinking, if your nonna only made those artichokes on special occasions, then this needs to be a special occasion."

She lifted her head up and cocked it toward me. I'd apparently piqued her interest. "Oh, yeah?"

My breathing was erratic, and I could hear my pulse in my head. "Autumn," I reached for her hand, nestling it between my own, "I know this is sudden, but I've fallen in love with you."

She sat up and smiled. I could breathe again. But then her smile faded, and she looked down at her lap.

My heart sank.

19

AUTUMN

*H*e loved me. I should be over-the-moon ecstatic — because I felt the same way — but I wasn't. He couldn't love me if he didn't know the truth. And it was time for me to tell him.

A tear escaped my left eye, trailing down my cheek. It was the moment I'd been dreading, the moment our perfect relationship would irrevocably change. And I was terrified.

Dylan dropped his arm from the back of the couch and put his hand on my thigh. He interrupted my mental assault. "Why are you crying?"

Here we go. Point of no return.

"Because I love you, too."

He smiled, and my heart broke a little.

"But also, because I don't want to cause you more pain."

His smile dropped, a look of confusion bubbling up in its wake. "Why would you cause me pain?"

I took a deep breath and fiddled with the hem of my shirt, knowing I had to come clean, but terrified of how he'd react. "I have to tell you something — " I was interrupted by the buzz of the intercom. The man at the front desk announced that my parents were on their way up.

I flew off the couch and charged the door, slamming my back against it as though that would keep them out. "Oh, my God! No!"

Dylan stood. "Autumn, relax, it's just your parents."

"You don't understand. I can't...not now..."

I'd told him before that I didn't have the best relationship with my parents, but he didn't know the half of it, and they were about to give him a live demonstration.

There was a knock at the door followed by my father's irate voice. "Autumn Josephine Bianchi, open this damn door."

I could feel the fear rush through me, chilling my limbs. Dylan must have sensed it as concern filled his eyes. I tried to remind myself to breathe.

This can't be happening.

He knocked again. More like pounded.

Dylan came up beside me and pried my frozen body away from the door. "Hey, it's okay. Whatever *this* is, I'm here. I'm on your side."

Dylan was perfect. And I didn't deserve him.

He wrapped his arm around my waist and pulled me against his hard body as he opened the door, smiling, just to be greeted by the very angry faces of Joseph and Valentina Bianchi.

I hadn't seen them since Christmas. Even though they lived in Connecticut, about forty minutes away from me, I only saw my parents five times a year. If that. They never made an effort to see me, beyond what was *required* of them, and that had been fine by me.

"Who are you?" my dad asked Dylan, his tone devoid of all amusement. My father's stern, dark eyes bore into Dylan, but he didn't waiver.

"Mr. and Mrs. Bianchi, I'm Dylan Hogan." He glanced down at me for a second before returning his gaze to my parents. "Autumn's boyfriend."

I didn't argue.

"Her boyfriend?" my mother erupted dramatically. As usual, not a single dyed-blonde hair was out of place on her head, and her face was expressionless. The result of years of Botox. "Does Drew know about this?"

My chin dropped to my chest. I felt like a child. Any progress I'd made to claim my power was suddenly shot to hell. I might as well have gotten down on the floor in a fetal position right then and there.

Dylan picked up on my reticence and took over. He stepped us to the side and motioned to my parents. "Please, come in."

Without hesitation, they stomped through the doorway.

Dylan closed the door behind them. "Can I take your coats?"

"We're not staying," My father snapped.

Dylan pursed his lips, and I could tell he was biting his tongue. He guided me to the big chair in my living room, and motioned for my parents to take a seat on the couch. And they did. Major points to Dylan for that one.

"Can I get either of you something to drink?" he asked, sounding overly nice.

"No," my father grunted.

Dylan squeezed into the chair beside me and put his arm around my shoulders, tugging me close.

My father redirected his death stare from Dylan to me. "You were in a fire?" he shouted more than asked. Clearly, he already knew the answer. I stayed silent while he continued his assault. "Young lady, would you care to explain to us why we got a phone call from Drew today telling us about it, *two weeks* later?"

I clenched the hem of my shirt in my fist as I opened my mouth to respond, but nothing came out. My vocal cords had obviously clocked out for the evening. Dylan glanced at me and must've noticed that I wasn't going to answer, so he spoke for me. "We're sorry you had to find out that way. As I'm sure you can imagine, things have been crazy for Autumn since the fire. She's doing just fine, though. I promise you she's in good hands."

My mother blinked at Dylan in stunned silence. She looked ridiculous sitting there in her fur coat. I'd never met a single person who could silence Valentina Bianchi. All I could do was stare at him in reverence.

My father, however, was a different story. "Oh, she is, is she? What are you, a doctor?"

"No, sir. I'm a firefighter. I was with Autumn that night. I can assure you, she made it out safely."

My father, seemed to not have a reasonable response, so he did what he did best and ignored Dylan, and continued on with his tirade. "Why did we get a panicked call from Drew saying you haven't been returning his calls, you haven't been at your office, and you refused to go to the hospital?"

That wasn't entirely true. Yes, I'd been ignoring Drew's calls, and I hadn't gone to the hospital, but I was still working. I'd lead Drew to believe that I wasn't simply to keep him from showing up at my office. But I didn't owe my parents an explanation.

My mother's silence was short-lived. "Have you been to the doctor?"

I shook my head, almost imperceptibly.

In her condescending tone, my mother replied, "No? Oh, okay, so you have a death wish then? You want your body to reject that stranger's lung, do you?"

And there it was.

My secret was out.

I couldn't bring myself to look at Dylan, but I felt him tense beside me.

"You put us through all those years of suffering with the cancer and the surgeries, just so you could destroy yourself, anyway. Is that it?" She fake-cried like the drama queen she'd always been. She was a master at it, after all. I'd known it was only a matter of time before she pulled that trick. Everything was always about her. How *my* illness affected *her*. My blood was rising rapidly to my head.

She wasn't done with her assault. "All those years we cared for you. All those doctor visits. The surgeries. The procedures. We put *our* lives on hold for *you* and you're just going to throw it all away like that." She snapped her fingers. "I don't think so. We are taking you to the hospital and you are coming home with us. Tonight."

"No," I shouted, jumping to my feet, surprising everyone — myself included. "You don't get to talk to me like that. I'm sorry I was an *inconvenience* for you, mother, but you don't get to say you put *your* lives on hold for me. You don't get to say you cared for me. Alma did that. Nonna did that. And you certainly don't get to barge into *my* apartment — uninvited — and berate me like this. I'm not a child anymore."

Wow. Where did that come from? That was new. I kinda liked it.

My father stood, towering over me with his presence, though he was only four inches taller. "Enough," he spat and pointed his finger in my face. "You are clearly too irresponsible to be out on your own. And you will not speak to your mother like that—"

"Everyone just stop." Dylan stood up, cutting my father off. "This fighting isn't going to resolve anything." He positioned himself between me and my father, protectively.

After everything he'd just heard, he was still there.

He was still on my side.

He knew my secret, and he was still there.

I really didn't deserve him, but I'd never wanted him more. My heart swelled.

"Now, I think the two of you should leave. Upsetting Autumn like this can't be good for her health." He glared at me, and I quickly averted my eyes. He wasn't happy. "When you're ready to sit down and have a civil conversation, give Autumn a call and schedule a time to *talk* to her."

My mother gasped, covering her mouth with her hands as though Dylan had slapped her. My father glared up at him, his lips pursed, and their eyes locked. My father was never one to back down, but it looked like Dylan wasn't going to back down either. Had my parents finally met their match?

20

DYLAN

I wouldn't say I *slammed* the door behind Autumn's parents, but I definitely closed it forcefully. Who in the hell did those people think they were, talking to their daughter like that? And what the fuck had I just witnessed?

Once the door shut, I heard Autumn take in a big gulp of air, and she let out a sob that I swear would haunt my dreams forever. I ran back to the living room and gathered her into my arms, telling her to breathe, fearful she would lapse into a panic attack.

I lowered her down onto the couch and tried to comfort her while she fell apart. I was conflicted I wanted to make her pain go away, but I also wanted to shake her. How could she have not told me? While she cried, questions circled through my brain. I wanted to know everything. Why had she needed a lung transplant? How long ago? Cancer? Was she still sick?

Finding out the way I had was far from ideal, but I paused the disappointment churning in my gut, to remind myself that two weeks ago, I hadn't even known that she'd existed. Could I really blame her for not leading with *I had cancer and a lung transplant*? No. That wouldn't be fair. But I thought I deserved answers.

I felt her starting to calm down in my arms. She stopped shaking and her breathing returned to a more normal rate. "Shh, it's okay, sweetheart." I held her and rubbed her hair to soothe her. Her sobs reduced to a whimper.

She wiped her face with her hands and leaned forward to sit on the edge of the couch. I went into the kitchen and poured her a glass of water.

"Here you go." I handed her the glass and napkin.

"Thanks." She rubbed her nose with the napkin before taking a long gulp of the water.

I stayed quiet, while I waited for her to fully compose herself.

After a few minutes, she put the glass down on the coffee table. "I am so sorry you had to witness that. I'm utterly mortified." She couldn't bring herself to look at me.

"It's okay. It's not like you planned to be ambushed," I reassured her. "You don't have to apologize for that. And you have nothing to be embarrassed about. Their behavior is not your responsibility."

"I don't deserve you," she whispered. She turned her head and I noticed that her hazel eyes had changed to a kelly-green. The leftover moisture from her tears made them glisten. "Thank you for standing up for me. No one has ever done that for me before."

That pissed me off. I couldn't imagine what life was like for her with parents who were so reactionary and hostile. She'd been on her own for so long, and I struggled to understand what that must have been like. My family had always been close, and I was saddened by the knowledge that she hadn't had that.

"And, Dylan, I'm sorry you had to find out that way. That's what I was trying to tell you. Before they showed up."

I nodded. "I figured. I can understand why you didn't tell me."

"You can?" She looked shocked.

"Yeah. I know we've moved this relationship pretty fast. We haven't known each other very long, so I can understand why you wouldn't want to talk about it. But I'm hoping you'll tell me now."

She nodded. "Of course." She leaned back on the couch, pulling her legs up to her chest, and stared off into the room, not at anything in particular. "I was sick a lot as a child. After what seemed like a year of endless bouts of pneumonia, my parents finally took me to see a specialist. That's when they found the mass on my right lung. It hadn't been visible in chest X-rays previously, so they'd kept treating me for pneumonia."

She took a deep breath and lowered her chin down to her knees. "I was eight years old. They did a biopsy, and it came back cancerous. Pleuropulmonary Blastoma or PPB. It's quite rare...guess I'm lucky like that," she said, apparently trying to make light of her condition. "So, I had surgery to remove the mass and it was successful. I was cancer-free."

Cancer at eight years old. Fuck.

"I got to go back to a real school after having been home-schooled for two years because I was sick, and I was really getting into it, too. I started middle school, got involved with a bunch of clubs, but halfway through sixth grade, I started to feel sick again. I was having trouble breathing. Again."

She paused as if to collect her thoughts. I was astounded by her strength. The worst thing I'd had to deal with in middle school had been wet dreams and my voice changing.

She reached for her water glass and took a sip before settling back against the couch. She balanced the glass on her knees, which she still had pulled up to her chest. "I went back to the specialist, and sure enough, my cancer was back. This time, it was *much* bigger. Because of the size of the mass, chemo wasn't an option, and neither was surgery. I needed a lung transplant."

Even though I knew it'd been coming, hearing her say it

was still shocking. I lifted my hand to my mouth and pinched my lower lip between my fingers.

Her jaw tensed and her tone was laced with bitterness. "I was pulled from school—again—and I spent the next year partially homeschooled and partially too sick to function until we finally got the call." She stopped and blinked her eyes rapidly, willing away the threatening tears. "I was twelve. Before I could really even process what was happening, I was being wheeled into surgery to get a new lung." She said that last part in a near whisper, and I could tell she was fighting back years of pain.

She scoffed. "My parents were on a two-week river cruise in the Mekong Delta because they, and I quote, 'had to get away from the stress for a little while.' They didn't even know I'd gotten the call until my new lung was already in place."

Tears stung my eyes. I thought of her as a twelve-year-old girl, wondering if she were going to die or if she would get a new lung and survive. I didn't think I would've been able to cope with something like that at twelve. And to have to go through it alone...

Fucking hell.

She was quiet, and I wasn't sure if she had more to say or not, so I asked, "If your parents weren't there, who took you for the surgery?"

"Nonna was there, and I had Alma."

"Alma was your housekeeper, right?"

She fidgeted. "Umm, actually, she was my in-home nurse." She looked up at me for the first time since she'd started telling her story. "I'm sorry I lied about that before. But the part about her teaching me to cook was true. Promise."

I believed her and shrugged it off. "I get it. What happened then? After the surgery."

"Obviously, it was a success since I'm here with you right now, but it took me a long time to recover, and I never returned to school. I had my own private teacher who understood why I threw myself into my schoolwork, wanting to graduate as soon as possible. She saw what I lived with. You just got a small taste of my parents."

All I could do was shake my head, at a loss for words.

"Once I had my new lung, they became helicopter parents. I was *expensive*," she said, her voice dripping with disdain. "And they never let me forget it. My private teacher, my home nurse, my doctor bills, my medications...that all adds up. And, don't get me wrong, I'm grateful they were able to provide that for me, but they'll never let me live it down. I was raised in a bubble."

It was a good thing I hadn't known that before my encounter with her parents. I wouldn't have been so kind.

"That's why I was never allowed to travel with them; why I pushed myself to graduate early so I could go to college. I knew that was my ticket to some kind of freedom."

She let her legs fall to the side. "Then when I was seventeen, the doctor's found a tumor on my healthy lung, and I was terrified that I'd have to go through it all again, but thankfully it was benign. I've been healthy ever since. Well, with the exception of one scare I had about two years ago when I got sick." She paused, and I couldn't help but notice the pain wince across her brow. "But I got through that. My new lung has lasted me almost thirteen years, which is a really good success rate. It's inevitable that I'll need another transplant at some point."

She let her legs fall to the side and looked me square in the face. "That's why when you told me you loved me, I started to cry." She squeezed her eyes shut and when she opened them, beads of water dotted the corners, but she'd kept herself from crying again. "You lost your father and your girlfriend so traumatically, and I simply can't bring myself to put you through that kind of pain again." She reached out and grabbed my hand. "I love you, Dylan, and that's why I can't be with you.

The odds of you losing me as well are high. I can't do that to you. Not again."

I pulled her into a hug, as I swallowed the emotion in my throat. "Oh, sweetheart, please don't feel that way. I think I love you even more because you're trying to protect me, but don't keep us apart because of that. Just because you were sick doesn't mean you don't deserve to be happy and loved."

She gazed into my eyes, repeating what she'd said earlier. "I don't deserve you."

It broke my heart. "Don't say that, sweetheart. You're beautiful, inside and out. You're brilliant, and you're definitely the bravest person I know. You, going through all that...you amaze me. If anything, it's me who doesn't deserve you."

She kissed me softly on the lips. "Thank you."

I brushed her hair out of her face and tucked it behind her ear. "Thank you for sharing your story with me. I'm not gonna lie, I'm a little hurt you didn't tell me, but like I said, I can understand why."

"I felt awful lying to you. When I told you my scar was from a car accident, and you told me about your girlfriend, I was so mad at myself. I just...I was afraid you would leave me if you knew the truth."

That stung. *Could she possibly think so little of me? Of herself?*

"Why would you think that?" I asked.

"Let's just say it wouldn't be the first time I had my heart broken because a guy couldn't handle my condition."

I stared at her in disbelief, wondering what kind of man would do such a thing. "Well, that's his loss. He never deserved you."

"I won't argue with you there. But, if I'm being honest, life with me is *different*. I have to take extra precautions and sometimes can't do things everyone else does."

The magnitude of what she was saying suddenly dawned on me. "Fuck. Autumn, the alcohol. You're not supposed to drink."

She nodded almost imperceptibly and fiddled with the hem on her shirt. "I didn't know how to tell you."

"Seriously?" I was stunned. "You put yourself at risk because you 'didn't know how to tell me' you can't drink? Why the hell would you do that?"

"I know it wasn't smart. I just…I really wanted you to like me. Things were going so well with us, and I didn't want to mess it up by telling you I can't enjoy that part of life."

The veins in my temples throbbed and I clenched my jaw. "That was foolish, Autumn. How could you think so little of me? You think I'd leave you because you don't drink?"

"It isn't a reflection on you. I swear–"

"Well, I don't know how else to interpret it. And besides that, as much as I don't want to side with your parents, did you really not go see your doctor after the fire?" The thought alone blew my mind. She was too smart for that, and couldn't possibly have been so careless, right?

She stared down at her lap. That was all the answer I needed. My anger propelled me to jump up. My hands balled into fists at my sides. I was concerned for the woman I loved and dumbfounded by how she could be so irresponsible. Maybe I didn't really know her after all.

21

AUTUMN

I didn't like seeing Dylan angry, and I was beyond pissed at myself for causing it, but I was tired of letting other people tell me how to live my life. It was bad enough I had to deal with that from my parents and my friends. Even Drew had done that sometimes. I hated it. And I hated that Dylan had started doing it, too.

He paced in my living room. "I know you're smarter than that. You inhaled smoke. With a donor lung, for fuck's sake. Why wouldn't you go get checked out?"

That was it. I wasn't going to let Dylan become like everyone else in my life who felt entitled to tell me what to do. "Because I felt fine! Because I didn't want to go. Because I'm sick and tired of everyone treating me like I'm fragile. That's why!"

He recoiled, surprised at my outburst, no doubt. "Do you hear yourself right now? You didn't go to the doctor after being in a *fire* because you 'didn't want to go' and you got *drunk* because you 'didn't know how to tell me' you don't drink. That's so irrational."

His air quotes were infuriating. "Don't throw my words back at me. You don't understand—"

"I do understand! I lost my father to heart disease because he pushed himself too far. You say you don't want to be with me because you don't want to hurt me. Well, hell, Autumn, if you're looking to kill yourself, you're certainly going about it the right way. So don't tell me I don't understand or that you don't want to hurt me when your behavior indicates that you want to hurt yourself. And that? *That* hurts me."

His words stung. Mostly because I knew he was right, but I was too agitated to concede. So I did what I had to do to protect myself. "I think you should leave."

He huffed and shook his head. "I just told you I love you. Like it or not, I care about your well-being and since your actions have been so irresponsible, I feel like I need to call you out on it *because* I love you. So think of this as a wakeup call." He knelt down in front of me, so we were closer to eye-level. "If you want me to go, I'll go, but not until you promise me you'll get over yourself and go to the doctor."

I was seeing a new side of Dylan, and it was both maddening and hot as hell. My breath hitched and my girl parts tingled. I hated that my body responded to him favorably when my brain was pushing him out the door and throwing away the key.

I ignored my body and got up from the couch. I walked around him and went to the door, opening it. Glaring at him, I told him to go with my eyes.

He sighed heavily and stood before meeting me in the entry. He grabbed his jacket off the hook. "Promise me," he breathed out, standing inches from my face.

The musky smell of his cologne was intoxicating. My sex clenched, only making me infuriated.

"Fine," I uttered, mainly to placate him.

He leaned his forehead against mine for a brief moment and I thought maybe he was going to kiss me, but instead, he took a deep breath before backing away and going through the doorway. He paused and turned back to look at me. "The ball is in your court."

I watched him walk down the hall to the elevator, my frustration building with each step he took. I heard the ding of the elevator arriving, and I slammed my door in response.

He left. He actually left. And there I was, the fragile, broken-hearted, sick girl—all alone. Again.

I knew I was the one who told him to go, but I didn't actually *want* him to go. And I was scared. One of my favorite things about Dylan was how he treated me like I was normal, and I knew it would never be like that again. I never wanted him to look at me in the way he had before leaving—like I was broken. I wanted him to love me as a strong, confident woman, not as the meek girl I tried hard to keep hidden inside. Because that girl—she was unlovable.

I knew this to be true because I'd experienced it. First, my parents never let me forget that I was too fragile to have a normal life. Then, Drew showed me I was too much to handle. And everything with Dylan was ruined because of it.

I snatched my cell phone off the counter and dialed Drew's number. He answered on the second ring.

"Autumn, thank God. Are you all right? I've been trying to reach—"

"How dare you," I hissed through my teeth. "You called my parents? Are you out of your fucking mind?" I knew Drew would immediately understand how angry I was from my choice of words.

"Whoa, baby, I was worried about you. You haven't returned any of my calls. I've been calling your office and your assistant keeps saying you aren't in. I don't know where you live so I couldn't come check on you. How was I supposed to know you hid the fire from your parents?"

"It's none of your business! I didn't respond because I didn't want to talk to you. You hurt me, Drew. You don't get to come back into my life all this time later and expect me to just welcome you with open arms. You have no right to be concerned about me anymore."

"I'll never stop caring about you, baby."

"I AM NOT YOUR BABY," I screamed before jamming my finger against the hang-up button on my cell phone. It wasn't nearly as gratifying as slamming a real phone down on the receiver, so I threw my cell across the room and watched it smash into pieces.

I collapsed against the kitchen island, buried my face in my hands and cried. I cried because I wasn't allowed to live a normal life.

Because my parents were detached assholes.

Because I felt betrayed by Drew all over again.

Because I never wanted to hurt Dylan.

Because I hated feeling the way I did when he looked at me with pity.

Because I loved him.

Because I'd screwed it all up.

After allowing myself to have my pity party for a little bit, I went to the bathroom and examined my reflection in the mirror, repulsed by how dreadful I looked. My eyes were puffy, my hair was a bird's nest, and I felt like I'd been hit by a truck. I forced myself to shower and pull myself together. All I wanted to do was throw on my sweats, curl up in a ball, and never leave my bed.

The only problem was, that wouldn't get me Dylan back.

His words—*the ball is in your court*—echoed in my head. I had to swallow my pride and fix things, except my only means of communicating with him lay in pieces on my living room floor. I piled my wet hair into a messy bun on top of my head, brushed on a layer of powdered foundation to hide the red blotches on my face, and swiped a few strokes of concealer under my eyes in a futile attempt to hide the puffiness. In my bedroom, I grabbed the first pair of jeans in the drawer and slipped those on with the sweater I'd worn to work earlier. I put on my coat, wrapped a scarf around my neck, slipped on gloves and a hat, then grabbed my keys and made my way out the door.

As I walked the six blocks to Dylan's firehouse, I tried to convince myself not to sound crazy and desperate when I got there. It was a long shot, but I needed to see him. I knew he wasn't working, but I hoped someone there could help me find him. I knew he lived in Yonkers, but I'd never been to his house before. Since we both worked in the city, it had made sense for us to always stay at my place, so I didn't have his address.

Since the doors were shut this time, I rang the bell. A voice came over the intercom. "Can I help you?"

"Um, hi, yes, I'm Autumn Bianchi. Dylan Hogan's...girl-friend." It felt good to say that for the first time. I just hoped it wasn't too late for it to still be true. "I'm sorry to bother you, but I, umm, I broke my phone and I don't have any other way of getting in touch with him so I was hoping someone here could help me."

"Be right there."

A moment later, a man opened the door. "Come on in."

I followed him into the dark truck house. I didn't recognize him as one of the guys I'd met the last time I'd gone by there. He was also very attractive. Muscular, with caramel-colored eyes and a killer smile. It really must be part of the job requirement. *FDNY seeks attractive men with obscenely large muscles and the ability to put out fires in buildings, but start fires in women's panties.*

He broke me from my delusion. "I'm Ewan, but everyone calls me Frisco, on account of me being from San Francisco."

"Oh, Dylan told me about you. You were with him during the fire in my building, right?"

"Yeah, I was. Glad you're doing okay."

"Thanks. For everything."

He shrugged. "No sweat."

"I'm really sorry to bother you this late. I was worried I'd wake you guys up."

"Everyone else is sleeping, but I've got the night watch tonight, so it's just me."

I exhaled in relief. "I'm glad. It makes this a little less embarrassing, not having to be in front of all the guys."

He waved me off with his hand. "Don't worry about it. No need to be embarrassed. How can I help?"

"Well," I twisted the hem of my coat. "I really need to get in touch with Dylan. We kind of got into a fight and I told him to leave. I didn't actually mean it, but he left anyway and then I got mad and threw my phone, which exploded, and now I have no way to reach him and I really need to see him and apologize."

Oh, my God. My face heated, and I slammed my hand over my mouth. "I'm so sorry. I don't know why I just told you all that."

He smiled. "Don't sweat it. I'm married. Trust me, I've definitely screwed up before. I can give you his address if you want."

"Yes, please. Thank you. That would be great."

"Wait here, I'll be right back." He went into the booth and came out a minute later with a piece of paper containing Dylan's address.

"Thank you again."

He nodded. "Autumn, a little advice: Dylan can be a bit hot-headed, but he's mostly a reasonable guy. And I know he cares about you. He's been walking around with this goofy grin ever since he met you."

That brought a much-needed smile to my lips. Maybe there was hope for us yet. "Thanks, Frisco. I mean it."

He showed me out the door. "Anytime. Good luck."

With Frisco's blessing and Dylan's address in my pocket, I walked to the corner and stuck my hand out to hail a cab. I was going to Yonkers.

22

DYLAN

What the fuck had just happened? I laid in bed, staring up at the ceiling, trying to figure out how our evening had started out so perfectly, but ended so horribly.

As scary as it had been for me to tell Autumn I loved her, it had also made me happier than I'd been in a long time. Too fucking long. To hear her say she loved me too had made me feel like I was on top of the world. I was really lucky that a woman like her could even like me, let alone love me.

Yet, she did.

And I loved her so much more for it.

As I reflected on the way we had left things, I wondered if she was still my girlfriend. I was angry with her, yes, but I still wanted to be with her. It pained me that she had hidden such a big part of herself from me—and it infuriated me that she'd taken the risks she had just because she didn't want me to know the truth. That stung.

While a part of me understood her reasoning, I still couldn't condone the risks she'd taken. It was my job to keep her safe, and I had failed.

I had failed her.

Maybe she was better off without me. If she hadn't been

trying to act normal for me, as she'd put it, then she wouldn't have put herself at risk. Hell, I'd actually put her in more danger by loving her. I needed to apologize.

I grabbed my phone off my nightstand, opened my messages, and clicked on her name.

Me: I'm sorry

I didn't hit send. I stared at the screen. That wasn't enough. I deleted it.

Me: Please forgive me

Delete.

Me: I love you

I stared at those three words, unable to bring myself to hit the send button because I didn't deserve her.

Just as I was hitting the delete button again, I heard a knock on my door. *Who could possibly be visiting me at this hour?* I ignored it, figuring someone had the wrong address. I started to type out a new message.

Me: You were right to tell me to leave. I'm not good enough for you. I'm sor

I heard the knock again. After putting my phone down, leaving my text unfinished, I went to the door. Through the peephole, I saw Autumn hugging herself out in the cold. *What the hell?* I opened the door.

"Autumn? What—how?"

"I'm sorry to just show up like this, but I really need to talk to you."

I stepped aside to let her in. "How did you even find me?"

"Don't be mad, but I went to your firehouse and Frisco gave me your address."

I stared at her, not knowing whether I should be freaked out or impressed. "You could've called."

"I would have." She dug into her purse and pulled out several pieces of metal and glass. "But I may have taken my anger out on my phone."

I smirked. She was so damn cute. "Did it make you feel better?"

"Worse, actually." She let out a sigh.

"Let me take your jacket." I hung it up on the hook by the door and ushered her through the hallway and over to the black leather couch in my living room. "I can't believe you came all the way up to Yonkers in the middle of the night. How'd you even get here?"

She took a seat in the middle of the couch and I found my place next to her.

"I took a cab. I couldn't just leave things with us like that. The only way I knew how to reach you was through your firehouse. I hope that's okay. I swear I'm not some crazy stalker."

I grinned. "I'm glad you're here."

And I was.

When I had left, I'd told her the next move was hers. I was happy that she took it, but it would be a million times harder letting her go face to face. Even if it was the best for her, having her near made me question my decision.

Her eyes fixed on mine. They'd returned to their normal hazel color, but the lids were swollen and they were bloodshot. "I'm sorry, Dylan. I shouldn't have made you leave. I was angry and freaked out. I took my own insecurities out on you, and I shouldn't have. I'm sorry."

"I'm sorry, too. I shouldn't have yelled at you like that. But mostly, I'm sorry for putting you in danger."

"Putting me in danger?" She furrowed her brow. "You did nothing of the sort."

"Except I did. You wouldn't have been so reckless if it wasn't for me."

She stared at me for a beat. "Maybe not. But, that's not *your* fault. It's mine." She started fiddling with the hem of her sweater. "You're the first person who's treated me like I'm normal and not fragile. I didn't want to ruin that." She sighed. "I wasn't expecting you. When we met, there was this...thing between us. A spark. I've never felt that before. I liked it. I wanted more. So, I lied."

Her head drooped and she stared at her hands as they balled up her sweater. "I regret that. And I know my behavior was stupid, but I'm just so tired of people telling me what to do and how to live my life. I wanted to feel normal for once."

She swallowed. "I didn't want you to look at me the way so many others have." Her voice cracked. "I wasn't broken around you."

I put my hand on her thigh.

"But tonight, after you found out, you gave me that same darn look that everyone else has, and I knew the fantasy I'd been living was ruined. I told you to leave because I figured it would hurt me less now than when you'd leave down the road." Her voice lowered to a tone just above a whisper. "And I was letting you off the hook. No one wants to be with the sick girl."

"That's ridic–"

She put her hand up, silencing me. "Let me finish. I know what you are going to say, but trust me, I'm not just making this up. I've lived it." She stared off into the corner. "Drew was my first boyfriend. My only boyfriend, actually. We started dating in college, and he knew about what I'd gone through. He'd get frustrated sometimes when I couldn't go drinking with our friends or do certain activities, but we made it work."

My jaw tensed at the mention of her ex. From everything she'd already told me, he sounded like a real piece of shit. I knew this story would be no different.

"About two years ago, I got a bad case of bronchitis, which, for someone like me, could be a death sentence. He helped me through it, but the recovery was long and arduous. I spent a few weeks in the hospital, and even after I was released, I had to limit my activity and socialization. My immune system is already weak because of the immunosuppressants so I need to avoid big crowds as it is, but even more so when my body is fighting off an infection."

I listened intently as she told her story. Having a sense of where it was going, her behavior made a lot more sense.

"At the time, I knew it was frustrating for Drew to have a girlfriend who was too sick to leave the house, but I thought he loved me. I thought he felt like I was more important than," she paused, "his social activities."

Her voice cracked, and I instinctively covered her hand with my own to comfort her.

She took a deep breath as if to collect herself. "He started acting a little strange. I talked to my friend Britt about it, and she put this idea in my head that he was probably going to propose and that he was just acting weird because he was nervous. I mean, we'd been together for five years at that point, and I had almost just *died*, so I really started to believe he was going to ask me to marry him."

The thought of Autumn marrying anyone other than me made my stomach turn. But it was too soon to be thinking about marriage. Wasn't it?

"One night, about a year and a half ago, I was finally starting to feel better, so Drew made plans for us to go out for a nice dinner at this new restaurant we'd been wanting to try. That was it. I thought for sure that was the night we were getting engaged. Britt came over and helped me curl my hair and I was so excited. When Drew and I got to the restaurant, it was crowded, like *really* crowded even by Manhattan's standards. I knew I probably shouldn't be packed into a place with all those people, but I was *not* going to ruin his proposal so I kept quiet."

She clutched the bottom of her sweater in her fist. "We eventually got to our table, and it was obnoxiously loud in there, we could barely speak. I was also getting super nervous because there was this guy at the table next to us—which was literally so close we might as well have been at the same table—and he kept coughing. I tried to hide my fear, but Drew saw right through me and we ended up leaving after only having appetizers. I asked if he wanted to go somewhere else, but he said no, and we just went home. I could tell he felt defeated, and I was frustrated with myself for being so darn fragile. We didn't say a word to each other the entire cab ride back to our apartment."

I wanted to punch that guy for making her feel that way. She'd used the word *fragile* several times, and I hated that she felt like that defined her. With everything she'd been through, she was far from fragile. Hell, she was the strongest person I knew.

Her voice pulled me back from my fantasy of putting my fist through that guy's face. "We got home, and the second we closed the door, he just blurted out, 'I can't do this anymore.' At first, I didn't know what he meant. I thought we were getting engaged that night, I never expected he'd been acting the way he was the few weeks prior because he wanted to break up with me. But that's exactly what he did."

Tears fell down her cheek. "He 'couldn't handle being with a sick girl anymore.' He said he 'wanted a normal life.' And being me with 'wasn't enough for him.'"

I squeezed her hand tightly. The way she quoted him told me that she'd spent entirely too much time mulling over his words. She'd gotten to a point where she believed them. And because of him, I'd almost lost her.

She wiped the tears from her face. "I left right then and never looked back. I didn't see him again after that until the night of the fire. Then I ran into him in Herald Square and he had the audacity to tell me he made a mistake and wants me back. He sent me flowers, called my office when I wouldn't respond on my cell, and then tonight—my parents." She shook her head. "After all the hurt and pain he put me through, he has the nerve to act like what he did was as mundane as, oh, I don't know, forgetting to get something I asked for from the grocery store."

She looked deep in thought.

"I'm sorry, Autumn. I'm sorry he treated you like that. He never deserved you, that's for sure."

She shook her head adamantly. "I didn't tell you all that just to make you feel bad because I got my heart broken. I felt like I had to tell you because it explains—or at least I hope it does—*why* I hid my condition from you. Like I said, this thing between us, I don't know, it's special. And I loved being treated like a normal girl for once in my life. You never looked at me with pity. You didn't treat me like I was fragile. And it felt good. So. Flipping. Good."

God, she was adorable. Even though she was sad. I pulled her hand up to my lips and kissed the back. "I get it now, sweetheart. And thank you for sharing that with me. But I need you to promise me something, okay? Please, don't let that dickhead's immaturity make you believe things about yourself that simply aren't true. Stop calling yourself fragile because you are far from it. You fought cancer *twice*—and won. While other kids were being stupid teenagers, you had a lung transplant, and not only survived, but you graduated high school *early*. At twenty-five, you are a director in your company. And you just told me that story about how you faced death—again —and survived. Hell, two weeks ago even, *you* got yourself out of a burning building."

I cupped her face in my hands, forcing her to look at me. "You are *not* fragile." I punched my words out to make sure they really got through to her. "Sweetheart, you are a strong, brave, bad ass woman."

The corners of her lips curled upward.

"I love you. I need you to understand that I'm not Drew. I'm not going to up and leave simply because things are *different*. Okay?"

And just like that, my plan to leave her was shot to shit. It was clear that I needed her, and I was pretty sure she needed me, too.

She nodded almost imperceptibly before throwing her arms around my neck. I pulled her as close to me as I could get, and it still wasn't close enough. Close simply wasn't enough. I needed to merge with her, to be a part of her. I wished so badly I could take the pain from her.

"I love you, too. So much."

I let out a breath and pulled back slightly, just far enough to take her lips in between mine. I kissed her with a passion uniquely our own. Kissing Autumn had always been intense, but this kiss was earth-shattering. This kiss screamed desire, love, *need*. I needed her, and she needed me, too.

As our tongues danced, she pressed her body against mine, and her fingers ran through my hair. The warmth emanating off her body blanketed me, and I realized she was it. She was the woman who was going to heal my heart. In a way, she'd already begun to do so. The brick wall I'd built slowly began to crumble when she had come into my life. And I needed more.

23

AUTUMN

*O*ur kiss said it all. All the words we'd left unspoken, the desire we'd fought, the love we shared. That kiss — Dylan's kiss — breathed new life into me, and I knew I would never be the same.

I needed him. All of him.

I worked my hands up his shirt, nudging it over his head before yanking my sweater off. I craved his bare skin on mine. He must've felt it, too, because he wasted no time unhooking my bra and tossing it to the floor.

His warm skin pressed against my nipples, causing them to harden instantly. I ran my hand over his abs, feeling every curve of every muscle beneath my fingertips as I made my way to his drawstring. My fingers slipped under his waistband, and he lifted his hips, allowing me to pull his shorts down and discard them, freeing his erect member. He stood and reached his hand out to pull me up from the couch, his eyes burning with desire.

Instead of grabbing his hand, I looked him over for a moment, studying him. He was beautiful. His light brown hair was left disheveled from my fingers and the slightest hint of stubble concealed his chiseled jaw. His lips transfixed me—they glistened from our kiss. The bulge from his shoulder muscles continued to his biceps, reminding me of how safe I felt in his arms. The pink nubs on his smooth chest stood at attention and the sight made my own peaks crest.

I couldn't resist the urge to run my hand over his sculpted abs again, feeling each one contract beneath my palm. My fingertips traced his deep cut V, which led down to his swollen manhood. He was so hard, I could see the veins that ran through his shaft. I couldn't wait another second. I needed him. I leaned forward and took him in my mouth, eliciting a moan from his lips.

"Fuck. Autumn."

I loved the way he hissed my name.

I made a conscious effort to relax my throat and pull as much of him as I could between my lips. He fit me perfectly—everywhere. I cupped his balls as I pulled my head back, swirling my tongue around his shaft as I went. His legs trembled, and I felt a surge of power at knowing I could do that to him. I could make that big, strong man squirm.

I ran my tongue along the slit on his head, tasting the salty layer of pre-cum. Dylan let out this primal sound that I felt between my legs.

"You are so damn good at this." His words pushed me further, and I swallowed him to the hilt.

I needed this.

I needed him.

I needed to feel this powerful.

His hands worked their way into my hair as he pulled himself out of me. I went to protest, but he beat me to words. "You're gonna...make me...come. Not yet. I need to...be inside you first," he uttered between labored breaths.

Dylan shoved his coffee table to the side and pulled me to my feet, making quick work of my jeans. His fingers found my warm center, and he parted my lips, easily slipping inside. I tossed my head back as his mouth closed around my nipple.

This man made me feel sexy, which had never been a word I'd used to describe myself. He made me feel desired, as though his body had to feed off of mine to live.

"Dylan," I whispered, drawing out the vowels. His touch was beautiful torture. I needed more.

As though he could sense what I was thinking, he spun us around and lowered me on top of him as he sat down on the couch. His rod pressed against my slit.

"Fuck," he growled, drawing the word out. "You are so wet for me, sweetheart."

I bit my lip as I lowered myself, taking all of him inside of me. He tried to thrust upward, but I pushed his hips down, compelling him to stay still to prolong our pleasure. He stared into my eyes, and I just knew we were both feeling the same thing.

He was a part of me.

I was a part of him.

This was love. Not any kind of love. *This* was what you felt with a soulmate. I just knew.

My heart skipped a beat, and my breath caught in my throat. His eyes bore into mine, seeing me in a way I'd never been seen before. He saw my soul. And I saw his. We were both a little broken, and I swear I could feel my pieces being put back together in that moment.

He began to rock his hips beneath me, moving slowly at first, letting me savor every inch of him as he penetrated deeper between my walls before retreating.

Deeper.

And retreating.

Deeper.

He gripped the back of my head, and kissed me with a burning intensity. He filled my mouth as he filled my sex. We were one.

His fingers found my throbbing bud, rubbing me as I rode him.

176

I contracted my walls.

He increased the pressure with his fingers.

I rolled my hips, moans leaked from my mouth.

It took all of my willpower to keep my lips on his, because I so badly wanted to scream.

His hips thrust up to meet my own movements, and I could feel him twitch inside me, his release working its way to the surface.

I drilled down on him one more time, and that was all I needed. I tried to pull my mouth away from his, but his hand on the back of my head held me in place. My nerves fired and my muscles quaked around him as I screamed into his mouth, releasing all the pain and the anger and the hurt I'd been holding onto for years. Relief washed over me and I felt...free.

His own release followed mine, and his mouth vibrated from the guttural moans that escaped his lips as he came—filling me with his seed. He was letting go, too, of all the pain and loss he'd been carrying.

When we both descended from our euphoria, he finally released the back of my head and planted the softest kiss on my lips before letting me pull away. He held my face in his hands, forcing me to look at him, and we were both teary-eyed.

I swallowed the lump in my throat a few times, overwhelmed by my own emotions, not sure how to process what had just happened. It was in that moment I knew that, no matter what, Dylan would always be a part of me.

24

DYLAN

"How do I look?" Autumn stepped out of my bedroom wearing a sweater dress that showed off all her curves, and it took every ounce of my willpower to keep from grabbing her and tracing her sides with my hands.

"You look beautiful, sweetheart."

"You think? Or should I try that other top on again with my jeans instead of that skirt?"

I laughed. This was the third outfit she'd tried on so far. She was cute when she was nervous. I take that back. She was always cute.

I got up from the couch and went to her, putting my hands on her hips. "You're perfect. It doesn't matter what you wear, they'll love you."

"Oh, yeah? Well, in that case, I did get some new lingerie the other day. Maybe I could—"

I planted a kiss on her lips. "Okay, maybe it matters a little bit what you wear. I don't need my brothers fighting me for you."

She patted my chest, and I took a step back. "I just want to look good for your family. I want them to like me."

A smile escaped my lips. "They will. I'm sure of it."

"I'm going to grab my boots, then I'll be ready." She returned to my bedroom.

I called after her, "About this new lingerie, if you're looking to show it off, I'd be more than happy to volunteer."

She appeared in those knee-high boots that reminded me of our first time. My dick jolted at the memory.

"Good. Because I'm wearing it under this dress." She winked as she brushed past me to get her coat.

I groaned. "You're killing me, sweetheart." I opened the door for her, leading her to my car.

It'd been a month since we had fought and I'd almost let her go. I was thankful every day that I hadn't pushed her away. I loved that woman something fierce, and I was jumping out of my skin with excitement over introducing her to my family. As we drove to my mom's house for dinner, I held Autumn's hand, always wanting to be close to her. The only girl I'd ever brought around for family dinner was Jenna. Until then.

Sure, I'd had girlfriends meet my family, but I had never brought them to my mom's. That family time was not for outsiders. It was always just us. But it finally felt right to bring Autumn home. It was only a matter of time before I officially made her my family as well.

I watched from the corner of my eye as she slid lipstick onto her lips in the visor mirror of my Dodge. I was jealous of that lipstick.

She smacked her lips together. "Okay, so remind me again, Kyle is your older brother, and he works in Manhattan, too. He's the one I met."

"Correct."

"And then it's you, then Jesse?"

"Yup."

"And he works in...Brooklyn?"

"Right again."

"Then there's Ryan—the youngest. He's in Queens?"

I chuckled. "You know there isn't gonna be a test, right?"

She sighed. "I just like to be prepared."

I squeezed her hand tighter, lifting it to my lips and planting a kiss on the back. "You're adorable."

She smiled. "I love you, Dylan. You know that, right?"

"Yeah, sweetheart, I do. I love you, too."

"Okay, good."

A minute later, we turned onto the street where I had grown up. "Here we are," I announced as I pulled into the driveway. I put my car in park and went around to the passenger side to open the door for Autumn. I offered her a hand and pulled her in for a hug and a quick kiss, trying not to mess up her lipstick. "Don't worry. You're going to do great."

She smiled up at me. I grabbed her hand, and we made our way to the door, but before we could get there, my mom came scurrying out. "Dylan, I'm so glad you're here!"

"Hey, Ma."

She pulled me into a hug. "And this must be Autumn."

Autumn extended her hand to my mom. "It's a pleasure to meet you, Mrs. Hogan."

My mom swatted her hand away, pulling Autumn into her arms. "I'm a hugger, dear. And please, call me Ann."

Jesse poked his head out the door. "Mom, would you let the poor girl get in the house before you accost her?"

She pulled back, releasing Autumn. "Yes, yes, of course. I'm sorry, I'm just so excited to meet you. Come on in."

I smiled down at Autumn, who returned a big grin of her own as we followed my mother into the house.

"Boys, Dylan and Autumn are here," my mother announced as we entered, though there was really no need to because my brothers were all in the room.

"Yeah, we see that, Ma." Ryan stepped forward and shook Autumn's hand. "Hey, I'm Ryan. Let me take your coat."

"Thank you." Autumn let Ryan help her out of her jacket.

At six-foot-six, he towered over her, but she didn't seem phased by his size. "It's nice to meet you, Ryan."

"And this is Jesse," I said as Jesse stepped forward to shake her hand.

"Hey, good to meet you. Dylan's told us so much about you."

"All lies, I'm sure." She laughed.

"And you remember Kyle." I pointed to my brother who was perched against the kitchen wall.

He waved, but made no effort to move to greet her. "Hey." I scowled.

"Yes, hi, Kyle. It's nice to officially meet you. And under much better circumstances."

He nodded in response, and I glared at him in return. He ignored me and took a swig of his beer.

"Want a beer, Autumn?" Kyle asked.

Autumn stuttered. "Oh, uh —"

I cut in. "Autumn doesn't drink, Kyle. I told you that."

"Right." He nodded. "My bad."

"Autumn, I got you some sparkling cider," my mom interjected. "Why don't you pour her a glass, Kyle?"

Her shoulders dropped, releasing some of her tension. "Oh, thank you, Ann. That's very kind of you."

My brother made a show of putting his beer down on the counter while he reached for a glass from the cabinet. Ryan must have seen the daggers in my eyes because he took the glass from Kyle. "I've got it." He poured Autumn a glass and handed it to her. "Autumn, why don't you come sit with Jesse, Mom, and me in the living room? We're dying to show off all the embarrassing pictures of our brother."

"Hilarious, Ry," I jested, but I was thankful that he was giving me a much-needed moment alone with Kyle. "Go ahead, sweetheart. I'll be right there."

Once Autumn was gone, I cornered Kyle. "What the hell was that?"

He threw his hands up. "What?"

"You know what. Don't act stupid. I told you Autumn can't drink. I also said it's a sensitive subject, so there was no reason for you to bring it up except to make her uncomfortable."

He shrugged. "I forgot."

"You *forgot*?" It took all my energy to keep from screaming at him. "You forgot my girlfriend had a fucking lung transplant? Seriously, bro, what the hell is going on with you? Would it kill you to be nice to her?"

"I'm gonna say exactly what I've been saying since you met her. Never date a victim. It's not smart."

"This is different. Besides, I didn't save *her*. That's not what this is. She's special, man. I don't know how else to say it. Would it kill you to give her a chance? Try to get to know her tonight—you'll see what I mean."

Kyle took a long pull from his beer, while he seemed to contemplate my request. "Fine."

"Is it seriously too much to ask you to be happy for me?"

Kyle sighed and handed me a beer from the fridge. "I do want you to be happy, Dyl. That's exactly why I'm concerned. I don't want to see you get hurt if things with this girl turn out to be a case of hero worship."

I might not have agreed with the way he handled his emotions, but I could appreciate that my big brother was looking out for me. "I'm telling you, it's not like that with Autumn. She's the most incredible person I've ever met. And she makes me happier than I've been in a really long time. Ever since—" I didn't have to finish my sentence for Kyle to know I meant Jenna.

Kyle patted my shoulder. "Then I'm happy for you, man. Truly." He held up his beer bottle, and I clinked it with mine.

Jesse poked his head in the kitchen. "Yo, Dylan, you might want to come in here and save your girl. Mom just pulled out the baby book."

I rolled my eyes. "Great."

Kyle and I followed Jesse back into the living room. "Mom, don't bore Autumn with that nonsense. We finally get Dylan to bring a girl home and you want to scare her away so soon?" Kyle laughed, and I nodded at him in appreciation.

Autumn glanced up from the photo album. "You were such a cute kid, Dylan."

I smiled at my girl, and she returned a smile of her own, a mischievous gleam in her eye. "What happened?" she jested.

My brothers broke out in laughter. Even my mother chuckled.

Ryan put his hand up to high-five Autumn. "Nice. I like this one, bro."

The oven timer buzzed. My mom stood. "Time for dinner."

I took Autumn's hand and led her to the dining room while my brothers brought everything to the table. "Told you they'd love you," I whispered to her as I pulled out her chair. She looked up at me with adoration in her eyes, and all I could think about was how lucky I was that she was mine.

25

AUTUMN

"*W*ait, so you're saying he has *three* brothers and they're all single?" Britt looked at me, wide-eyed, over the rim of her wine glass.

We met for Happy Hour at The Monterey Club at least three times per month. Britt loved it because they had seven-dollar wine specials. I liked it because it was nice, but low-key and it never got too crowded. We sat at one of the high-top tables against the wall in the bar area, amongst a plethora of business men in suits.

I took a sip of my iced tea. "Yup."

"And I'm just finding this out now because…?"

Because there's no way I'd set you up with one of my boyfriend's brothers. But I didn't say that.

"Britt, I just met them a few days ago. Maybe give me a little time to get to know them better before I go setting you up with the wrong brother."

She twirled her long blonde hair around her finger. At least it'd been blonde that day. "Right. Good idea. But, just pick the hottest one and I'm sure he'll be right." She winked.

I laughed at her. Britt was relentless. She was what you'd

call a serial dater. Every weekend, she dated someone new that she'd met on one of those dating apps. It really was impressive that she hadn't found the right guy yet. She'd practically dated half of the eligible men in Manhattan...and even a few not-so-eligible. I loved my best friend, but we couldn't be more different.

"There's more to a relationship than just being attracted to one another."

"I know, I know, but it's certainly an important aspect."

I shrugged. "I suppose."

"Oh, shut up. Your boyfriend is *hot*, Autumn. Don't try to tell me that's not part of why you're into him."

I sighed. "Yes, it's important to have physical chemistry, but what I have with Dylan is so much more than that."

"Yeah, yeah, I know, he's your soulmate, blah, blah, blah. I'm just saying, it doesn't hurt to have a guy who's nice to look at while you're underneath him."

I rolled my eyes. I hadn't expected her to understand. Britt was two years older than me, but I'd always felt like the older one in our relationship. We had been in the same English class our freshman year at NYU. On the first day of class, she had walked into the lecture hall with her head held high, as if it'd been her own house. I had watched as she scanned the room before finding a seat over by a group of guys. I'd later found out they had all been on the basketball team. Britt had flirted with them effortlessly. A few weeks into the semester, she and I'd been paired up for a group project. When she'd found out I was sixteen, she'd decided to take me under her wing, and we'd been best friends ever since.

Britt and I were rather different, but her friendship had been exactly what I'd needed to come out of my shell.

I spread some of the homemade apricot jam onto a cracker. "Don't you want something more than just sex, though?" I asked, before popping the cracker into my mouth.

"Eventually. Maybe. Guess I haven't met someone worth keeping around for more than that."

"Well, maybe you should stop going out with all those guys you swipe right on, and try meeting someone the old-fashioned way."

"Get with the times, Autumn. Most people meet online these days."

"Perhaps," I conceded. "All I'm saying is maybe you should try to have a real conversation with a guy before you jump into his bed."

"I like sex." She shrugged. "Nothing wrong with that."

"Not at all. Just trust me, sex with someone you love is *so much* better."

Britt lifted her wine glass. "Cheers to sex!"

She always had a way of making me laugh. Britt was unapologetically herself, and I loved her for it. She'd had an interesting upbringing. She'd never met her father and her mother was hardly around. Her older sister basically raised her, and she had done her best, but she'd been merely a child herself. Britt had never had a strong example of a healthy relationship, so it hadn't been much of a surprise that she was more into casual dating.

She popped a piece of cheese into her mouth from the platter we were sharing. "So, tell me more about these sexy firefighting brothers."

"Sorry, but I got the sexiest one."

"Damn. Okay, fine, I'll settle for the next best. Which would be…?" She dragged out the last vowel, waiting for me to finish her sentence.

"Ryan is super tall and has a bit of baby face. He seems like a lot of fun. Jesse is built like Dylan and he is hilarious. Kyle looks like a cross between Dylan and Jesse, but you can tell he's older. He's…" I tried to think of the best adjective to describe him. "Kind of moody."

"Ooo." She tapped her fingers on her glass. "The brooding type, huh?"

"He's just, I don't know—troubled? I actually met him before the dinner. He was there the night of the fire, and he really laid into Dylan. Right in front of me. Then, the other night, I could tell he had an issue with me being there at first. I think Dylan talked to him because he started being nicer, but I could tell he's the one I had to impress. Dylan worries about Kyle. He's very serious all the time."

Britt nodded inquisitively. "Interesting."

I put my hand up. "I'm not trying to paint him as a challenge for you to conquer."

"Sounds like *someone* needs to loosen him up."

"Britt—" I warned.

"Okay, fine. Not Kyle, got it." She popped a cube of cheese into her mouth. "So, do you think you won him over?"

Had I? I considered her question for a moment. It had seemed like he'd warmed up to me after a while, but he'd been hard to read. He hadn't been as welcoming as the others had been, though. By the end of the night, I'd felt like Ryan and Jesse were friends I'd had forever, whereas Kyle and I hadn't really connected. He's seven years older than me, so I presume that could have had something to do with it. He hadn't exactly been friendly to me the night of the fire either, though.

I tapped my fingers on the table. "Not sure. The other guys were really nice to me, and his mom is so sweet. Kyle just kept his distance a little more. Like he was trying to evaluate everything. While we were cleaning up from dinner, he pulled me aside and asked me why I was dating his brother."

"And what'd you say?"

I blushed. "I said because he made me feel like the person I've always wanted to be."

Britt dabbed at her imaginary tears. "So sweet."

"Shut up." I swatted her with my napkin. I often got sappy

when I talked about Dylan. I couldn't help it, though. I was happy. Extremely happy.

"What'd Kyle have to say to that?"

"He asked me another question."

"Oh?"

"He asked me if I was with Dylan because I think he's my hero."

"Interesting." She raised an eyebrow. "How'd you respond to that?"

It had felt strange when he asked, and I hadn't been able to tell where he'd been going with it. Had it been a trick question? Or had he been trying to gauge my level of affection for his brother? I'd had no clue, so I'd answered honestly.

"I said that every little girl dreams of her knight in shining armor, so, yeah, Dylan is my hero. But that's only part of why I'm with him. While, I love that he protects me, and that he has my back, there's so much more to our relationship. We just click."

She brought her hands up to her chest. "Aww."

"Cliché. I know."

She shrugged. "A little, but seriously, I'm thrilled for you. True talk: you've had me worried since Drew—you know."

I nodded. "Yeah. I know. It feels good to be alive again." That's what it felt like being with Dylan. He'd breathed new life into me.

"Speaking of Drew." Britt propped her elbows up on the table. "Any news in that department?"

"He has *finally* stopped calling me. I never want to speak to him again." After that night with my parents, Drew had tried to get a hold of me for two more weeks before he'd finally given up.

"Good. I'd hate to see you fall down that rabbit hole."

"I think I'm finally rid of—" I stopped mid-sentence as my gaze met a very familiar pair of eyes across the bar. I swallowed hard and choked out, "Drew."

"You all right? You look like you've seen a ghost."

Drew lifted his arm and waved in my direction. I quickly looked away. "Drew's here."

"Seriously?" She looked around. "Where?"

He started in our direction.

"Oh, good lord, he's heading this way." I bent my head, as though I could possibly hide from the inevitable meeting.

Britt stood up. "I'm not going to let him ruin our girls' night! P.S. We totally summoned him. This is like that night with the Ouija board—"

Drew came up from behind Britt and placed a hand on her shoulder. "Hey, Britt." He stared in my direction. "Autumn. Hi."

Britt scowled at him. "Drew."

"Autumn, can we talk?" He seemed sincere, but I wasn't buying into it.

Britt answered for me. "I think Autumn has made it very clear that she wants nothing to do with you, Andrew."

Drew ignored her. "I just wanted to apologize. Again. I meant no harm in calling your parents. I was worried about you. I'll always worry about you because I love you. I know it's not what you want to hear, but that doesn't mean it isn't true." He sighed. "Just know I'm here for you. Always. No matter what."

"Thanks," I choked out, not knowing what else to say. My skin flushed.

He bowed his head and said, "I'll let you ladies get back to your evening," before walking away.

I felt jittery and I hated that he had such an effect on me.

"You okay, love?" Britt asked, looking at me with concern.

"Yeah. I will be."

She took a sip of her wine and shook her head. "Rabbit hole."

I sat up straight and flattened out the hem of my sweater

that I'd been fiddling with. "I'm in love with Dylan. Drew isn't going to ruin that."

"Good. Because I don't want to have to help you pick up the pieces *again* after he breaks your heart a second time."

"You won't. There won't be a second time." I looked her dead in the eyes. "I mean it."

26

DYLAN

"No fucking way I'm eating this." Frisco looked down at the bowl of stew in front of him, repulsed. "It smells like feet."

"Yo, new guy, did you use your sweaty socks to make this broth?" Palmer hollered from the table, dripping the liquified slop from his spoon.

Hart, the newest member of Truck 64, shrugged and responded from where he stood at the kitchen counter beside us. "Told you guys I'm not much of a cook."

"Well, you better learn, new guy," Lieutenant Brewster chimed in. "You're on kitchen duty until we get a new new guy."

Hart groaned.

"Pizza, anyone?" I asked as I went from the table over to the kitchen and pulled the menu from the drawer. I gave Hart a pat on the back. "New guy is buying."

He threw up his hands. "All right, fine. Whatcha guys want?"

Keith Hart had joined our crew fresh from the academy. This was his second shift ever on the job. He was a good kid, eager to learn, but he was green. I had worked with him on his first shift, too, and had gotten to see him in action. He'd done all right, clearly worked hard to try to prove himself, but the kid was cocky. That needed to change.

While we waited for dinner to be delivered, I took advantage of the extra downtime and snuck into the bunk room to call Autumn.

"I was just thinking about you," she answered on the second ring.

"Oh, you were, huh?"

"Yes, sir. Although, what I was thinking about involves you actually being here."

"Naked?" I asked suggestively. I was insatiable when it came to her.

"Maybe," she teased in return.

"Sweetheart, I'd give anything to be with you right now."

"I miss you."

"I miss you, too." I sighed. "It's been too long. I hate going an entire week without holding you." It'd been two weeks since she'd met my family, and I'd only gotten to see her three times since then. "I'm sorry my schedule has been so crazy lately. Working that side job with Palmer and those overtime shifts have been keeping me away from you too much."

"Stupid jobs. We should just quit."

I imagined her wrinkling her nose, and it made me smile.

"We're still on for tomorrow night, though, right?" she asked.

"Absolutely. I get off at six pm. I'll meet you there. Wouldn't miss it for the world."

"It's just Britt's birthday party. You make it sound like we're going somewhere special."

"Anywhere with you is special."

She giggled, and I felt it in my heart. "Good line, mister."

"I bet you're blushing right now."

"Maybe I am," she teased. "Are your brothers still coming?"

"They are."

"Britt will be thrilled."

I couldn't help the smile on my face. Merging my world with hers made us feel more official.

We talked for another ten minutes before dinner arrived.

After dinner, I sat in the lounge with Palmer and Frisco while texting Autumn.

Me: I miss your cooking
Autumn: I still owe you mofongo
Me: That's the chicha-pork skin dish right?
Autumn: Haha, yes. And it's chicharrones.
Me: Whatever it's called, I want it. Man, you're making me hungry again.

Palmer's voice pulled me out of my bubble. "Dude, you've had this goofy grin on your face for the past five minutes."

"He's *in love*," Frisco mocked.

I shook my head, unable to hide my smile.

"Seriously, man, I'm happy for you. Autumn's a great girl."

"Thanks, bro."

Palmer cut in. "Yeah, yeah. But more importantly, does she have any hot friends?"

"Actually, she's got this one friend, Britt. From what Autumn's told me, the two of you would probably hit it off." They both seemed to have the same "fun" vibe about them. "We're going to her birthday party tomorrow night at Gypsies on the East Side. You can come if you want."

"I'm in." Palmer shouted.

I regretted it almost immediately. "Remember, she's my girl's best friend. Don't screw it up."

Palmer threw his hand over his chest in mock offense. "I can't believe you think I'd do such a thing."

"How's Tanya?" Frisco asked.

"Who?" Palmer replied.

I coughed in an attempt to disguise my words. "Last" *Cough.* "Thursday." *Cough.* "Night."

"Tanya?" Palmer looked at us seriously. "I thought her name was Tammy."

"And that's why I don't set you up with friends." Frisco tipped the bill of his San Francisco Giants cap in my direction. "Good luck, Hogan."

"Look, I said you could come, Palmer, all I ask is that you don't put me in a position where I have to answer to my girlfriend when you break her friend's heart."

Palmer made a cross over his heart with his finger. "I'll be on my best behavior."

The rest of our tour went pretty smoothly. We'd actually gotten some sleep, which was great because going out to a bar on little-to-no sleep would've been rough. The day shift was pretty quiet, too. We had less than an hour left before I could leave and finally see my girl. I couldn't wait.

As though dispatch could hear my thoughts, the tones went off. "Ladder 64, Engine 13. 10-75

Lieutenant Brewster jumped up from the table as dispatch relayed the address. "That's the fire E11/L171 got called out for a little bit ago. Must be good. Mount up!"

E11 was Kyle's company, but he wasn't on shift. I raced to the rig, and we were out the door within thirty seconds. As I buckled my SCBA to my back, listening to all the chatter over the radio, I cursed under my breath, knowing I would be late to the party. We were going to work—and it was a big one.

When we pulled up to the scene, the street had already been closed, and flames were blowing out all the windows of the warehouse.

Lieutenant Brewster barked orders. "All right, primary

search. Use your search ropes, this place is huge. No one is getting lost on my watch. Palmer, Frisco—you two head right. Hogan, you take Hart straight through to the rear. We have reports of multiple people trapped. Be smart. Go!"

I grabbed a set of irons and directed Hart to grab a hook and a can. As we approached, I noticed smoke billowing from the front entrance.

I masked up before hooking my carabiner to the main search line and hollered to my partner. "Hook on and stay close to me."

The heat of the flames wasted no time assaulting us upon entry. Sweat beaded on my brow almost instantly. Our gear was made to withstand up to a thousand-degree heat, but it didn't exactly keep us cool. With the new guy at my back, we followed the search line to the middle of the building where it ended.

We still had further to go. "I'm hooking my bag to the main line so we can get to the back." I pulled the end of my search rope from the bag hooked to my hip, tying it off to the main line. "Hart! Feel this knot." I grabbed his hand and placed it on top of the knot I'd just tied. "Feel how it's different from the others? When we have to get out of here, you feel this knot and know there are three more knots between here and the exit, every twenty-five feet. Got it?"

"Got it, Hogan."

"Good. Right hand on the rope at all times. Follow me. Stay close."

We made our push to the back of the warehouse, the rope unfurling from my bag as we went.

"Fire department, call out!"

Visibility was poor, even though we were on our hands and knees, beneath the worst of the smoke. Fires like that were nightmares. The rows of cardboard boxes made it easy to get lost, and they also made the perfect fuel for the flames. There was a faint "Help," in the distance, so we pushed forward faster.

We came upon a man, face down and coughing. He was conscious. That was good. I positioned him between me and Hart. "Sir, cover your face with your shirt and grab this rope. Follow him." I pointed to Hart. "We're going to get you out."

"No, wait!" the man protested. "Tricia! You have to get Tricia. She's in the back office."

I looked in the direction he was pointing, but couldn't see much. If I made the man wait while I pushed forward to try to find the other victim, he'd be unconscious by the time I got back. Then we'd have to carry out two victims while trying to stay on the search line.

"Okay. I'll go back for her. You follow him and get out. Hart, take him. Now!"

"I'm not leaving you, Hogan."

"Not a request, Hart. Get him out of here."

When he hesitated, I snapped, "Go, dammit!"

That's when all the sirens and horns went off, signaling an evacuation. The Battalion chief came over the radio a moment later. "All units, evacuate the building. We're moving to an exterior attack. All units, evacuate."

"Hogan, we gotta go!"

"I'll be right behind you," I lied.

I watched them crawl away while I pushed forward. I knew how deep the building was from the assessment I'd done while we were outside. I quickly calculated how much rope we'd used and realized I couldn't be more than forty feet from the back wall. I crawled further into the inferno, using my tools to sweep the floor around me.

"Fire department, call out!"

I listened for screams, but heard nothing other than the roar and crackle of flames. I saw the outline of an office door ahead of me and I surged forward, but was quickly tugged back by the rope on my hip. I was out of line. Fuck. I looked toward the door and figured it was about ten feet from my current position. What was that woman's name?

"Tricia?" I screamed. "Fire department, call out! Tricia!"

I listened for a response, but heard nothing. It was decision time. Either I followed the evac order, turned around, and took the lead line out like my training dictated I should, or I unclipped from the line, did a quick search of the office, then got back on the line and headed out.

I shouted a final time. "Tricia!"

A knocking sound came from the office ahead, and my decision was made for me. I ignored the evacuation order — and my training — as I unclipped the carabiner from my pants, counting my movements to the door. I reached up to try the handle, but it was locked, so I jammed my Halligan into the crack between the door and the frame, then pushed all my weight into it until it popped open.

It was getting noticeably hotter, and the roar of the fire behind me got louder. As I pushed open the door, flames rolled overhead. I had to locate the victim and get her out.

"Tricia!" I screamed as I made my way around the perimeter of the office.

A bang came from the desk, so I crawled my way over to it and found a woman lying underneath, her fist knocking on the desk leg. I noticed her burns immediately. She was barely conscious. I wrapped my webbing around her, creating a harness I could use to pull her out, and dragged her back toward the door.

I had to move fast.

I pulled the victim behind me as I made my way back into the main part of the warehouse. The thick, dark smoke was banked down to the floor, and visibility was zero. The heat was almost unbearable, so I knew the fire was right on top of us.

But I couldn't see it.

I tried to count my movements to get back to the line except when I got to where it should have been, I felt nothing.

I moved about five feet in each direction, searching for the line, but came up empty.

Stay calm, Dylan. I reminded myself of my dad's words: *Fire doesn't kill firefighters, panic kills firefighters.*

I felt the rumble of the collapse before I heard it. Boxes crashed down in front of me. I threw myself on top of the victim and waited for the movement to stop. When it did, I took a moment to reorient myself, totally blind, and headed back in the direction of the office. I needed an anchor point. Staying out in the middle of the warehouse was a death sentence.

Once back in the office, I shut the door and tucked the victim against the exterior wall with me, as far away from the bulk of the fire as possible. I got on my radio and made the call no firefighter ever wanted to make. "Mayday, mayday, mayday. Dylan Hogan, Ladder 64. I'm trapped in a back office on the three-side with a victim."

My lieutenant came over the radio in response. "Stay put, Hogan, we're sending Squad in. Any specifics you can provide?" Squad was trained specifically for cases like this. Getting trapped firefighters out of bad situations was part of their job.

"Follow the center lead rope to the end. My rope is hooked onto it. I ran out of rope one hundred and fifty feet in, so I'm about ten feet past the end, inside the office. Victim has severe burns and just lost consciousness. Be aware there was a material collapse about a hundred and forty-five-feet in."

"10-4, Hogan. Stay put," Lieutenant Brewster ordered.

I was going to get my ass chewed out, but I couldn't think about that just yet. First, I needed to survive. I looked around the room, assessing my surroundings. There was another door diagonally across from me, so I went to check it. Closet.

My radio beeped. "Hogan, this is Captain O'Conor. We followed the lead line in, but we've run into a roadblock about a hundred-and-twenty-five-feet in. We're going to have to let the engine try to knock down some of these flames before we can push forward. Do you see any other means of egress from your position?"

I scanned the room again, already knowing the answer. "Negative, Captain."

My SCBA alarm went off, warning me that I was low on air. I had maybe five minutes tops before my tank was empty. I didn't have time to wait for Squad to get through.

If I didn't find another way out of that room, I was going to die.

I went back to the closet and felt the wall inside. It was warm, but not hot. Chances were that the adjacent room wasn't on fire. I pulled out the small filing cabinet inside and took my ax to the closet wall. It took some effort, making me use up more air than I would've like, but I was able to break through to the next room. As I pushed through the hole, I did a quick scan of the room and noticed a few small windows about twenty-feet up. Too high to get to on my own, but with a ladder, it was an exit.

I went back to the other room for the victim and dragged her through the wall with me. My face mask started vibrating. I was on my last breaths of air. I held my breath and pushed down the button on my radio. "Captain O'Conor, I was able to get into an adjacent room. There are three small windows about twenty feet up. With a ladder, we can use it as an exit."

"10-4, Hogan. We're sending a truck company to get a ladder up in the back. Are the windows intact?"

I looked at the windows closely. "Yes, Captain, they are."

"Look for something you can use to throw at them and break them. When I give you the signal, I want you to go ahead and do so, then we can see which windows you're at."

"Got it, Cap."

I looked around the small office, hoping to find a paperweight, then I saw a signed baseball in a case up on a shelf. *Perfect.* I reached for it, and as I did, my tank emptied. I pulled off my helmet, tugged down my hood, and lifted my mask from my face. I held my breath and pulled my hood back up, making sure it covered my mouth and nose. I replaced my helmet and did my best to hold my breath.

The captain came over the radio. "Hogan, go ahead and break the window."

Once I stood up, I wouldn't have a clear view of the windows through the smoke, so while on my knees, I calculated the distance I had to throw. I stood up, said a prayer, and chucked the ball toward the window. I heard it bounce back.

"Fuck!" I cursed and gulped in smoke, causing me to cough. I felt around, trying to find the ball. My eyes were burning, making it nearly impossible to see. I was getting dizzy.

Dad, please help me. I need to find that ball. I need to get out of here. I need to get back to Autumn.

I swept my hand under the desk and connected with the ball. After wrapping my fingers around it, I stood and lined up my shot again.

Please, Dad.

I pulled my arm back and released the ball. I heard glass break. I dropped to my knees.

"We got you, Hogan. Throwing a ladder up now."

I crossed to the victim and dragged her to the center of the room, closer to where the ladder would come down. There were noises above me, but my vision was gone. I wasn't sure if it was just from the smoke burning my eyes or from the lack of oxygen. Probably both.

I heard the familiar clank of metal on cement, and I knew Squad had dropped a ladder in. "Hogan!" a voice called out.

I tried to respond, but all that came out was a cough. I wrapped my arm around the victim and pulled her toward where I thought the ladder would be. My hand made contact with the metal, and I was so grateful.

I felt a pair of boots land next to me. "Take her," I choked out. The victim's body was lifted away from me, and I heard the creaking of the ladder as our rescuer ascended.

"Hogan, it's about to flash, get out!"

I looked up out of instinct. Though I couldn't see anything, I heard it. The whoosh a fire made when a new fuel source was introduced. Breaking the window may have created an exit for us, but it also fed the fire. The flames were licking overhead, salivating at the chance to consume the oxygen and grow. A flashover was imminent.

I reached my hand up, feeling for a rung on the ladder, willing myself to garner the strength I needed to ascend it. Using the ladder to help support my weight, I pulled myself up to my knees. I tried to stand, but my legs gave out beneath me.

Come on! This couldn't be the end. I wasn't ready. There was a woman I loved that I had to get home to.

I tried to stand again, using more of the ladder for leverage. I got my toes up on the first rung and willed my muscle memory to take over. I'd climbed ladders hundreds of times. I could do this.

Slowly, I ascended the ladder, feeling the metal beneath me —my guide to safety. As I approached the top, I felt the heat. The fire rolled over, and the flames breached the window. I'd have to push through them to get out. Once I got over the sill, I'd have to feel for the ladder on the outside. Since I couldn't see it, I'd be relying on touch to get me through—otherwise I'd fall twenty-feet onto the pavement. I had to move fast because I wouldn't be able to withstand those flames for long.

I counted the rungs. I was only a couple from the top when I heard my best friend's voice like he was right next to my ear. Then I felt his hand on my shoulder. "Dyl, I've got you. Come on!"

With Palmer's assistance, I flipped over the windowsill and onto the exterior ladder. He helped guide me down so I wouldn't fall. When we got to the ground, I spun and hugged him.

Or, more like, fell into him.

"Fuck, bro," Palmer emphasized. "You scared the shit out of me. Out of all of us."

I coughed and fell through his arms to my knees. My helmet and hood were ripped off my head, and an oxygen mask was put over my face. Someone unbuckled my bunker coat, then the cold metal of a stethoscope was pressed against my chest.

"I—I can't see," I stuttered in a higher pitch than usual.

My heart raced in my chest as the dizziness intensified. The last thing I remember was hearing the medic say, "He's tachycardic. Let's get him in the ambo!"

Then the world went quiet.

27

AUTUMN

The jazz band pumped loudly through the speakers, giving the bar an upbeat New Orleans vibe. Well, at least what I imagined New Orleans would be like, never having been there myself. It was only seven-thirty and Britt was already on her third martini.

"I love you *and* your boyfriend, Autumn," she declared.

I sniggered, knowing there was more to it. "I love you, too. And you haven't even met Dylan yet."

"Don't need to." She tilted her martini in the direction of the Hogan brothers who were getting beers at the bar, spilling some of the pink concoction over the rim. "His brothers are delicious. All I need to know to love him."

"Down, Britt," I warned.

Jesse caught us looking at them from the booth we'd reserved across from the bar, and he flashed a smile back in our direction. It was my first time actually hanging out with them. It meant a lot to me that they came out that night. Once my nonna died, I basically lost my family, and seeing how close Dylan and his brothers were, made me envious. I'd hoped I could be a part of their family, too, one day.

"Let's dance!" Britt's yelling startled me out of my fantasy.

She slammed her martini down on the table, spilling more of it out of the glass. I swear she spilled more than she actually drank...probably not a bad thing. She grabbed my hand, pulling me toward the center of the bar by the stage. Our friends Michelle, Tia, Hollie, and Joelle stayed behind at the table, giving me a look of pity, grateful they had gotten out of that one.

There wasn't exactly a dedicated dance floor, more like a little extra space that could've probably fit a table or two, but was left vacant to give the band some room. Britt shimmied her butt into the section, staring at the saxophonist with puppy dog eyes as she swayed to the music, hips shaking and arms waving like she was at Coachella. I felt the eyes of all the other patrons on us, and I wanted to sink back into our booth and hide.

Don't get me wrong, I loved dancing. I just felt out of place in that jazz bar with Festival Barbie (aka my best friend). We should've been sitting and sipping fancy drinks while we gently swayed along like all the other people at the bar. But Britt was never good at subtleties.

While I tried to formulate a plan to get Britt back to our group, our little space suddenly got crowded. I turned around to see Jesse and Ryan dancing along. They smiled at me, and Ryan winked. I was so grateful to them for saving me from the embarrassment. We were no longer a spectacle, merely a group of friends dancing and having fun.

I let my guard drop a little and began dancing along to the music, enjoying the rhythmic, bluesy notes. Ryan grabbed my hand and swung me around while Jesse did the same with Britt. I had to admit, they were good dancers, and I assumed it was a family trait, remembering my first date dancing with Dylan.

I was having a blast, but the thought of Dylan made me miss him. According to the guys, Dylan's firehouse had caught a late run, so he was behind schedule getting to the party.

Kyle's firehouse was also on the call, so he was getting updates. He said it sounded like a big one.

Out of nowhere, this odd feeling hit me in the gut. You know, like when you know something is off or wrong? I chalked it up to being my typical worry for my boyfriend. He was meant to have been there by then, and I missed him. I hated that he had such a dangerous job, but he seemed to genuinely love it.

He had the whole weekend off, which rarely happened, and I was so looking forward to spending both days with him. We'd planned to leave for upstate the next morning to go skiing at Hunter Mountain. It would be our first trip together, and I couldn't contain my excitement. While I'd never been skiing before, I was willing to give it a try (although, if I were being honest, I planned on spending more time in the hot tub at our resort than I did barreling down a snowy slope at high speed in the cold). Either way, I knew the trip would be one of those defining moments in our relationship. Years down the road, we'd look back at our first trip together and fondly recall the memories, a part of us wishing we could go back and relive it all over again.

Britt and I had gone shopping earlier in the week, and I'd bought a whole ski outfit, which she said was "tres chic." Apparently, that was a good thing. Britt didn't actually speak French, she just knew some key French phrases, which she'd drop at opportune times to make herself sound sophisticated and alluring. It was part of her charm.

Ryan whirled me around, spinning me behind his back, and that's when I caught sight of Kyle barreling toward us, fear plastered across his face. I froze, causing Ryan to stumble and look down at me in concern. Tia breezed past me and grabbed Britt as Kyle made it over to us.

"We gotta go. It's Dylan," he shouted over the music. Jesse, Ryan, and I barreled outside behind Kyle. That sinking feeling in my gut returned with a vengeance.

The cold air hit me like a brick wall as we exited the bar. While Kyle attempted to hail us a cab, Hollie busted through the door. "Autumn!"

I turned back to her, completely numb—and not from the cold.

"You forgot your jacket." She had to help me into it because I'd forgotten how to move. "It's going to be okay, Autumn. Just breathe."

Jesse put his arm around me and swept me into the waiting cab. Kyle directed the driver to take us to the emergency room at Mount Sinai Hospital, then jumped on his cell phone.

"Mack, what happened?" he bellowed into the phone.

I watched him intently while he listened to this Mack guy, and his skin visibly turned red from his neck up to his ears. I managed to find my voice again. "What's going on?"

My head swiveled to the brothers on both sides of me. Jesse put his arm around my shoulders, and Ryan placed his hand comfortingly on my knee.

"Something happened to Dylan at the fire," Jesse said calmly, which I found strange given the fury resonating off Kyle in the front seat.

"Is he—is he…?"

"We don't know," Ryan said softly. "Kyle is trying to find out what happened. His company was also on the scene, so he's getting all the details."

I nodded. *Please be okay, please be okay* became the internal mantra on repeat in my head.

My pleas were interrupted by Kyle, who had hung up the phone and turned back to look at us. "He got trapped in a warehouse fire. They got him out, but he'd run out of air. He collapsed on scene. That's all they know so far."

I gasped, and my hands flew up to cover my mouth. Ryan tilted his head back and sighed, his eyes boring into the roof of the cab. "Fuck."

Jesse squeezed my shoulder. "Dylan's tough. We have to think positive, okay? He's going to be fine."

I bit my lip, willing myself not to cry. In a matter of weeks, I'd fallen so in love with that man. I couldn't picture living the rest of my life without him. He had to be okay. He just had to be.

When we pulled up to the emergency room, Kyle flew out of the cab before it came to a full stop, tossing cash at the driver in his wake. By the time I got out with Jesse and Ryan, Kyle was already causing a scene at the nurse's station. "He's my brother and I demand to see him, now! Dylan Hogan. Hogan. H. O. G. A. N. He's a fireman, came in on the ambo not too long ago directly from a fire scene."

Kyle looked like he was about to climb over the desk and commandeer the computer if the nurse didn't give him an answer within three seconds. Jesse must've taken notice as well because he grabbed Kyle by the shoulders and pulled him back.

"Please, ma'am," Jesse pleaded with the nurse. "Just tell us where he is."

With that, a familiar voice beckoned from the intersection of the adjacent hallway. "Lieutenant Hogan." Kyle's head whipped around, and I was sure he'd pulled a muscle. I looked over to where the voice came from and saw Frisco standing there in his turnout gear, hair disheveled, with soot dirtying his face. "I'll take you to him."

We all hastily followed Frisco down the hallway. My brain immediately started overanalyzing his words. He said he'd take us to Dylan which probably meant he wasn't dead because if he was dead Frisco probably would've told us to follow him to a place where he could break the news in private at least that was what I would do if I were in that situation unless he knew we'd figure out something was really wrong if he didn't say anything about Dylan so he just told us he'd take us to Dylan to keep our minds at ease a little longer.

My head spun.

The guys probed Frisco for answers, and I tried to listen, but my mind was clogged with worry, so I only caught bits and pieces. "...in there a while...couldn't get to him...no air...victim...burned badly...collapsed on the ground..."

We made it to a waiting area where a dozen firemen stood anxiously. I took in the sight of them, several of whom I'd met before, but I was seeing them in a different light. They all matched Frisco's level of dishevelment and were still wearing their gear. I could smell the char of smoke emanating off them, which made me realize how nauseous I was.

A few of the guys walked over to Dylan's brothers and gave them friendly pats on the back. The Hogan brothers erupted into a chorus of "Where is he?" and "What the hell happened?" They weren't getting answers. Granted, Kyle was rambling about what he'd already heard so no one could really get a word in.

Bile rose to my throat as I summoned all my inner strength to fight off the ensuing panic. I needed to see Dylan. Now.

"Excuse me," I shouted, louder than intended, but my fear propelled the words out of me. The group grew silent, and Kyle stared at me, stunned. "Someone is going to tell me what is going on. Right now!" I pumped my fists down at my sides for emphasis. "And I want to see Dylan."

The man I recognized as Jace Palmer stepped forward and put his hand on my shoulder, steadying me. I hadn't even realized I was shaking. He bent down so he could look me directly in the eyes. "He's all right, Autumn."

Relief suddenly flooded me, and my muscles turned to jelly. "Oh, thank goodness," I exhaled.

Jace continued. "They're treating him for smoke inhalation, and he has some minor burns. Dylan was without oxygen for a little while so that, plus the irritation from the smoke exposure, caused him to temporarily lose his vision. They're doing a CT scan just in case to make sure that's all it was. You can see him once they finish."

I nodded, grateful for the answers and to hear my boyfriend was safe. Willing myself not to cry in front of them, I bit my lip. Hard. I sniffled, trying to recall the tears welling up in my eyes.

Jace pulled me into a hug. "Hey now, it's all right. Dylan's okay. He was actually asking for you before they took him in for the scan."

I pulled back and looked up at him, hope filling my voice. "Really?"

Jace smiled down at me. "Really."

I answered him with a small smile of my own. "Thanks."

Ryan addressed the group. "We heard he collapsed on scene."

Another man stepped forward with an air of authority. "That's correct. Likely from the smoke inhalation. He held on just long enough to get the victim and himself out. He was lucky. Real lucky. Another thirty-seconds in there and we'd be having an entirely different conversation."

My hands flew up to my chest, as though they could protect my heart from the news that Dylan could've died.

"This victim," Kyle asked, "she make it?"

The other man shook his head. "She died on the way to the hospital. Her skin was charred, and her airway was badly burned. She'd inhaled too much smoke."

Kyle pursed his lips before addressing the man. "Lieutenant, can you run me through what happened?"

The man detailed the course of events. My heart flopped around in my chest as I imagined Dylan being in that burning warehouse, trapped. Obviously, I knew what his job entailed, but hearing about it in such detail made me queasy. I looked around at all the men. It could've been any of them laying in a hospital bed. They all went to work every day, fully aware that they might not make it home. At that moment, I developed an acute hatred for his job. I deplored knowing he was in that kind of danger

Kyle looked like he was about to explode, and my fear *for* Dylan transformed to fear *of* his brother. He addressed the crowd. "Hart?"

A young guy stepped forward. He looked to be about my age, and he seemed timid. "That's me, Lieutenant Hogan."

Kyle nodded slowly, studying the man standing before him. "You went in with my brother?"

"Yes, sir."

"Then why is it Dylan got caught in the collapse, but you didn't?"

The guy looked around erratically. "Uh, I was taking out a victim."

"So you left my brother behind?" Kyle asked.

"Firefighter Hogan told me to." His eyes darted around. "Sir."

Kyle slowly nodded again, clearly contemplating something. "When you heard the evacuation order, were you still with him?"

"Yes, sir."

"What happened after that order was given?"

Hart shuffled his left foot and hesitated before answering. "Well, um —"

"Tell me the truth, Hart. Don't lie, thinking you're protecting him."

"When we found the male victim, he said there was a woman still trapped in the office. Dylan ordered me to leave and take the guy out while he went to look for the woman — and then the evacuation call came over. I told him we had to go and he said he'd be right behind me."

"But he wasn't, was he?" Kyle interrupted.

"I thought he was. I swear. The victim was following me on the rope, and I thought Hogan was right behind him. It wasn't until we got out that I realized he wasn't. Before I could say anything, though, the mayday call came over the radio. Conditions were brutal, lieutenant. We couldn't see shit, so I had no way of knowing he wasn't behind me. Honest."

Dylan's lieutenant chimed in. "Hart, are you saying Dylan Hogan disobeyed the evac order so he could go find that victim?"

Hart gave a tiny nod. "It appears that way, Lieutenant Brewster."

I looked around the room, taking notice of everyone's reaction to this news. Ryan laced his fingers over his head, eyes closed, neck tilted back. Jesse had his fists on his hips, his knuckles white, and the look on his face made him appear as though he wanted to punch something. Palmer cradled his forehead in his hand, his head shaking back and forth. Frisco threw up his hands, looking pissed. Lieutenant Brewster pursed his lips, his nostrils flaring. And Kyle...Kyle looked murderous.

I was trying to process the information. I remembered back to our first date when Dylan had told me he'd gotten into trouble after the fire in my building because he'd taken a risk to save Eli. I'd told him I was glad he did it, unknowingly encouraging what appeared to be a problematic behavior of his. He'd ignored orders — again — putting himself at risk.

And this time, it had nearly killed him.

Lieutenant Brewster spoke first. "I'll have to suspend him. He's been warned about this behavior before. Clearly, warnings were not sufficient enough."

Kyle growled, low and ominously. "You go ahead and suspend him. I'm going to kill him."

At that moment, a doctor came into the waiting area and addressed the group. "We just finished the CT Scan. Everything came back normal. We'll monitor him overnight, and keep him on oxygen, but he should be able to go home tomorrow."

"Can I see him?" I pleaded, probably sounding a little desperate, but I didn't care.

"Are you family?"

Jesse answered for me. "She's his fiancée."

I couldn't deny I liked the way that sounded.

"Okay, sure, you can follow me back."

Kyle pushed in front of me. "I'm his brother. I'm going, too."

The doctor must have sensed Kyle's combative tone because he hesitated, but before he could answer, Jesse got in his way. "No, you need to calm down first. Let Ryan go with her. You wait here with me and we'll go after them."

Kyle started to protest, but I felt Ryan's hand on my back, pushing me forward and down the hall behind the doctor.

When we got to Dylan's room, I shuddered at the sight of all the machines, remembering my many hospital trips. Dylan's eyes were closed, so I approached the bed slowly, not wanting to startle him. I placed my hand on his forehead and ran it up over his hair, which was matted and reeked of smoke, but I didn't care. His eyes flickered open, and he smiled. "Hi, sweetheart."

I threw myself across his chest, hugging him fiercely as the tears finally fell.

"Shh, don't cry. I'm okay."

"I was so scared, Dylan. I thought I lost you."

"I'm really sorry I worried you. I'm fine, though. Promise." He cradled my head in his hands and gently turned my face up to look at him. "Look at me." He stared into my tear-filled eyes. "I'm right here with you."

I sniffled as Dylan wiped the tears from my cheeks. "I love you."

He kissed me on the forehead. "I love you too, sweetheart. So much."

"You really had us scared, bro," Ryan said from the doorway.

Dylan nodded. "Guess this one just got away from me. You know how that goes. Conditions can turn so fast," he said, as though he were trying to make light of what had actually happened before changing the subject. "Thanks for taking care of my girl." He kissed the top of my head.

Ryan nodded, and I could tell he was biting his tongue. The guys were mad at Dylan, but he didn't need the added stress while he was healing. I was grateful Ryan was holding back.

"Your brothers were great. Ryan here is a pretty good dancer."

"Dancer?" he asked, confused. "Oh, yeah, Britt's party. I'm so sorry I ruined your evening."

I gave him a reassuring smile and patted his hand. "Don't you worry about that. There will be more birthdays."

He smiled up at me, and I wanted so badly to pull him in for a kiss, but then I heard the commotion behind me, and Dylan's smile faded away. I turned to see Kyle and Jesse piling into the room with us.

Anger radiated off Kyle, instantly changing the energy in the room. Not wanting to upset Dylan, I spoke up. "Please, Kyle, he's been through a lot. Be easy on him."

"Be *easy* on him? Are you fucking kidding me? He nearly got himself killed because he's ever the hero. Aren't you, Dylan?"

"Don't speak to her like that."

"We've got bigger problems than how I speak to your rescue crush."

"Rescue crush?" I asked, perplexed.

"Now wait a minute—" Dylan sat up.

"Kyle, enough. This isn't about Autumn," Jesse interrupted.

Kyle addressed me while staring Dylan down. "Autumn, you need to go. We have to talk to our brother."

I wanted to argue, but knowing what was probably coming, I didn't really want to be there. This argument between them was inevitable, and nothing I said would put a stop to it. At that moment, Jace poked his head in. "Guys, we can hear the yelling down the hall. They're gonna kick you out."

Ryan turned to the doorway. "Palmer, can you take Autumn back to the waiting room? We'll be there shortly."

I looked at Dylan, and he squeezed my hand. "It's okay, sweetheart. I'm just going to talk to my brothers, then you can come back and see me."

I gave him a kiss on the forehead and reluctantly left. I could hear the yelling behind us as we walked away.

"Jace, what's a rescue crush?"

He looked at me funny. "It's when someone we help on a call ends up developing a crush on one of us because we saved her. Why do you ask?"

"Oh. Kyle said something about it."

"Don't listen to him. Kyle can be a real dick."

"Yeah," was all I could say while I contemplated the meaning. Dylan had a thing for saving people. What if he only liked me because I was a victim? Like a reverse rescue crush.

"This is a problem for him, right? Being reckless?"

Jace stopped and leaned up against the hallway wall. He let out a sigh, and his face said he was really contemplating what he was going to say next. "Dylan takes risks, yes. We all do. But with Dylan, it's different."

"How so?" I asked as I leaned against the wall next to him.

"I'm not gonna lie to you, Autumn, our job is dangerous. That fire tonight…" He ran his hand through his hair. "It was bad. Three people died. We probably shouldn't have gone inside in the first place, but we did because it's our job and there were people who needed us."

He sighed again, tucking his thumbs behind the suspenders holding up his bunker pants. "When the chief made the call to evacuate, it was because he knew conditions were about to take a turn for the worst. And they did. Dylan got trapped behind a collapse because he disobeyed the evacuation order. Did he do it for the right reason? Arguably, yeah. He was trying to save someone, but the real shitty part of this job is that sometimes we can't save them all. We put our lives on the line every single day, but there are some risks that aren't worth taking because if one of us dies, that's one less firefighter on earth to make a difference."

He turned, putting his shoulder against the wall so he could look at me. "Dylan prioritized that victim's life over his own tonight, and it nearly got him killed. Then she died, anyway. This isn't the first time he's done something like that. Hell, it isn't the second or third time either."

He looked down to his feet as though the weight he was carrying on his shoulders was forcing his neck to bend. "As I'm sure you know, Dylan experienced two significant losses when he was younger. He hardly talks about them, but he's my best friend so I know that, while he might not admit it, it's like because he couldn't save them, he's spent his entire career trying to save everyone else. Like he believes that if he dies, it's his punishment for having survived."

Jace lifted his gaze to meet mine. "He's been this way for as long as I've known him, and I don't think that'll ever change. So if you're going to be with him, Autumn, you need to seriously think about whether you can handle this." He gestured to the hospital around us. "Because this isn't gonna be the last time he ends up here as the result of him taking a stupid risk."

I stared at him for a few silent moments as I processed everything he'd said. He hadn't told me anything I didn't already know, but the way he presented it made me think. Unless Dylan moved on and stopped blaming himself for his father's and his girlfriend's deaths, he could very well get himself killed. Nausea rolled through my gut.

"Thank you for speaking so candidly, Jace. I appreciate it."

"Dylan's like a brother to me. I love him and I want the best for him. He's been happier than I've ever seen him since he started dating you. You're good for him. That being said, you deserve to know the truth. What you do with it is up to you, but you needed to know."

I nodded in agreement. "Thank you."

We rejoined the others in the waiting area, and I found myself a quiet corner to sit in and think. What Jace had said made a lot of sense. Dylan made a habit of being reckless. Could I really be with someone who had a high probability of dying due to his own risk-taking behavior? Someone who prioritized the lives of strangers over his own? What if we got married and had kids?

I'd accepted that the man I loved had a dangerous job, but knowing that he willingly added another level to that danger of his own volition...

Like Jace had said, I really needed to consider whether or not I could accept that part of him. On top of all that, Kyle's rescue crush comment burned in my mind. I knew I was with Dylan for the right reasons, but maybe Dylan was with me for the wrong reasons. Maybe there was some merit to the argument that Dylan was only dating me because he felt like my hero. How long could our relationship really be sustained on that kind of foundation?

I loved Dylan, but if we were going to make things work in the long run, he'd have to make a change.

28

DYLAN

"Kyle, please, I don't need a lecture. I was putting on a face for Autumn. I feel like crap and I'm fucking pissed that I lost that victim, so I don't need to hear it from you right now."

"Oh, you don't need to hear it from me?" Kyle spat. "Well, *I* don't need to rush to the fucking hospital on a Friday night, wondering if my brother is in the burn unit, or a coma, or the goddamn morgue because he did something stupid! Again!"

I squeezed my eyes closed and rubbed my temples with my fingertips. "I'm sorry. To all of you. I wasn't trying to end up here, you know. It wasn't my goal to get trapped in that fire. I heard a woman in that office, and I just couldn't leave her. She was alive. When I found her, she was alive." A single tear fell down my cheek. "But it wasn't enough. *I* didn't do enough. I couldn't save her."

Jesse put his hand on my shoulder. "Dyl, we're just worried about you. We don't want to lose you because you decided someone else's life was more important than yours."

Ryan whispered, "You can't save them all."

My eyes sprang open. "Yeah, but I sure as hell need to try."

"If no one else is gonna say it, I will." Kyle slammed his fist into his hand to emphasize his point. "Dad couldn't be saved."

I grumbled in protest, but Kyle cut me off. "No, you're going to listen to this. Even if we'd found him sooner, there's no guarantee he would've survived. He had a bad heart that was going to kill him eventually, anyway." Kyle crossed closer to the bed and sat down by my feet, looking me in the eyes. His tone softened. "Jenna couldn't have been saved either."

"Don't you dare talk about her," I warned through clenched teeth.

Jesse cut in. "What happened to Jenna was tragic, but, Dylan, it was an *accident* and you've been beating yourself up ever since."

I looked away from my brothers. "I'm not talking about Jenna."

"Fine," Ryan said. "But these risks you've been taking your entire career need to stop. Saving those victims won't bring Dad and Jenna back."

"You think I don't know that?" The vein in my temple throbbed. "I'm a fireman for fuck's sake. We all are. It's our damn job to save people, and I will not lie here and let you guys beat me up for doing my job."

Kyle stood. "Well, you won't have to worry about doing your job for a while. You're suspended."

I recoiled. "You have no authority to suspend me."

"I didn't make that call. Lieutenant Brewster did."

"You're lying."

"He's not." Ryan sighed. "Your lieutenant found out you disobeyed the evac order. He's suspending you."

I resisted the urge to punch something. "Get the fuck out of here. Now. All of you!"

My brothers turned away from me to exit, all but Jesse, who stayed by my side and said, "We're really glad you're okay, Dyl. I'm not ready to bury my brother." He went to the door and shut it behind him.

My stomach was in knots, and my skin felt like it was on fire. I ripped the sheet off my body and tossed it to the floor, not feeling the satisfaction I'd hoped for. I couldn't be suspended. Being a firefighter was all I knew. It was who I was. Having that taken away from me was the last thing I needed.

I shook my head erratically, trying to erase my brothers' words from my mind. I didn't want to think about my dad or about Jenna. It was bad enough that I couldn't get the image of that victim out of my head without also seeing my father lying dead in our driveway. And Jenna's big blue eyes as the life faded from them.

My mouth was dry, and I tried to force myself to swallow. My heart trembled in my chest, and the beeping of the monitor I was hooked up to quickened. I wasn't stupid. I knew losing victims was as much a part of the job as saving them was, but it still crushed me, to say the least.

A soft knock sounded on my door, and when it crept open, Autumn's head poked through. My beautiful girl. I forced a small smile. "You can come in, sweetheart."

Autumn wasted no time and sat down on the side of my bed, placing a kiss on my forehead. The familiar scent of gardenias wafted my direction. God, she smelled good.

"How are you feeling?" She looked at me, her eyes soft with concern.

"Better now."

She fiddled with the hem of her shirt. I hated that I'd caused her to worry. She deserved so much better. I was damaged, but her? She was so damn strong. Stronger than me.

"What's wrong, sweetheart?"

She shook her head. "Nothing."

I didn't believe her. I cocked my head and pressed her for an answer. "Autumn..."

She ignored me and got up to grab some tissues, then sat

back down on the bed beside me and brought one up to my face.

"What are you doing?"

"Cleaning you up a bit. Your face is coated in soot."

I studied her as she did it. Her brows were scrunched toward her nose and she was frowning. The sparkle in her hazel eyes was missing, and I knew I'd caused that. I reached up and wrapped my fingers around her wrist, stopping her mid-swipe.

I received a blank stare from her in return. Something was up.

"I'm sorry I worried you, sweetheart."

She continued to stare.

"Autumn, what's going on?"

She shook her head and dropped her eyes. "Nothing."

"Please," I begged. My patience was wearing thin. "Don't make me ask again."

"Let's focus on getting you better, so we can go home, okay?"

Her avoidance was irritating. "I know you. I can tell something else is bothering you, besides you being worried."

"Not now—"

"Yes, now," I snapped.

"You've had a rough night. We can talk in the morning."

I wanted to pull my hair out. "I'm. Fucking. Fine," I gritted through my teeth. "Would you just talk to me?"

She stood up and faced the wall, then she sighed heavily before turning back around to face me.

"Why did you want to go out with me?"

I certainly wasn't expecting that. I narrowed my eyes at her. "Excuse me?"

"What made you decide to go out with me?"

Was she doubting my feelings for her? I scooted myself up further on the bed. "What do you mean?"

"I mean are you sure you aren't just dating me because of some reverse rescue crush?"

My jaw unhinged. "What? Where did you get that idea?"

"Well, Kyle—"

"Don't listen to him. My brother is an idiot." I rolled my eyes.

"Okay…"

I could tell she had more to say, but for some reason, she didn't want to. "What else?"

She folded her arms across her chest. "Just forget it. Now's not the—"

"Dammit, Autumn. What the hell is going on?" I pounded the mattress with my fist, making her jump.

"Can we just forget I said anything?"

"No. We cannot." I wanted to shake her.

She paced beside me. "Look, I've learned some things tonight. Things about you. I guess I'm concerned that you only wanted to date me because I made you feel like a hero. Because you have a thing for needing to save people."

I snorted, completely exasperated. "That's utterly ridiculous."

"Is it? I love you, Dylan. I know your job is dangerous, and I accept that." She sighed deeply. "But, I'm really worried that you take more risks than you should. Tonight, when I thought I lost you—" She shook her head and swallowed hard, trying to hold back tears.

I hung my head. "I'm sorry, sweetheart. I never want to make you feel like this. You're right, my job is dangerous. Sometimes, the good guys get hurt."

She pursed her lips. "But you make it more dangerous than it inherently is, don't you?"

I glanced sideways at her. "Where are you going with this?"

She ran a hand into her hair and twirled a piece between

her fingers. "You've had a rough night. We don't need to have this conversation—"

"I don't know how else you need me to say this, but I am not putting this damn conversation off, so you're gonna have to fucking talk to me right now, woman."

She pointed her finger at me. "First off, you will not speak to me like that. Ever. Second, I'm having doubts. And I don't think *now* is the right time to discuss this, but since you're giving me no choice, tell me: did you think you were going to die tonight?"

I closed my eyes and pinched the bridge of my nose. I'd screwed up again. "I'm sorry. You're right, tonight's been rough, and I shouldn't take it out on you." I opened my eyes and my stomach rose to my throat. "Yeah, sweetheart. There was a point in that warehouse when I thought I might not make it. But when I was trapped in that room, I knew I *needed* to get out of there, so I could get back to you. You gave me the strength to fight for my life."

She stared at me for a beat before taking a seat on the foot of my bed, facing me. Her voice was soft, but serious. "Then I need you to think about that feeling when I say this next part."

I leaned forward and waited, bracing myself.

"Do you remember the night of our first date, when you told me about saving Eli?"

I nodded, not sure where she was taking the conversation.

"You said that your job requires taking calculated risks and that saving Eli was a risk you shouldn't have taken. And I told you that I was glad you'd done it." She took a deep breath. "But I realize now that was a mistake. At the time, I didn't understand the implications of my encouragement. I hadn't known that those risky behaviors were part of a pattern for you. A problematic one."

I bit the inside of my cheek.

"You need to change. I can't worry every single time you go to work that you're going to do something reckless and get yourself killed. I think it's beautiful that you have this desire to save people, Dylan, but you need to make *yourself* a priority, too. You need to make coming home to me, as you put it, your priority."

"Autumn, this is my job. It's dangerous—"

"Let me finish." She held up her hand to interrupt me. "I understand that. But you're important, too. The night you found out about my transplant, you became angry at me for drinking, remember? You said that my wanting to hurt myself, hurt you. This is so much worse than that."

That had been different. Hadn't it?

She looked me square in the face. "So you have a choice to make. It's them...or me."

I gaped at her, wide-eyed. "You can't possibly ask me to choose between you and my job."

"That's not what I said. Either you prioritize the victims or you prioritize yourself. I want you to come home to me, too. Always. You know that saving these victims isn't going to make up for having lost your dad and your girlfriend."

My vision began to tunnel as rage flooded back to the surface. I threw my hands up. "For fuck's sake, not you, too."

"You need to accept that they're gone, and yes, that's sad and awful, but there's nothing you can do about it—no one you can save—that will bring them back."

"Did my brothers put you up to this? Is that what this is about?"

"Your brothers? No. I—"

"Dammit, Autumn. I really can't do this right now."

"You're the one who insisted on having this discussion." She threw her hand sup. "All I'm saying is that you need to be more careful—"

"You think I don't know that?" I shouted. "You think I want to get myself killed? I was just doing my damn job."

"You don't need to yell—"

"I'm sick and tired of everyone telling me why I do the

things I do. I'm a fireman. My *job* is to save people. That's the end of it. I'm not going to stop doing my job, and I can't believe you would even ask me to."

"That's not what—"

"You need to go. Now."

"Dylan—"

"Now!"

She opened her mouth as if to say something, but instead she nodded and stood up. I watched her walk away from me. She stopped with her hand on the door and, with her back to me, said resolutely, "I love you, but you need help. And I can't help you if you won't let me." She opened the door and took a step through it. "Goodbye, Dylan."

Just like that, she was gone, and I was left to wallow in a hell of my own making.

29

AUTUMN

I forced myself to hold it together as I made my way down the hallway and to the waiting room. The nurses bustled past me, each on a mission of some sort. The soundtrack of beeping machines played in the background and the sterile smell of chemicals and latex gloves permeated the air. I hated that smell. I'd lost track of how many days I'd spent in hospitals, but the familiarity of it all told me that it had been too many.

All eyes turned to me when I entered the waiting area. My chest rose heavily with each shallow breath as I tried to keep the panic at bay.

"I'll be going now," I announced to no one in particular, my chin held high, my shoulders pulled back. I may have been freaking out inside, but I would not let all those men see me like that. I wasn't fragile anymore.

Ryan stepped forward from the crowd. "What do you mean, you're going?"

Deep breath, Autumn.

"Dylan told me to leave. So I am."

I could hear some of the guys mutter curses under their breath.

Jesse moved toward me. "I'm sure he didn't mean it. We got him riled up. It's our fault if he's being an idiot."

I smiled at him. Jesse was a good guy. "I appreciate that, but this isn't because of you. He isn't ready to be helped, and I'm not going to stand by silently and wait for him to kill himself."

I snuck a look at Jace, and his face blushed as he stepped forward. "I'll take you home."

I shook my head. "No, that's okay. You stay. I can find my way home."

"At least let me walk you out."

I nodded. Jesse, Ryan, and even Kyle gave me hugs good-bye. Each of them uttered an apology of some sort on behalf of their idiot brother—their words, not mine (although I was inclined to agree). Dylan had shown me a side of him that completely contradicted the kind, loving man I knew. And I hadn't liked that side one bit.

I'd had no intention of having that discussion with him then, but he'd been insistent. I worried about him and that was all I'd been trying to say, but he hadn't heard me. He immediately went on the defensive and concocted his own narrative. I loved him, but I wasn't stupid. If we had any chance of working in the long run, he had to change, but he hadn't even been open to having a conversation about it, let alone actually putting in the work to resolve his issues.

Jace led me down the corridor toward the main lobby, and the moment we were away from the group, he grabbed my hand and stopped me.

"This is on me. I never should've opened my mouth. I was the one who pulled him out of that building tonight and it freaked me out. I let that get the better of me and—"

I put my hand on his bicep to stop his diatribe. "This isn't because of you. You were right. I needed to hear what you had to say, but truthfully, I already knew everything you told me. I had my blinders on when it came to Dylan, but you helped me take them off. Thank you."

He shook his head. "I still feel guilty."

"Don't. Dylan doesn't see things the way we all do, and unless he does, you're right—he'll keep taking these risks. Then one day, he might not be so lucky. I can only imagine what a tough night you guys have had, but the way Dylan spoke to me was inexcusable." I took a breath to steady myself. I was shaking from the emotional roller coaster I'd been on that evening. "I love him and I want to help him, but he made it perfectly clear that he doesn't want my help."

A lone tear escaped and rolled down my cheek, settling at the corner of my mouth. Jace pulled me into a hug.

"Take care of him, okay?"

He nodded, then walked me to the lobby, and I saw a line of taxis outside. I just had to hold it together for a few more yards. I gave him another hug goodbye before pushing through the doors toward the assault of the cold.

When I got outside, instead of heading toward the taxis, I turned the other direction and started down the street. I felt like I was suffocating in my body, and I just needed to walk it out. I made it three blocks before ducking into a doorway to get away from the world.

Tears stung my eyes as my breathing became shallower, and I sunk to the ground. There I was, heartbroken and alone in a doorway in the middle of Manhattan. My vision blurred, and I flung my head back. I was done fighting it. I'd left my heart back in that hospital, and I felt empty. My tears turned into full-blown sobs as the world disappeared around me.

"Autumn?" a familiar voice called out, and a moment later, his arms were around me, soothing me. "You're okay, shhh. Just try to breathe. Count with me. Inhale. One, two, three, four. Exhale. One, two, three, four."

I felt myself calming. My heartbeat slowed, my breathing

became deeper, and the sobs reduced to tears. I nuzzled myself against his chest without thinking.

"You're okay, baby. I'm going to get a cab, and I'll take you home."

Drew walked away from me, and I watched him hail a cab. He poked his head in, saying something to the driver, before turning back to collect me. I slid into the cab first, and he followed, grabbing my purse and pulling my ID out of my wallet. He read off my address to the driver and put his arm around my shoulder as we drove in silence back to my place.

Sitting on the couch in my living room, I still hadn't said a word. Drew was in the kitchen making me tea. My head was spinning from simply thinking about the events of the evening. I stared off in the distance, trying to figure out how I had gotten here. Earlier that evening, I couldn't have been happier, but then I felt like someone had thrown a giant grenade into my life, blowing it to pieces.

Drew handed me my mug and sat on the couch beside me. I willed myself to find my voice and croaked out, "Thank you."

"Happy to help. I'm glad I found you." His voice was gentle and full of concern.

I nodded slightly.

"Do you want to talk about it?"

I considered my response. I didn't really want to talk to Drew about what had happened, but I needed to talk to somebody. My only other option was Britt, but she'd been drunk when I'd left her hours before, which meant she was either passed out or delirious by that point.

"My boyfriend was almost killed tonight. In a fire."

"Oh, God. I'm sorry. Is he all right?"

"He will be."

"That's good."

"But I think we may have broken up."

His brows peaked. "You did?"

"Yeah. It's complicated."

"Well, whatever it is, he's a fool. It's his loss." He looked down at his hands, which were bunched in fists on his lap. "Trust me, I know."

I studied him, really seeing him for the first time since we'd reconnected post-breakup. He had a few fine lines in the corners of his eyes and around his mouth that he hadn't had when we were together. He was different. More serious. Mature.

"You really have changed, haven't you?" I asked, more of a statement to myself than a question to him.

"Yeah, Autumn. I have. I've already told you that letting you go was the biggest mistake of my life. I was a jerk. I know I don't deserve you, but that doesn't make me love you any less."

For so long, I'd waited for the moment when he would come groveling back to me. Autumn from six-months prior would've forgiven this Drew and we would've ridden off into the sunset together. But that was before.

He brought his hand up and cupped my cheek, a simple gesture that used to comfort me. "I'm too late though, aren't I?"

"Drew…" When I looked him in the eyes, all I could picture was Dylan.

He hung his head and let his hand fall from my cheek. "It's him, isn't it?"

"Yeah," I whispered. "It is."

"You're in love with him."

I nodded. "Yeah, I am."

He looked me dead in the eyes. "Then I hope he doesn't make the same mistake I did and let you slip through his fingers."

I sighed, feeling badly that I was the cause of the sadness in his eyes. "Thank you. I'm sorry things had to end this way with us."

"Don't be. This is my doing." He leaned forward and gave me a soft kiss on the forehead before he stood. "I'll go. You should get some sleep."

As if on cue, I yawned, overcome with exhaustion from the emotional ride I'd been on. I watched from my seat on the couch as he went to the door and shrugged on his jacket. I'd needed closure with Drew—and I finally had it.

He put his hand on the knob, but didn't turn it. He glanced over at me and said, "I hope you have the best life, Autumn, filled with all the love and happiness you deserve."

I gave him a lopsided grin. "Thank you. I hope you find your own happiness, too."

He let himself out. I settled further into my couch and Lily curled up against my chest. Everything about the kitten made me think of Dylan, and I desperately wished that I was in his arms.

30

DYLAN

That entire week without Autumn had been the longest of my life. I played it off like I was upset about my suspension, but everyone saw right through that excuse. I sat in a lawn chair in Jesse's garage, sipping a beer as he worked on his motorcycle. I'd been suspended for one pay cycle and was only a week into the fifteen days, so I'd taken to hanging out with either my brothers or Palmer on their days off to help pass the time. Honestly, I was desperately trying to keep it together and not spiral into despair.

"Pass me the wrench," Jesse said, reaching behind him and waiting for me to place the tool in his hand.

"Man, I don't know why you still have that thing. You spend more time fixing it than you do riding it. Besides, it's winter. You're not taking it out anytime soon."

"I wouldn't expect you to understand. Stop stomping on my passion just because you're miserable."

I took a swig of my beer. "Touché."

Jesse looked up from what he was doing. "Dude, when are you going to call Autumn and apologize?"

"She doesn't want to hear from me."

"That's bullshit and you know it. She was hurting, and you

were caught up in your own rage." He pointed the wrench at me. "Get over yourself and make it right." He made a few more adjustments before putting the wrench down. "I'm gonna take a shower before our hot date."

I shook my head and laughed as I followed him inside. While my brothers and I had fought the night I'd been in the hospital, we'd made up shortly afterward. That was how it'd always been with us. They were right, of course. I'd known it deep down, but I'd never wanted to hear it, much less accept it. But when Autumn said the things she did in my hospital room, it really hit me.

Granted, I didn't react well to her words, falling back on my go-to: anger. That being said, I had spent the rest of that evening sulking and reflecting on what Autumn and my brothers had said. I had to make a change, and as hard as that would be for me, it was unavoidable. And until I was able to do that, I didn't deserve a woman like Autumn. She deserved better, and I planned to work hard to become that man for her.

At family dinner on Monday, I'd apologized to my brothers. I'd told them that losing Autumn had been a wake-up call and I knew I had to adjust my "savior complex," as they called it. I'd been holding onto my dad's and Jenna's deaths for too long. I had to finally let them go, but I didn't know how I was going to do that yet.

I finished my beer and was putting the bottle in the recycle bin when Jesse came out of his bedroom, dressed to go. "All right, brother, let's do this."

Truthfully, I was in no mood to go on that date, but I didn't have much choice, and I couldn't remember the last time I had eaten dinner at five thirty. I already knew I'd be looking for a second dinner before bed.

· · ·

I parked by the restaurant and we made our way inside. Our auction dates, Betty and Kathy, were already seated at the table.

"Hello, ladies," Jesse said as he greeted each of them with a kiss on the hand. I followed suit, just to be nice. I never would've thought a double date with women older than our mother would be fun, but they were really sweet, and it felt more like we were out with our grandmas.

They had similar haircuts, both short and teased high on their heads, but Kathy's was gray, while Betty's was dyed red. They were a little overweight in the way that inevitably happened once your metabolism slows down as you age, but it suited them. Kathy wore an understated black sweater, whereas Betty's glittering top matched her hair. They were an interesting duo.

After dinner, I excused myself to use the restroom, and when I came back, dessert was on the table. Tiramisu. The sight of it transported me back to my first date with Autumn and just like that, I sunk into a shit mood.

I didn't say much as everyone finished off the dessert. I couldn't bring myself to have any, even though it was one of my favorites, and Jesse gave me a side-eyed glance. We left the restaurant and headed to a piano bar around the corner. I forced my feet to move in the opposite direction of my car, despite the overwhelming desire to go home and sulk.

Once we were inside the dark bar, they seated us in a horseshoe-shaped booth, and I sat on the end, next to Betty. The stage was in the middle of the room, not far from us, and the music made it hard to talk across the table to Jesse and Kathy. I cursed under my breath, knowing I would have to force myself to carry a conversation.

The waiter brought us our drinks. Jesse and I had both ordered the IPA on draft while the ladies got hot tea. I took a sip of my beer and watched as Betty pulled a flask out of her bag, emptying caramel-colored liquid into her mug. She caught me looking and winked. "Hot toddy." I couldn't help but laugh.

She picked up her mug and clinked it against my glass. "Now, will you tell me why you came back from the bathroom in such a sour mood?"

I took a long pull of my beer before responding. "My girlfriend and I broke up a week ago today. We had tiramisu on our first date."

Betty playfully slapped me on the arm. "You mean to tell me I'm your rebound?"

I joked back. "Something tells me I couldn't handle you."

"Right you are, boy." She took a sip of her spiked tea. "Now, tell me about this girl of yours."

"She's perfect. She's brilliant and beautiful and successful." I was glad to gush about Autumn. *My* Autumn. "My favorite part about her, though, is her strength. She fought cancer as a child, and as if that weren't enough, she also had a lung transplant. Her resilience is inspiring. She makes me want to be better." I sighed. "And I failed at that. I screwed it up. I never deserved her."

Betty studied me for a while, and I shifted in my seat, waiting for her to respond after having just let my guard down. Finally, she did. "Something tells me there's more to this story."

I went on for probably twenty minutes. I told her *everything* and she sat there, listening intently, her kind eyes watching me as I unloaded my baggage.

"I want her back. I love her more than anything, but in good conscience, I can't pursue her until I'm deserving of her. I owe her that. Now I need to figure out how to let go of my ghosts so I can be the man she deserves."

Betty poured a little more whiskey from her flask into her now-empty mug. "Let me tell you something, honey. When my husband died, I thought my life was over. After forty-years together, I had to learn how to continue on without him." She took a sip and didn't flinch in the slightest. "I won't say it was easy, because it was the hardest thing I've ever had to do, but I did it. I think about my husband every single day, and I'll continue to do that until the day I die. I never let him go because that's not what it's about."

She reached over and put her hand on top of mine. "You don't have to let go of your father, and you don't have to let go of your high school girlfriend. It's not about letting them go, it's about allowing yourself to move on. To live your life because that's what they'd want you to do."

I thought about that for a moment. I'd spent half my life in mourning, afraid to move on because I thought that in doing so, I'd forget about them. I carried survivor's guilt with me every single day. I wasn't letting them go, and I certainly wasn't allowing myself to move on.

"I never thought of it that way. They would want me to live my life for me, not for them."

"And one way for you to do that would be to fall in love and allow yourself to be happy without sabotaging it."

I nodded. She'd hit the nail on the head. "I love Autumn, but there's this part of me that holds back because of the guilt." I'd never admitted that out loud before.

"Just because you loved that other girl, doesn't mean there isn't space in your heart for Autumn too."

Autumn already had my heart, and I had to stop trying to kick her out of it.

"And, since we're discussing your survivor's guilt, while it's admirable that you push yourself so hard to save victims, Autumn is right. Your life is important, too, and you need to realize that."

"I know I haven't made the smartest decisions. Even if I save every single victim the rest of my career, it's not going to be enough. I'm more likely to die trying in the process."

"Probably," she said matter-of-factly. "Is that worth losing Autumn over? Worth dying over?"

I drained the rest of my beer. "No. It absolutely is not. I never used to care about myself. If I went to work and didn't make it home, then so be it. But now? Now I have a reason to care. Autumn's my reason."

"Then what are you waiting for? Go tell her that."

"You're right. I don't want to live this life without her." I leaned in and gave Betty a big hug and a kiss on the cheek. "Thank you."

"Thank me by getting the girl. Go. I'll explain it to them." She gestured to my brother and Kathy. "And don't worry, we'll take him home."

I ran down the street to my car. Thankfully, it was still early. Perks of dating older women, I suppose. I could be at Autumn's apartment by eight-thirty.

Despite Friday night traffic, I managed to make it there in just over an hour. I parked in the garage of her building, waved at the doorman like I belonged, and got in the elevator. My heart pounded with excitement. I couldn't wait to see my girl. I got off on her floor and made a beeline for her door. I took a breath to steady myself and knocked.

I waited a minute and knocked again. Still no answer.

My excitement started to dim. It was almost nine on a Friday. She was probably out. I would've called her, but I doubted she would've taken my call, so I parked myself in front of her door, hoping she'd come home.

After about twenty minutes, my phone rang, and Kyle's picture popped up on my screen. Wasn't he working?

"Hey, Kyle."

I recognized the worry in his voice immediately. "Dylan, it's Autumn —"

I was in the elevator before he could even finish his sentence.

31

AUTUMN

I sat across the table from my best friend at The
Monterey Club, which was quickly filling up since it
was a Friday night. It was hot in there, so I tugged the sleeves
up on my shirt. I hadn't been feeling the greatest all week, as it
was. The intensity of everything had caught up to me. I hadn't
been sleeping well, and I'd had another hospital nightmare. I
hadn't had one of those since the night of the fire. I guess
visiting Dylan in the hospital had brought it back to the
surface.

Britt's mouth was moving, but I wasn't listening. I checked
my phone for the hundredth time that evening, and we'd only
been at happy hour for forty-five minutes. Still nothing. It'd
been a week, and Dylan still hadn't reached out to me. I guess
we really were over.

Britt reached across the table and smacked my hand.
"Phone away. This is girls' night. We're here to get your mind
off of him, not to sulk. You've done enough of that."

She had a point. I'd spent the previous weekend crying in
my apartment and cuddling my cat. On Sunday, Britt had
come by with groceries and had forced me to eat. And shower.
She had her quirks, but she also had a heart of gold. I was

fortunate to have her in my life. After she had left, I'd felt a little better. I had woken up the next morning and promised myself that I was done grieving over Dylan Hogan. I was moving on.

That lasted about two hours.

All week, I'd anxiously waited to hear something—anything—from Dylan. Radio silence. I felt like a fool for loving that man, for thinking he could actually be the guy I'd spend the rest of my life with.

Britt tapped on the table. "Earth to Autumn."

I tried to shake the thoughts of Dylan from my head. "Sorry."

She rolled her eyes and flung her long blonde locks over her shoulder. "Okay, fine. Let's do this so we can put it to bed. I know you've explained, but I just don't understand why you're not trying to make things work with Dylan. You can't deny that you're in love with him."

I leaned back in my chair and crossed my arms over my chest. "I told you, he's seemingly incapable of change." I took a breath. "I can't be with a man who goes to work not caring if he winds up dead."

"That seems a bit dramatic." She popped a cheese cube into her mouth.

Was it?

"I love him too much to stand by and watch him get himself killed. If he had said *anything* the other night that indicated he would consider changing, then I would fight for us, but he just got mad at me and told me to leave. He was incapable of even having the conversation. If he can't simply talk about it, how is he going to change?"

She side-eyed me. "I suppose."

"Besides, he hasn't reached out to me at all, so obviously, he has no intention of making us work." My skin flushed and I tugged on the neckline of my favorite gray cashmere sweater, trying to get some air down my shirt.

"Why don't you reach out to him?"

"He was the one who told me to go, so it's up to him to tell me to come back."

Britt reached for her wine glass. "I can see how you would feel that way, but what if he's waiting for you to make a move?"

I shook my head vehemently. "Not a chance. That night with my parents when I messed up and told him to leave, he said the ball was in my court. So what'd I do? I picked the darn ball up and ran with it all the way to Yonkers. It's his turn." I took a gulp of my water.

"I'm no expert in relationships, but I don't think it's about taking turns."

My chest hurt. "Look, he clearly didn't love me as much as I thought he did. He chose to stay stuck in his past over having a future with me. I need to accept that and move on."

Britt sipped her wine, eyeing me over the rim. She placed the glass back on the table and laced her fingers. "If that's what you really want, I'll support you, but I don't think you mean that."

I dabbed at the sweat on my forehead with my napkin. "Of course, that's not what I *want*." I tried to take a deep breath. "But it's what I have to do." I finished off my water.

Britt scrunched her nose. "Are you feeling all right? You've had three glasses of water already and you look a little clammy."

I fanned myself with my hand. "Yeah, it's just hot in here. So, tell me, how was your date last night?"

She went on to tell me all about the new guy she'd met online. I know it made me a bad friend, but I didn't want to hear it, even though I'd asked. I thought about what Britt had said, and I wondered if perhaps she was right. Maybe he was waiting for me to call him. Even though it hadn't been my intention, I'd made him angry that night. What if he was waiting for me to apologize?

I knew I could be stubborn sometimes. Okay, a lot of times. If I reached out to him and he rejected me, it couldn't be any worse than what I was already going through. At least then I'd know for sure where I stood. If he told me that he didn't want to be with me, at least I could walk away knowing I'd done everything in power to make it work. No regrets.

Our server came over and refilled my water glass and I reached for it the instant she put it back on the table. I was feeling worse by the minute and I just wanted to go home.

I interrupted Britt. "I'm sorry, but I think I need to go. I'm not feeling so great."

"Yeah, you're not looking too good." She finished off her wine. "I'll go with you."

"No stay." I waved her off. "Hollie and Tia will be here any minute. I'm sure I'm fine. It's just hot and I could use some fresh air."

"You sure?"

"Yeah." I smiled like it was no big deal. "It's been one of those weeks. I think I just need to go lie down."

She gave me a hug goodbye and made me promise to text her when I got home. I swiped my jacket off the back of my chair and draped it over my arm. It was too hot to wear it. I weaved my way through the crowd, and took a deep breath when I finally made it to the sidewalk. There was a sharpness in my chest when the cold air penetrated my lungs. I ignored it.

It was cold, but walking had always helped me organize my thoughts. I told myself that when I got home, I'd call Dylan. I was mad at him, but I loved him, more than I've ever loved anyone, and I wasn't ready to throw in the towel just yet. Maybe he was, but I had to try one more time to make it work. If I didn't, I'd spend the rest of my life wondering what could've happened.

I'd made it two blocks when I felt the pain in my chest again, and my breathing intensified. I'd been having a little trouble breathing all night, but I'd honestly thought it was just because my nerves were shot and it was warm in the restaurant. Going from hot to cold was probably making it worse, so I put my jacket on, but by the time I got to the end of the third block, I knew it was something else. Something bad.

I looked down the street to my right and saw a firehouse half a block away. I clutched my chest in a futile attempt to make my lungs work, and stumbled against the building beside me. I willed my legs to move. *I can do this.* I attempted to pull in a breath, but I felt like I barely got any air. I put one hand against the wall beside me, and used it to keep me steady on my feet as I pushed closer to the firehouse.

When I finally arrived at the door, I found the intercom and pushed on the buzzer for longer than was polite.

The man who answered the door looked irritated. "Can I help you?"

"I need—help," I choked out.

His demeanor changed and he guided me in with his hand on my back. "What's wrong?"

"I'm—having—trouble—breathing," I forced out between breaths. I wasn't sure if it was actually the pain or my ensuing panic, but breathing was becoming increasingly difficult by the second.

"Okay, sit down here. I'll be right back with the medics, and we'll get you checked out."

I nodded, not having the breath to beg him not to leave me, for fear I'd be dead before he returned. Dramatic? Maybe, but fear breed irrationality. Seconds later, a woman came in with a big bag of medical supplies.

"I'm Sadie. What's your name?"

"Autumn." I looked at her with desperation.

"Okay, Autumn, I hear you're having a hard time breathing, so I'm going to take a listen with my stethoscope, and then I'll get you on oxygen, okay?"

I nodded again. I had to tell her about my transplant, but I couldn't get the words out. A few more people came into the truck house, and I recognized one of them right away. Kyle Hogan.

He ran over and knelt beside me. "Autumn, what's going on?"

My eyes filled up with tears because when I saw Kyle, I saw Dylan, and I was suddenly terrified that I was dying, and I'd never get to actually see the man I loved again.

"You know her, lieutenant?" Sadie asked as she poked and prodded me with various things.

"She's my brother's girlfriend. Is she okay?"

"She's got a temperature and she's definitely having some labored breathing. I want to get her on oxygen."

"Oh, shit." Kyle's mouth gaped open. "She had a lung transplant."

Sadie's eyebrows arched. "Recently?"

Kyle shook his head. "No, when she was younger."

Sadie placed her hand on my arm. "Autumn, we're going to take you to the hospital and get you checked out, okay?"

The hospital? It couldn't be that bad could it?

"I'll go with you, Autumn. You're going to be just fine, okay?" Kyle said.

Sadie pulled an oxygen mask over my face, and she and Kyle helped me over to the ambulance. I got in the back, and they laid me down on the stretcher. "Autumn, I'm going to get you started with fluid therapy before we go, just as a precaution." When she dug in a drawer and pulled out a catheter needle, my eyes bulged and my already shallow breathing grew shallower. It was worse than I thought.

Kyle sat next to me and held my other hand. "Do you want me to call–?"

I was nodding feverishly before he could even finish the sentence. He pulled out his phone and dialed his brother. "Dylan, it's Autumn. She's having trouble breathing. I'm in the ambo with her now, we're taking her to Mount Sinai." He paused to listen. "Okay, I will. See you soon."

Sadie got my IV started, then she closed the back of the ambulance, leaving me alone with Kyle while she drove us to the hospital.

"You're going to be all right. Dylan isn't far away, so he'll be at the hospital with us soon. All this is just a precaution because of your transplant."

A wave of relief rushed over me.

"I'm actually glad to see you. Not that it's like this, of course, but I wanted to thank you. You got through to Dylan after we failed to do so on many occasions."

Does that mean Dylan had actually considered what I'd said?

Kyle continued. "You're the best thing that's happened to him in a long time, and I'm sorry if I was an ass. I've always been extra protective of him. Of all my brothers, really, but especially Dylan. I was wrong—what I said at the hospital. It's you that's his hero, not the other way around."

I smiled and squeezed Kyle's hand to let him know I accepted his apology and appreciated his words.

"I really hope the two of you can work things out."

I leaned my head back and closed my eyes. *Me, too, Kyle. Me, too.*

They rolled me into the hospital where Dylan had been just a week before. In what I'm sure was record time, Kyle had a doctor by my side, and I was wheeled into an exam room. They stopped Kyle at the door, and I heard him shout, "Be strong, Autumn. You're gonna be fine."

"Ms. Bianchi, I'm Dr. Powell. I hear you're having trouble breathing?"

I nodded. A nurse was at my side, quickly replacing my oxygen mask with a nasal cannula. I was feeling a little better already, though I suspected part of it was knowing Dylan would be there soon. She then started pulling blood from the catheter Sadie had placed in my right arm.

"I'm told you had a lung transplant," the doctor said as he looked at the numbers corresponding to the pulse oximeter on my finger.

"Yes, twelve years ago. The right one only."

He nodded, but he didn't have to say anything for me to know what he was thinking. It was the same thing I woke up thinking every day. *Is today the day my donor lung stops working?*

I knew the statistics. Only half the people with donor lungs survived more than five-years post-transplant. Only having had one lung transplant instead of two increased my odds some, but I was still pushing it at twelve-years.

"I want to get you in for a chest X-ray and a CT scan to see what's going on in there. You just hold tight, we'll be back to get you shortly."

He left the room with the nurse in tow, and I was alone in that hospital bed with my thoughts. That was a dangerous place to be. Maybe this was it for me. The doctors had told me that this lung wouldn't last forever. Hopefully, at that time, they'd be able to remove it, and I might survive with just my remaining lung. It had some slight damage to it, so it wasn't perfect, but it should work as long as no further damage had been done. I'd been in remission long enough to mitigate the risk of living with one lung.

I had a benign tumor on my left lung. They found it when I was seventeen, but the doctors left it in, not wanting to put me through yet another surgery. They said it shouldn't cause me problems, but there was no guarantee. As I lay in that hospital bed, I prayed that if my time with my donor lung was up, my remaining lung would be strong enough to keep me alive.

"Let me in. I'm her fiancé," a familiar voice shouted in the hallway outside my door.

"Oh, thank God." I actually said out loud to myself, relieved that he had come. I instantly felt more at ease knowing Dylan was there.

A few seconds later, my door pushed open, and he was at

my side. He pulled my hand into his and used his other hand to brush the hair away from my face. "Hey, sweetheart." His smile broke me, and I began to cry.

"No, no, don't cry," he shushed me. "It's okay. I'm here. Everything's gonna be okay." He kissed my forehead and wiped at my tears.

"I've…really missed…you," I coughed out, realizing at the sight of him just how much I had actually missed him. I'd tried to fight it, but there was no denying it. I loved him.

He flashed his teeth as a smile stretched across his face. "I've missed you, too. So much. I'm really sorry. I was a total jerk, and you didn't deserve any of that. I'm ashamed of my behavior that night."

I squeezed his hand and my tears subsided. "Yeah…you were…a jerk."

He laughed.

I smiled. "But…you're…here now."

"I am. And I'm not going anywhere."

"I'm sorry…too. I…shouldn't have—"

"Shh." He ran his hand over my hair. "I know we have a lot to talk about, but let's figure out what's going on with you first, okay? There will be plenty of time for us to talk after that."

I nodded, hoping he was right about us having plenty of time. The nurse came in then to take me for my CT scan and X-ray. Dylan bent down and kissed me softly on the lips. "I'll be right here when you get back, okay?"

I forced a smile, trying to pretend like I wasn't afraid that it was the end for me. "I'll see you soon."

They returned me to my room just over an hour later, and within that first minute, Dylan was back by my side. I took in the sight of him. His face was laced with worry, and he had dark circles under his eyes that matched my own. He must not have been sleeping well either. The love in his eyes was undeniable though, and I couldn't believe I'd doubted he loved me.

"How are you feeling?" Concern was etched on his face.

"A little better. They gave me some steroids to help with my breathing."

"Good." He went to grab the chair in the corner and drag it over to my bed, but I stopped him.

"Sit here with me." I scooted over to make room for him. I wanted him close. I needed him to be. I'd done some thinking while I was getting those tests done, and if things were about to get bad for me, I had to lay it all out there with Dylan.

Warmth spread into my heart as he took a seat beside me, tucking my hand between his. I rubbed my lips together, trying to calm my nerves for the conversation we were about to have.

"Dylan, I—"

"I'm so sorry, sweetheart."

We spoke over each other, but I could tell he had no intention of letting me speak first. He was itching to get out what he needed to say, so I let him.

"This week has been brutal without you. Shortly after you left me at the hospital last week, I realized you were right. I made a vow to myself that I would figure out a way to let go of my dad and Jenna."

"Jenna?" I asked, my interest piqued.

"My high school girlfriend."

"Oh, you've never mentioned her name before."

He sighed. "I guess I didn't want you to know it. In a way, I felt like I was cheating on her with you."

"Oh." I slid my hand out of his and gripped the top of the sheet with my fingers.

He rubbed his hand over his head. "That sounded bad. I... you see..." He sighed. "I'll get back to this, just hear me out."

I nodded, urging him to continue.

"What you said to me the other night made a lot of sense—even if I hadn't wanted to hear it—you were right. I need to change. So, I told myself I'd figure out a way to do that so I could be the man you deserved, and then I would fight like hell to make you mine again." He paused and rubbed his hand over his head. "But then, I went on this date tonight."

I narrowed my eyes at him and scooted away. That certainly wasn't what I'd been expecting. First, he told me I was basically his second choice, then he admitted to dating again a week after we'd broken up. To say I wasn't thrilled with him just then would be an understatement.

"It was that double date with those older ladies from the firefighter auction."

My mouth eased into a smile and my shoulders relaxed.

"I had a really great conversation with Betty. She's a widow, so she understood what it was like to move on after death, and she gave me some great advice. She said that it isn't about letting them go, but about moving on because they would want me to. Their lives may have been cut short, but they wouldn't have wanted mine to be, too."

His voice shook with emotion, but he was resolute in his words. "And that's how I've been living since they passed. Or how I've been *not* living, I guess would be the more appropriate thing to say. But I realize that, no matter what I do, nothing will bring them back."

I placed my hand on his forearm. I was finally understanding how hard those losses had been for him all those years.

"And she also made me realize that you were never in a competition with Jenna for my love. She's my past." He pulled my hand back into his. "But you're my future."

I fought the urge to pull him to me for a kiss.

"Betty helped me see what an idiot I was for letting you go. So, I left our date and drove straight to your apartment. I was sitting outside your door when Kyle called."

"Oh, Dylan." My heart throbbed.

"*You* are my life now, and there's no risk worth taking that's more important to me than you. I'll do anything for you. I'll quit my job if that's what you really want. Anything."

I scrunched my nose. "Why would you quit your job?"

"Because you asked me to."

I shook my head. "I never asked you to quit your job."

"Yes, you did. That night, in the hospital—"

"I never asked you to quit. I simply asked you to stop being so reckless and be more calculated with the risks you take."

He furrowed his brow. "I thought you were trying to make me choose."

I shook my head exaggeratedly. "I know how much being a firefighter means to you. It's much more than a job, it's part of your identity. I would never ask you to give that up. I simply needed to know that when you go to work, your main goal is to come home safe, not take whatever risks necessary to help others, potentially killing yourself in the process."

He let out a breathy chuckle. "Wow, I'm an idiot."

I gave him a reassuring smile. "You must've been pretty upset with me that night if you thought I was making you choose between me and your career."

"I was." He nodded. "But I would do anything to be with you. I want to spend my life with you, and I promise I'll never make another reckless decision again. Coming home to you will always be my priority."

I lifted my hand to rub his cheek, and he leaned down to kiss me, quickly but tenderly so as to not hinder my breathing. He'd said everything I needed him to say, but the nagging in my stomach wouldn't quit because I knew what I had to do next.

"I love that you've come to this realization, and I'm so proud of you…"

"Why do I feel like there's a 'but' coming?" Dylan asked nervously.

I took a steadying breath. "I know we've talked about me being sick before but being here makes this even more real." I couldn't bring myself to meet his gaze. "There's a chance that my lung is failing." I let my words sink in—for both of us.

"I could potentially live with one lung...but that's not a guarantee. It might be damaged, and with my history of cancer..."

My head fell forward. The reality of my mortality was hitting me hard. A tear dropped onto my chest. I hadn't even realized I was crying.

"Like I said before when I told you about my condition: it would be selfish to put you through a relationship with me. If you really want to be with me, you need to understand that it's highly unlikely I'll live a long life like you will. The last thing I want is to be the cause of more pain and anguish for you."

I felt Dylan's fingers beneath my chin, forcing me to look up at him. "Hey, don't you talk like that. You're going to be just fine, I know it."

I shook my head, my heart breaking of my own doing. "You don't know that."

"And you don't know that it's not." He kissed my forehead and let his lips linger there. "Besides, I don't care how much time I get with you, as long as I get whatever is left."

The amount of love I felt rendered me speechless. I blinked through the pool in my eyes and noticed that Dylan was shedding tears of his own.

"Sweetheart, I know you're scared. And I love you so much for wanting to protect me from any more pain because of what I've been through. Yes, life was difficult after I lost my dad. Then, watching Jenna die next to me in the car *I* was driving." He shook his head, clearly trying to dispel the image. "It broke me. But, for once—in a very long time—I feel whole again, and that's because of you."

He kissed the back of my hand, leaving it wet from his tears. "I can't give up on you and I won't let you go through this alone. I love you."

I threw my arms around him. "I love you, too. So much."

We held each other as we cried, releasing all the emotions we'd been holding back—from ourselves and from each other.

Dylan mourned the loss of his loved ones, and I could feel the heaviness of the guilt he'd been carrying on his shoulders all those years finally release. He was finally free to truly live his life, and he wanted to live it with me.

I sobbed into his shoulder because, for the first time, despite being sick, I felt I was worthy of love, and that allowed me to open my heart completely to the man wrapped around me. I was still scared, but I was going to be okay because I wasn't alone anymore. I wasn't going to die alone. No, I was going to live out whatever time I had left with the most amazing man in the world by my side. And, for that, I was eternally grateful.

When we finally pulled away, we looked into each other's eyes and smiled, our faces coated in salty tears, our noses running like faucets, in a way that was only possible after a hard cry. Dylan grabbed the tissues from my bedside table and used one to help wipe my face before using another to wipe his own.

"Wow." He let out a half-suppressed laugh. "I didn't know I had that in me."

I returned with laughter of my own. "Yeah, me neither."

He planted a kiss on my forehead. "I know you're a little scared right now, but let's not get ahead of ourselves, okay? We'll see what the doctor says and go from there, tackling each challenge as it comes. Together. There's no reason to get all worked up over something that may or may not be happening, right?"

I nodded, knowing he was right. "Thank you."

"For what?"

"For being you." My voice hitched in my throat, but I had no more tears to shed. Dylan flashed me a big smile, and my heart swelled with the love we shared.

The doctor walked in, interrupting our moment. I was certain we looked ghastly, but Dr. Powell pretended not to notice, sparing us any embarrassment.

"All right, Ms. Bianchi, I was able to look over your results, and it appears you have an acute case of bronchitis."

I released the breath I hadn't realized I'd been holding since the doctor returned. Bronchitis certainly wasn't good news, but it wasn't the worst either.

My lung *wasn't* failing.

"Have you been in contact with anyone who was sick recently?"

I racked my brain, trying to think of where I could've possibly contracted bronchitis, but I came up empty.

Dylan swooped in. "Oh, man, it's my fault."

"What? How?" I cocked my head at him.

He addressed the doctor. "I'm a fireman, and I was hospitalized after a fire last week. She came to visit me."

Dr. Powell looked at me, and I knew what he was going to say before he even said it. My palm met my forehead.

"Did you wear a mask?"

I shook my head. "No. I was freaking out about Dylan being okay, and I, uh, I didn't think about that."

"I'm so sorry, sweetheart."

"It isn't your fault." I put my hand on his forearm. "I should have known better."

"You said you had bronchitis a couple years ago, right? It was bad, right?" His Adam's apple bobbed as he swallowed.

I rubbed his arm to soothe him. "I can fight this."

Dylan grinned at me. "Hell, yeah, we can." He turned back to the doctor. "What are our next steps?"

I loved that he included himself in my treatment plan.

"I'm going to send you home with a steroid prescription and an inhaler. Get lots of rest and stay home for the next week. No crowds, no visitors."

"I can be with her though, right, doctor? To take care of her."

"We'll do an examination and make sure you're healthy before we discharge her. If you are, then yes, that'll be fine.

Ms. Bianchi, I want you to follow up with your doctor in a week and make sure your healing is progressing. It's an acute infection, so I anticipate you'll be all right in a few weeks as long as you don't push yourself."

Dylan and I both relaxed a little at his words.

"We're going to keep you here until the morning for observation. If you don't have any more questions for me, I'm going to leave you to get some rest." He turned to Dylan. "Sir, I'll send a nurse in to get you started with an exam shortly."

"Thanks, doctor," we said in unison.

Dylan brushed the hair that was matted with my tears back from my face. "See, sweetheart, I told you you'd be just fine. Now try and get some rest."

I smiled up at him before closing my eyes and drifting off to sleep, knowing I was safe with Dylan there to watch over me.

32

DYLAN

I never imagined I'd say this, but I was grateful to be on suspension. It gave me the opportunity to stay with Autumn and take care of her for eight days before having to go back to work. Whether she liked it or not, I wasn't leaving her side until she was better. Actually, I might not leave then either. I loved sharing a home with her.

I'd spent the first two nights after she had gotten out of the hospital watching her sleep just to make sure she was still breathing. There was nothing I could do about Autumn being immunocompromised on top of the complications with her transplant, but I was determined to do anything in my power to make sure whatever life she had left was special and filled with love. I refused to live in fear of the end, but rather chose to live for every moment.

I unpacked the groceries, having just returned from the store, then went to the bedroom to check on my girl, but the room was empty. I noticed the light on in her office, so I opened the door and poked my head in. "Hey, you. Feeling better?"

She looked up at me, startled. "Oh! I didn't hear you come home."

I loved hearing her refer to her place as our home—I wanted it to be ours. I was ready for that with her.

"I was trying to be quiet in case you were asleep." I pushed open the door and sat in the armchair across from her desk. She had a stack of files on the floor in front of her. My interest was piqued. "What are you doing?"

Her eyes darted around nervously. "I, um, was just looking for something." She clutched what looked like a newspaper clipping to her chest.

"What's that?"

She pursed her lips. I rose from the chair and knelt on the floor next to her. "What's going on?"

She took a few deep breaths. "There's something I need to tell you. It's big."

I fell back off my knees and sat cross-legged beside her, steadying myself for a blow. I couldn't imagine what else she could possibly have to tell me that was heavier than everything we'd already been through.

"You said something the other night at the hospital that got me thinking. I wanted to mull it over a little bit before telling you, just to make sure."

I placed my hand on her thigh, seeing she was just as nervous as I was, more even.

"I told you I was put on the transplant list after my cancer came back. At the time, only one of my lungs was affected, and I could've potentially lived with one lung, but the doctors were worried about leaving me with just one given my medical history." She bit her lip. "If they removed the bad lung and then the cancer ended up coming back in the good lung, it would've been a death sentence."

Her breathing grew shallow, concerning me. "Breathe, sweetheart. Whatever this is, you can tell me. I'll help you through it."

"Finding a matching donor was a long shot as is, but in my case, it was even harder because I only needed one lung. So if a donor died with two healthy lungs, those lungs would be donated as a pair. I basically needed someone who was a match to die with only one healthy—or undamaged—lung to donate.

"I'd been on the transplant list for a year with no success. My condition was worsening, and my doctors decided I was better off taking the risk of living with one lung, so they scheduled my surgery. A few weeks before they were going to remove my lung, I got the call that they found me a donor."

She was shaking uncontrollably.

I put my hand on her shoulder. "Sweetheart, you're scaring me."

She ignored me. "When I was lying there after having been prepped for surgery, I overheard one of the transplant guys tell a nurse that he was delivering a few different organs from a teenager who had died in a car accident in Westchester. After my surgery, I did some research and I only found one article about a teenager who died in a car accident in Westchester that fit with the timing of my transplant."

My heart sped up, and my breathing shallowed, too. *It couldn't be. Could it?*

Tears streamed down her face, and though her voice was shaking like the rest of her, she continued. "The article mentioned she was an organ donor, and I just *knew* I had her lung."

Sweat dripped from my brow, but I ignored it. I was paralyzed, hanging on every word she spoke.

"According to this, she was in the passenger seat of her boyfriend's car when they hit a tree."

Autumn pulled the article away from her chest and laid it on the floor in front of me. I gasped, like I'd just been punched in the gut and had the wind knocked out of me.

"Your girlfriend was Jenna Lawson, wasn't she?"

I stared at the article, which had a photo of my car wrapped around that tree next to Jenna's senior picture. My mouth felt like cotton, and my mind was spiraling. Forming words was an impossible feat.

"Oh, Dylan." She pulled me into her arms and held me while I processed the shock.

The veins in my temples throbbed.

Jenna was Autumn's lung donor?

Jenna was *Autumn's* lung donor.

Jenna.

Autumn.

Fuck.

I pulled myself out of my girlfriend's arms and placed my hand over Jenna's picture.

Autumn let me have a moment before she spoke again. "The first time you ever mentioned her name to me was a couple of days ago in the hospital. I knew my donor had died in a car accident, and while I'd forgotten the details after all these years, I'd never forgotten her name. People die in car accidents all the time, so when you told me about what happened to your girlfriend, I didn't think twice about it. But when you mentioned her name, recognition hit, and I knew it had to be her." She covered her chest with her palms. "I felt it."

I stared down at Jenna's photo. It'd been a long time since I'd seen her face. As the shock started to wear off, I was filled with this sense of peace. I looked up toward the sky. "Thank you, J," I muttered, almost inaudibly.

I turned toward my girlfriend. "Do you remember the day I came over here to help you set some stuff up after you moved in?"

She nodded.

"I realized then that whatever was going on between us was powerful. It freaked me out a little bit. I went into your bathroom, and I talked to Jenna. I asked her to send me a sign if you were *the one.*"

Autumn's hands flew up to her mouth. "Oh, my God."

Chills stretched over my body. "I always knew you were

special. This just solidifies what I already knew. You and me, sweetheart, this is the real deal. You're it for me." I swallowed the giant lump in my throat. "The girl I loved in my youth died so that the woman I was destined to be with forever could live."

"Oh, Dylan —"

My mouth was on hers before she could say anything more. I tasted coconut on her lips from her lip balm, a flavor I'd become addicted to over the last two months. My tongue danced with hers, and I sucked on her lips with the sole intention of telling her she was mine forever. Her kisses gave me life, and I needed her more in that moment than I'd ever needed anything before.

Once satisfied that my pledge to her was clear, I pulled away, allowing us both a chance to catch our breath.

"I love you, Autumn."

She looked up at me with that sparkle in her eyes. "I love you, too."

EPILOGUE - JESSE

There were very few people I'd leave the beach for, especially since surf season had begun again, but my brother was one of them. Ryan and I had driven the four hours up to Hunter Mountain together and checked into the room we were sharing at the lodge.

"I still don't get why people stay at a ski lodge in the spring. There's no snow." Ryan tossed his bag onto the bed by the window, claiming it.

"Dylan said he and Autumn were supposed to come up here for a weekend trip a few months ago, but that was right after he ended up in the hospital, and then she got sick, so it never happened. He's making it up to her now."

"Yeah, yeah." He waved. "I get that, but how can he make up for their ski trip when there's no actual skiing?"

I shrugged. "Apparently, there's other stuff to do here."

"Like what?"

I picked up the guidebook perched on top of the dresser, flipping through it. "Like hiking, rafting, horseback riding. Hell, this all sounds better than skiing to me, anyway."

"How you played hockey all those years astounds me."

I shrugged. "The waves sing my song, bro. I don't know

what else to tell you." I hung the garment bag containing my suit up in the closet. "Ry, where's your suit?" He unzipped his duffle, felt around the sides, and eventually pulled out a very wrinkled suit. "Really?"

I snatched it from him, shaking the pieces a few times in an attempt to release the wrinkles, before hanging it in the closet next to mine. "You realize you're going to have to wear this in a few hours, right?"

He lifted his shoulders to his earlobes. "Mom and Kyle should be here soon. I'm sure she'll iron it for me."

I shook my head. My little brother was the epitome of the baby of the family. We had a few hours to kill before the big surprise, and we were under strict instructions to stay in our rooms until Dylan told us we could leave so Autumn wouldn't see us and effectively ruin the surprise.

I stepped out onto the balcony and closed the door behind me so Ryan wouldn't hear my phone call.

"Hey, you!" she answered on the first ring.

Lana's voice never failed to make me smile. "Hi there."

"I take it you made it to the mountains safely."

"We did. I'm standing on our balcony now."

"I'm sure it's beautiful."

"Not as beautiful as you."

I could practically hear her rolling her eyes. "You and your lines."

"It's true," I retorted. "Wish you were here."

"Me, too. But that would require us telling people we're actually dating."

I raised my eyebrows. "Still ashamed of me, I see."

"You know that isn't it. I swore —"

"I know, I know, you were done dating firefighters. Yet, here we are." I knew I shouldn't push her. I had my own reasons for wanting to keep our relationship secret, but she couldn't find out about that. It was in both of our best interests if I kept letting her believe that we were keeping things quiet for her sake.

"Here we are," she echoed, and I could picture her sexy smile clear as day.

Ryan slid the door open behind me. "Dude, what are you doing?"

I gestured to my phone, annoyed by the interruption. "Talking to someone."

"A female someone?" he teased.

"It's Chris —"

In an instant, he swiped the phone from my hand before I could react. "Chris, my man! How's life in paradise treating you?"

I couldn't hear what was said on the other side of the phone, but Ryan got quiet and his face flushed pink. I bet mine was redder. I grabbed the phone back from him before he had a chance to respond to her.

"Chris, huh?" he goaded me.

I wanted to wipe that smug expression off of his face so badly, but my priority was getting back to Lana. "Inside. Now!"

I helped him not-so-gently back through the slider into our hotel room, closing the door behind him. "Sorry, beautiful, my brother is an idiot."

"That's all right. I may have led him to believe you're paying by the minute for this call, though."

I couldn't help but laugh. "You didn't."

The sound of her dying of laughter on the other side of the line was contagious. "Your brother might be talking about this one for a while."

I shook my head, knowing I'd have to deal with that mess later. I heard voices in the background and looked at my watch. She was probably still at work.

"Sorry, Jesse, but I've gotta go."

"Have a good night, beautiful."

261

"You, too. And don't forget to send me some photos of you looking all hot and distinguished in your suit." She blew me a kiss and was gone.

I shouted at my brother through the closed bathroom door, "Ryan, come on we're gonna be late."

"Be out in a sec."

Fuck, he took forever to get ready. We had four minutes to get down to the lobby. Kyle and our mom stood in the hallway, holding the stack of signs, threatening to leave.

Ryan opened the door, and Kyle spat, "So kind of you to finally grace us with your presence."

As always, our mom came to his defense. "You know Ryan is always late. It's part of his charm." She handed Ryan his suit jacket, which she'd ironed for him. "Here you go, dear."

"Great, let's go." I shoved Ryan out the door, pulling it closed behind us.

When we got to the lobby, we found Autumn's parents over by the fireplace. I'd only met them once shortly after Autumn was sick. There was a story there, but Dylan said they were trying harder to be better for their daughter. He didn't have to say it, but I knew my brother played a big part in that. It was just who he was.

As a group, we followed Kyle to the chairlifts. Kyle had competed in the FDNY Ski Race for a few years. It was always held at Hunter Mountain, so he knew where he was going. We rode up to the summit, where we got off and positioned ourselves how Dylan asked us to. If all went according to plan, we had ten minutes before they'd arrive.

Kyle handed a sign to each of us, and we lined up, waiting for the moment. We saw them before they saw us. Kyle gave the cue, and we each held up our signs.

Autumn

Will

You

Marry
Me
?

From the chair lift, Dylan glanced our direction, looking nervous, but he had the biggest smile on his face. It was refreshing to see how happy Dylan had been since meeting Autumn. She fit into our family perfectly, and we were all excited to officially make her a Hogan.

They hopped off the lift, and Dylan grabbed her hand, pulling her in our direction. And then she saw us. Her hands flew up to cover her mouth, and we heard her gasp even though they were still twenty or so feet away. Dylan's hand went to her back, nudging her forward.

When they reached us, my brother dropped to one knee and said, "These past few months, we've gone through some serious stuff, and I know we haven't been dating that long, but I'm confident that together, we'll make it through anything. You are not only the love of my life, but you are so much more. And I can't wait another minute longer to spend forever with you."

He reached into his jacket and retrieved the ring box. My mom was standing next to me, already shedding happy tears. My brothers and I all had the biggest smiles on our faces. Autumn's parents, too.

"Autumn Bianchi, will you marry me?"

Autumn hopped up and down and screamed, "Yes!" as she dropped to her knees, throwing her arms around Dylan. He pulled her back up and kissed her passionately while we all cheered. As he slipped the ring on her finger, one thought popped into my mind: Lana.

Want a Bonus Epilogue from Dylan and Autumn?
Get in now for free by going to www.
kayekennedy.com/autumn

Help others fall in love with Dylan and Autumn by leaving a
review on Amazon and Goodreads.

Your reviews also help me bring you the content you want
most. I look forward to hearing your thoughts!

***

Ready for Jesse & Lana?

Read the first two chapters of Jesse and Lana's love story for
free! Go to www.kayekennedy.com/jesse

Get the book now at www.kayekennedy.com/books

***

You can interact with Kaye, chat all things romance, and get
access to freebies in her exclusive **Facebook Group:**
Romance Reads that Kiss & Tell
https://www.facebook.com/groups/kayekennedy

Kaye Kennedy

BURNING FOR THIS

Will these star-crossed lovers beat the odds, or will the odds beat them?

Lana

She'd dated her fair share of New York City firemen, but after being burned one too many times, she swore she'd never date another one.

Enter Jesse Hogan—she certainly had a type and he was it—tempting her to bend her rules for one night. He was just a volunteer fireman, there had to be a loophole for that, right?

Wrong.

He wasn't only a volunteer, he was a lieutenant in the FDNY. A fireman twice over. So she told herself to forget about that feeling in her chest (and that mind-blowing orgasm) and move on before he bulldozed her heart. Easy, right?

Wrong.

Jesse

One nighters were his specialty. After meeting Lana though, he was left wanting more. She was an enigma for whom he was committed to changing his ways.

Except she refused to date him. But he was determined to wear her down. His "let's be friends" routine seemed to be working. Great, right?

Wrong.

He discovered something that threatened to not only destroy his chances with the only woman to ever make him want to settle down, but also send his career up in smoke. He could keep that secret from getting out though, right?

Wrong.

ACKNOWLEDGMENTS

Without the following people, this story may never have been told:

- My husband, who sacrificed our time together so I could hole up in my office to write
- My fairy godmothers for encouraging me, for being some of my first readers, and for making sure the cocktails kept coming
- My grandmother for fostering my love of reading from a young age and for her recipes (yes, the artichokes are real! And you can get the recipe on my website)
- August Head of Walter's Writing Emporium for guiding me to make this story the best it could be
- Sara Burgess of Telltail Editing for being my cheerleader and policing my affinity for em dashes
- Jaycee DeLorenzo for bringing my vision for the cover to life
- My beta readers for handling my drafts with care and helping me make this story better

- My street team for being awesome and for loving Dylan and Autumn as much as I do
- Authors Claire Kingsley, Maria Luis and Susan Stoker for being so encouraging and for sharing this story with their readers. If you haven't read their books, I highly recommend doing so!
- YOU for taking a chance on love with my characters

ALSO BY KAYE KENNEDY

Burning for the Bravest Series

If you like alpha males with soft centers who love hard and make love harder, then this series featuring New York City firefighters is for you!

Burning for More – Dylan & Autumn

Burning for This – Jesse & Lana

Burning for Her – Ryan & Zoe

Burning for Fate – Jace & Britt

Burning for You – Kyle & Allie

Burning for You: The Wedding – Kyle & Allie

Burning for Love – Declan & Gwen

Burning for Trouble – Mack & Tori

Burning for Christmas - Keith & Brielle
Standalone set in the same world

Flirting with the Finest Series

Follow the men and women of the Special Investigations Task Force in New York City as they fight crime and fall in love.

Flirting with Forever – Hunter & Lauren

ABOUT THE AUTHOR

Kaye Kennedy is a CEO by day and a romance novelist by night! She earned her degree in English Literature and taught college composition & literature classes before switching gears entirely and becoming an entrepreneur, starting three businesses. She writes steamy contemporary romances because who doesn't love love?

Kaye is originally from New York, but now lives on the Florida coast with her husband, who often inspires her characters (she's a sucker for an alpha with a soft side). When she isn't busy writing or running one of her companies, Kaye spends as much time as she can cuddling with her rescue mutt, Zeus, taking her standup paddleboard out on the water, or relaxing on the beach with a good book.

Made in the USA
Middletown, DE
11 July 2021